I0686009

THE HOT MESS

A Novel

by
Gayle Carline

This is a work of fiction. All characters, organizations, places, and events portrayed in this novel are either products of the author's imagination or are used fictitiously.

Cover art by Joe Felipe of Market Me (www.marketme.us).

ISBN: 0985506024
ISBN-13: 978-0-9855060-2-5

Published in the USA by Dancing Corgi Press

ACKNOWLEDGMENTS

Let the *thanks* begin.

To Tameri Etherton, Joanna Keating-Velasco, and Rick Ochocki: Thank you all for your invaluable insights, questions, and general slapping around. I needed it.

To Jim Thomsen: Thank you for your mad editing skills. When I think I might have sullied the title of a Steely Dan song, I could cry.

To Joe Felipe: Your cover art is the bomb. You're not allowed to retire. Or die.

To my family: Thank you for ignoring the mess while I write one more chapter.

Also by this author:

Freezer Burn (A Peri Minneopa Mystery)
Hit or Missus (A Peri Minneopa Mystery)
Clean Sweep (A Peri Minneopa Short Story)

What Would Erma Do? Confessions of a First Time Humor Columnist
Are You There, Erma? It's Me Gayle

To Placentia, from your grateful resident.

CHAPTER 1

The drugs pulsed through the teenager's mind and body, beating in time to the techno music in his head. Lying on the floor, Alex watched the ceiling above him swirl into a dark velvet expanse, dotted with stars. His arm stretched out to grab a handful but they eluded his grasp, settling on his fingertips. He smiled, the corners of his mouth stretching away from their usual pout.

Dad says I'm grumpy, but it's his fault. He barely speaks to me, anyway. Good thing. "Why can't you just" whatever, it's all he ever says. Straighten up, go to school, be normal. What for?

Mom yells at me to stop screwing up, then says that it's okay, she understands me. What does she know? She doesn't know what school is like, all those crappy teachers with their stupid crappy assignments. Homework is useless. I already know what I want to know. If I don't, it's because it's boring.

My friends are all I need.

He scowled, his hand lowering to his chest. His friends hung out with him because his parents were generous.

Mom and Dad fed them, let them swim in the pool, and were kind enough to leave beer where they could get at it. He supplied the video games and kept his parents at bay by apologizing each time the liquor cabinet was raided.

These drugs are fine. Def wicked.

For several minutes, he focused on his breath. He felt his bones move apart to give the air somewhere to go, then relax back into each other. In... out... in... out...

Dylan said it was some kind of cocktail. Alex giggled. *Cock. Tail. Cock tail.* He laughed out loud. That Dylan was a riot.

The inky darkness above him began to turn gray and dirty. The air coagulated in a brown haze around him. His ribs no longer spread, although his lungs fought for oxygen. The air they drew in smelled of smoke and stung all the way down. He coughed himself out of the dream and looked around.

The room was dark and unfamiliar. He remembered that he and his friends had broken into the place, thinking it was abandoned. Each over-filled room told them they were wrong, but no one was home, so they explored it before the pills and whiskey took effect. Alex had ended up in what looked like an old lady's bedroom. A vanity held fancy glass bottles, and a porcelain doll nestled in the pillows that were covered by a tufted bedspread.

He heard his name being called. "Alex. Hey, Alex."

Opening his mouth to answer, he coughed again. The air was getting thicker with smoke. He saw shadows pass by the doorway, and tried again, but his throat was too raw for noise. One of the shadows paused.

2

"Dude... we gotta... get... out of here." Whoever said it was coughing hard.

"Come on." Dylan's voice sounded hoarse but loud. "Alex is probably already out."

He didn't hear anything after that, so he rolled to his stomach and began to crawl. The smoke swirled around his body, much like the imaginary stars. He wished the smoke was the illusion.

Dragging himself around the corner of the bed, he peered down the hallway. Red-hot light sizzled upon his face, stinging his eyes. He backed into the bedroom again and saw curtains. With effort, he pushed to his hands and knees and scooted to the lacy ruffles. He pulled them open and yanked on the window. It was locked.

The room continued to fill with smoke and heat. He felt like a fish, gasping, out of water. His fingers moved around the frame, searching for a latch. Finding one, he slid it, the only direction it would go. The window sprung from its casing. He reached both hands forward to remove the screen and slide to safety.

Wow, am I going to have a story to tell the guys.

That's when he felt the security bars. With his last bit of strength he grabbed them and proved their immobility. He slid down to the floor beneath the window, and listened to the pretty glass bottles exploding on the vanity, as they shattered from the heat. Rolling to his side, he looked at the shards on the carpet, lit by the flames around the doorway.

He reached out his hand to them, sparkling like stars.

CHAPTER 2

Peri stood at the corner of Morse Avenue and Angelina Drive, gaping at what she saw. A house, previously aflame, now belched smoke and expelled rivers of murky water. The acrid smell ate at her sinuses and assaulted her eyes. It was not a good beginning to the day.

She'd started her morning with a two-mile run. It was not her favorite time of day, but she had a new client coming at ten o'clock and the southern California afternoon would be too warm for jogging. At fifty, she felt she sweated plenty without external encouragement.

The smell had hit her first, followed by the sight of smoke. A private investigator's job is to be curious, so she trotted toward the source and saw fire engines pulling out of Morse Avenue onto Kraemer Boulevard. Two police cars were at the corner, officers directing traffic away from the scene.

Fortunately, it was already mid-June; the elementary school down the street was out for the summer, so the police didn't have to re-route frazzled parents.

Now she stood and looked at the devastation. She wanted to cry and it wasn't even her house.

It belonged to Benny Needles.

Benny was a one-time client, part-time assistant, and full-time needy little man with a big obsession with Dean Martin. He had spent the last couple of years running through his inheritance, stuffing his house with Dino items he bought on eBay.

Peri was never sure whether he was actually a hoarder. While his house was so full it was difficult to move around, it was full of specific things. Tables, chairs, and sofas from the sets of Dean Martin movies littered the living room. Posters, and photographs, all signed, were on the walls. And then there were the tchotchkes—ashtrays, barware, even an ice cube tray that had been the center of Peri's first murder case.

She wanted to get a closer look at the damage, but she wasn't certain if the police would let her past the barricade. She knew everyone in the Placentia Police Department, so she surveyed all the uniforms, hoping to see someone who didn't view her as a buttinski private eye. Officer Chou was on his phone. A friendly face, he smiled and motioned her over.

She adjusted her ball cap over her blonde ponytail and approached the group.

"Hey, Peri," he said after he ended his call. "I was just talking to Detective Carlton. He's on his way here."

She smiled. If Chou couldn't let her pass, Skip Carlton might. For one thing, he was a reasonable man. For another, she'd been dating Skip for ten years. But why was he needed on the scene?

"For a house fire?"

"House fire's not the problem. The body inside is." Officer Chou looked worried. "I'm assuming it's Benny."

"No." Peri shook her head. "I happen to know he's out of town this week. It's Dean Martin's birthday, and he went with Phil and Nancy Nickels to some town in Ohio. Dino's birthplace and all that."

"It's nice you keep tabs on him."

"Not really. I'm watching the Nickels' cat."

When his owners died, the orange tabby named Mr. Mustard had been adopted by the Nickelses, along with Benny to some extent. In keeping with his Dino-centricities, Benny had re-christened the cat Matt Helm. They were ready to send Matt to a boarding facility, but Benny had insisted on keeping him at home.

"He'll miss his stuff too much," he told them.

When they wondered how he could stay alone in the house for a week, Benny had the answer at his fingertips: "Ask Miss Peri. She loves Matt Helm."

Peri moved past Officer Chou to take a good look at the house. The two-story home next to the church had fallen into disrepair, due to Benny's inattention. His mother had maintained an immaculate curiosity. Salmon pink paint with cobalt blue trim, its white picket fence enclosed a neat little garden, guarded by two rather whimsical gnomes. Since his mother's death, nothing had been painted, or even refreshed. Even the gnomes looked depressed.

Now there was a hole in the roof, over the living room, ragged edges tipped in black. The front window was shattered. Everything dripped of dirty water and debris. Black stripes tattooed the front door.

Peri couldn't help but think how lucky the neighbors were, that the fire department was on the scene so quickly. Years of seasonal heat and fires had taught southern Californians to replace their shake roofs with something less flammable. Benny preferred to invest in Dino over home improvement.

Benny. Peri thought about him on vacation with the Nickels, having fun, soaking up all the Dino-ness Ohio had to offer, not knowing all his precious Dino-stuff had gone up in smoke. If this didn't drive him mad, it might actually kill him.

"Hey, Doll." Skip's voice interrupted her thoughts.

After all these years, his deep bass still made her heart flutter. She turned and saw him, trim and handsome in khakis and a white polo shirt that accentuated his tan.

"I should have guessed you'd see the smoke and have to take a peek," he said.

"Oh, Skip, how are we going to tell Benny?"

The tall detective grimaced. "I can't imagine. Maybe we should meet him at the airport with a tranquilizer."

"We'll have to shoot him with a dart gun, like in those nature shows."

"Who's getting shot in a nature show?" Blanche Debussy, Assistant Orange County Coroner, walked up, carrying a large black case.

"No one yet, Beebs," Peri said. "But Benny will need it."

She chuckled. "No joke. In the meantime, someone mentioned a body."

"In one of the bedrooms." Skip motioned toward the door, then turned to Peri. "No, you can't come in."

7

Peri cocked her head and put her hands on her hips. "Who said I wanted to? I'll just hang out here for the report."

As he began to walk away, she stopped him. "Maybe you could find one or two small things in there that weren't burnt."

"Why?"

"I was just thinking, if we could give Benny something that was saved from the fire, it might mean the difference between a meltdown and a straightjacket."

"I'll see what I can do, but the fire chief may not want anything disturbed."

"Just try, okay?"

She resisted following Skip and Blanche as they walked to Benny's front porch. The battalion chief met them and began to talk. Peri assumed he was telling them where they could enter and how safe it was. She saw Skip say something to the chief. The chief nodded and swept his hand toward the door.

"Morning, Peri," Jason Bonham called as he ran past her to join them. Placentia's Crime Scene Unit of one, he would tag and bag any evidence surrounding the body in the bedroom, and document the scene. Peri watched the three of them put on suits and safety gear, for their journey inside.

"I'm really glad it's not Benny." Officer Chou had moved up beside her.

"I am, too," she told him. "Although, when Benny sees this, he might wish he was dead."

CHAPTER 3

Skip stepped into a jumpsuit and rubber boots, as did Jason and Blanche. They adjusted their goggles and mask before putting on hard hats and entering. The trio sloshed through the living room, toward the back bedroom.

"Wow, I remember when I was in here the last time. All this stuff—" Jason's muffled sentence went unfinished.

Skip looked around to see him taking pictures of the damage. The fabric on the couches had melted into gray wrinkles, and the wooden pieces were charred beyond redemption. The camera clicked a steady beat, as if counting each destroyed object.

The hallway and doors had been licked by the flames, but not burned to ash. Dark smudges lined the walls, forming a wavy landscape of points, like a painting of a pine forest if Salvador Dali had been the artist.

Skip paused at the doorway to the bedroom. This was probably Benny's mother's, he decided, looking at the feminine décor. Shards of glass sprinkled the carpet and a heavy smell of gardenia clung to the edges of the smoke. Looking toward the window, Skip saw an outstretched hand showing from the foot of the bed.

9

Blanche walked past him, along with Jason. She stood, quiet, her gloved hands adjusting her mask, while the CSU took pictures of the body from various angles.

"He's all yours." Jason stepped away and began to get photos of the rest of the room.

"Male. Looks young," she said, her throaty voice muted by the covering.

Skip watched her work. She was a model of efficiency and organization, prodding the body, checking off the list, speaking into the recorder. A few times she picked up her notepad and pen, scribbling.

"What time did the call come in about the fire?" She looked at the thermometer and wrote something down.

"About one a.m." Skip looked at his watch from the doorway, knowing that the fewer bodies that were in the room, the less chance of contamination. It was a little past eight.

"Liver temp puts death approximately eight hours ago." She stood up. "Body isn't burned. COD is probably asphyxiation due to smoke inhalation, but I'd like to get tox screens to rule out drugs. I mean, this kid looks barely eighteen, maybe less. I can't imagine why he couldn't get out of the room."

Skip agreed. "There are bars on the window, but they have an emergency release latch. Even if the flames trapped him in here, he could have figured it out, if he was conscious."

She looked down at the boy and shuddered. "Hand stretched out, like he was asking for help. Breaks your heart."

Her words stunned Skip. While Blanche was not an ironclad woman, he had never heard her muse about any of the bodies. He always believed she paid her respects to the dead by doing her job well. That's what they all did in this line of work. You showed your regard for the community, to the victims of crime, by knowing what to do and doing it. Sometimes the bad guy got away. Sometimes you couldn't give a grieving family closure. Sometimes there was no closure to give. But you tried your damndest, each and every day.

A throat cleared behind him, causing him to turn and step aside for the gurney. Two men accompanied the cart into the room, where they carefully lifted the body from the floor and put it into its black bag. All zipped up, with accompanying paperwork, they began their journey to the wagon and on to the morgue.

Blanche followed them while Jason remained in the room, bagging possible evidence. He picked up a piece of pink glass. At one time, it had been a cherub sitting on a plastic stopper, but half of the face and an arm were missing.

"Funny," Skip said. "The glass breaking, when the fire didn't even get to this room."

"But the heat did. This is really thin glass, maybe hand-blown." Jason held it up to the light. "Make a container so delicate, seal the top with a rubber stopper, and it doesn't take much heat for it to blow."

Skip looked up at the ceiling, watching the lines of water running toward a common bead, forming a ball and falling when they got too heavy. The battalion chief, Cornelius Danes, had warned him not to stay too long in the house. The fire department liked to err on the side of caution when it came to civilians.

"Finish up and let's get out of here. This might not be the safest place to be."

Jason nodded his answer. Skip watched him label a final bag, before turning toward the doorway.

"I hate unstable crime scenes," the CSU said, pointing to the bedroom ceiling. Skip followed his direction and saw the bulge in the drywall. The water was pooling here. It wouldn't take much to bring the ceiling down and ruin any evidence.

Both men turned and left, moving through the rest of the house at a quick pace. Chief Danes was waiting for them at the doorway.

"Get everything you need?"

Jason held up his camera. "Need a few quick pictures of the rest of the house." He disappeared down the hall toward the kitchen.

"Almost," Skip added, and did a quick visual sweep of the room. In the last, untouched corner of one of Benny's beloved end tables, he saw something he recognized. He pointed to the object. "Chief, can I take this with me? I may need it to help me with the homeowner."

The chief agreed, so he picked it up. It was the ashtray from the *Some Came Running* movie set. Skip recognized it because Benny had shown it to him numerous times. There were a few dark smudges, but it had survived the fire without cracking. He carried it outside and waved it at Peri.

"I'm hoping we got enough evidence to figure it all out," Skip said, stripping off his hazard gear. "We may not be able to get back in there."

"Wish I could tell you different, but it'll need a couple of days to dry out before anyone can assess the amount of damage," Chief Danes told him.

The chief was still in his yellow uniform, carrying his helmet under his arm. His stocky build, along with his six-foot-four frame, made light disappear from doorways when he entered a room. A few gray hairs at his temple teased at his age, although his coffee-colored skin showed no wrinkles.

Skip paused, scratching through his short, peppery hair. "Any obvious cause?"

"There are remnants of cans, looked like paint and turpentine, where the blaze was hottest, so I'm guessing the homeowner was going to do some painting. My gut tells me it's about the hoarding." He regarded the house. "Granted, there wasn't the kind of filth you associate with that kind of thing, but did you see all the furniture in there? All it took was a faulty wire, a can of turpentine and poof, it all goes up."

"Yeah, Benny's got a little problem."

"Well, now it's a big problem. We try to educate people but no one wants to think it could happen to them. This is gonna be an insurance nightmare."

Skip thought about Benny's obsessive need for his things. "I'm guessing the insurance will be the least of Benny's bad dreams."

He returned to Peri, who waited on the sidewalk. It amused him to see her attempting to look uninterested in what was happening. Her expression seemed almost indifferent, but her body was tense and restless, her fingers clenching and unclenching. He smiled and stretched his hand out as he approached, offering her the ashtray.

"His favorite ashtray," Peri said. "Perfect."

"Time for me to go to work." He took his notepad out and observed the audience standing at the police barricade. "Think the neighbors might know anything?"

He could see the wheels in her brain grinding as she scanned the crowd. "Are you working on anything right now, Peri?"

"I've got a meeting this morning with a potential client. Other than that, just finishing a background check on an employee. Why?"

"Because I wish you were too occupied to want to snoop into this thing."

She grinned. "Ah, Skipper, when do I snoop? Okay, forget I said that. All I want to know is, do you know who the body belongs to, and was it arson?"

"I don't know and I don't know. Chief Danes thinks it was probably faulty wiring and paint cans, compounded by classic hoarder's neglect. Fire started in the living room, body was in the back bedroom."

"Benny's mom used to be in the back bedroom." Peri frowned. "Paint cans? Why would there be paint cans in the living room?"

"Again, I don't know. Doesn't sound like our Benny, to paint anything. Body was a young male. Blanche couldn't determine cause but time of death is probably about the same time as the fire."

"This is all sounding weirder and weirder."

"It's too early to call anything weird. We on for dinner tonight?"

She ran her hand down his back. "I was thinking take-out and fool around."

He smiled. "I'm on board with that. Now let me get my work done."

14

CHAPTER 4

Two days later, Benny stood on the sidewalk, looking at the boarded-up remnants of his house, jerking and wide-eyed as he scanned the damage. In his hands, he clutched the *Some Came Running* ashtray, rubbing it as if he expected a genie to appear.

"Benny?" Peri put her hand on his arm.

"No." Life popped into his face as he pulled away. "No no no no *no*—"

Nancy Nickels rushed to embrace him. Petite to the point of birdlike, she could barely get her slender arms around his shoulders, but she still held him tightly. "Benny, dear, calm down."

He shook his head, although he didn't try to avoid her touch. Phil, Nancy's husband, also moved closer to him. A stout man who stood a few inches taller than Benny, Phil leaned over him in a concerned, paternal way.

Peri watched the trio. It was an odd combination. The Nickelses looked like a typical retired couple who might be headed to the golf course in their tailored shorts and polo shirts, Phil's thinning hair was hidden under a Lakers ball cap and Nancy's silver locks were in a short, stylish coif.

Between them stood a short, round man in slacks and a bowling shirt, having a nervous breakdown. They huddled together for a few moments.

She looked to her right, where Skip stood, looking at his notebook. He had agreed to interview Benny here, instead of asking him to come to the station. Benny didn't do well in formal settings. He had been known to hyperventilate during routine traffic stops.

Phil looked at Skip. "Do they know what caused the fire?"

"No. Their first guess is that faulty wiring caused a spark that lit some of the paint cans in the living room."

"Paint cans?" Benny's voice squeaked his denial. "Paint cans? Why would I have paint cans? They're liars. They're all liars. I would never let my house catch fire." He slumped forward, cradling his ashtray.

Peri tried to get his attention by touching his arm, but he shied away. "Benny? Listen to me. It's going to be okay. Not right away, but eventually, it's going to be okay. Skip grabbed the first thing he saw, but there may be more things in there that survived the fire."

Benny looked up at her, his eyes glassy. "Can we go see?"

"Not right now. Once the firefighters say it's safe to go in the house, we'll go look through it all, okay? It should only be a couple of days."

He nodded. "What time?"

Nancy chuckled and Peri glanced at her, wondering how she and her husband had handled Benny for an entire week, two thousand miles from home. "As soon as we get permission, we'll set up the time. Now, I've talked with your Aunt Esmy. She said you can stay with her."

"Her house is so creepy, Miss Peri." Benny's dear aunt had a penchant for taxidermy and had filled her home with as many stuffed creatures as he had Dino memorabilia.

"I know, but hopefully it will only be for a few days." She took a deep breath and exhaled slowly. "Benny, there's one more thing we need to tell you."

His face had that same puppy-dog look of expectancy as when he worked as her assistant. It was the innocence in his eyes that kept her from killing him most of the time. "They found a body in the house."

Innocence erupted into anger and fear. "Someone was in my house? Going through my things? Who? Who was in my house?"

"I don't know who it was. He was a young man, and he was in your mom's room. Do you know why anyone would be in your mom's room?"

He didn't appear to hear the question. "Why were they in my house? Maybe they were painting. Did they ruin any of my stuff? We need to go look inside."

It took all four of them to restrain him from breaking the police tape and barging through the door. After a few moments, he withdrew again and rubbed his ashtray.

"Benny," Skip said. "It doesn't sound like you let anyone in your house while you were gone, but do you happen to know any young men, around seventeen or eighteen years old?"

"No."

"Have you had any run-ins with teenagers, maybe an argument or something?"

"No."

Peri sensed a pattern here. Benny had shut down. She tried to get Skip's attention, but he was still looking at Benny.

"Is there anyone who might want to hurt you?" he asked.

"No."

Peri shot a look at Skip, then walked down the sidewalk, away from Benny's home. Benny followed, as she had hoped. Perhaps if she could get him to move his feet forward, his brain would become unstuck.

"Detective Carlton is just making certain that the young man they found was a stranger who broke into your house, and not a friend or the housecleaner or gardener," she told him.

"But I don't know anybody who was mad at me. And I didn't kill anybody."

"Well, of course not, dear," Nancy said. "You weren't even at home."

He giggled a little. "Of course not. I was in Steubenville, with you. It was fun."

"Yes it was. I wonder what Matt Helm got into while we were away."

"He tried to get into your sewing kit," Peri told her. "But I caught him in the act. And I changed the Dean Martin picture next to his cat dish every day, Benny, just like you told me."

Their conversation wandered to the happier subjects of the beloved orange cat, and the trio's trip to Steubenville for Dean Martin's birthday. Benny couldn't get the words out fast enough to tell Peri about the tributes and the tours and the souvenirs.

"I brought you a souvenir, too, Miss Peri," he said. "It's in the car." He raced ahead to Phil's old Mercedes sedan and opened the back door.

"How was it traveling with him?" Peri asked.

Nancy smiled. "Oh, it was fun. He reminds me so much of our grandson. He lives in Boston, so we don't see him very often, but he's an Aspie, just like Benny."

"Aspie?"

"Asperger's Syndrome. It's on the spectrum of autism. They can have repetitive patterns, obsessive interests, and usually have a hard time with social skills."

"I didn't realize," Skip said. "I just thought he was Benny."

Phil laughed. "Well I'm sure they didn't have a name for it when he was younger. I think if you're not diagnosed as a child, then as an adult, people just think you're weird. They don't try to pin the diagnosis on you anymore."

Benny scampered up to Peri, a wrinkled brown bag in his hand. He held it out to her, looked at it, and took it back. He spent several seconds smoothing the wrinkles as best he could, then handed it to her at last.

"Thank you," Peri told him, and reached inside. It was a Dean Martin bobblehead doll, his body bouncing as she held onto his oversized head.

"Do you like it? I figure you can put it on your dashboard. Or maybe on that shelf where the blue moose was."

The blue ceramic moose had been knocked from her curio shelf by Matt Helm while she was providing a foster home for him. Benny had been caring for the cat, and suggested several times that she needed more Dino stuff in her house. She guessed her gift was his attempt at starting the trend.

"Sounds like a perfect spot," Skip said.

Benny didn't seem to hear him. He was examining his ashtray again, fingering all the grooves and tracing the curves. He popped from his reverie to face her.

"Miss Peri, I want to hire you."

"To do what?"

He rolled his eyes. "To find out what happened to my house. Somebody must've killed that guy and tried to burn my house down to hide the body."

She looked up at Skip, who kissed the top of her head. "I got what I needed. You're on your own."

"Oh, I don't know," she said, watching the detective walk to his car and thinking, *coward*. "The fire chief says—"

"The fire chief is wrong." He cut her off. "I never bought a can of paint in my life, and I never put anything next to wires or outlets or the stove or matches or, or, or anything hot. My mom taught me better. I may have a lot of stuff in my house, but I know the rules. Somebody set the fire. And you can find out who."

"Oh, I don't know." Peri repeated herself, in an attempt to consider what he was saying. "I'm not a fire investigator."

"But you will talk to the investigator, just like you talk to the police officers and figure things out. I can help you, too, like I did before."

"You're finished with your community service hours, and I can't afford to hire you."

"Why not? In jail, we found out minimum wage is eight dollars an hour. Charge me eight dollars more than your regular fee, then when I pay you, you pay me my eight dollars."

"While mathematically correct, it sounds a little crazy," Peri said.

Phil agreed. "Sounds like you're paying to work for her."

"But I have plenty of money," Benny told them. "And when the insurance pays me, I'll have even more money."

Peri saw his hands massaging the ashtray. They worked together, kneading his stress into the glass. Here was a guy who could make it through life as long as there weren't any problems, but problems wouldn't leave him alone. She felt her heart soften. "Okay, Ben, I'll at least look into everything. But you don't have to help me."

"Oh, thank you. If you need my help, ask me." Benny turned back to the Mercedes, where Phil was helping Nancy into the front seat.

"And Benny..." Peri wanted to remind him the insurance money was to pay for fixing the house, not buying more Dean Martin posters. She watched him turn back to her, his face down. He was looking at his ashtray.

"I'll call you when I know something." She couldn't bear to force him into more reality. Not today.

Peri watched Benny hop in behind Phil. The older gentleman said something over his shoulder, and she saw Benny's head bobbing in agreement, while his body made the motions of stretching a seatbelt across his lap.

Walking to her own car, she thought about Benny's request. Fire investigations were not even on her menu of services. Still, she could use the money, she wanted to help Benny, and she was curious. Arson to cover the murder made no sense at all, since the fire was in one room and the body was in another. What had happened in Benny's house that night?

She got into the driver's seat, adjusted the steering wheel and set Dino the Bobblehead on her dash. Flicking his head once made it bounce in a perky, if chaotic, rhythm.

"I have no idea what I'm doing," she told the doll. "Ain't that a kick in the head?"

CHAPTER 5

As usual, Peri rang Blanche's doorbell once, and then walked into the house. Life in the rolling hills of Yorba Linda meant not worrying about locks, at least not before nightfall. The Debussy home was two large stories of brick and stucco, trimmed in white. Peri kicked her sandals off at the door and wandered around the staircase, from the foyer toward the kitchen. She swung a bag of limes in her hand as she walked.

"Knock knock. Anybody home?" She looked around the vacant kitchen and set the bag on the counter.

A door to her left opened and Blanche walked out of her office. The petite brunette, stunning yet casual in beige capris and a chocolate tank top, went to the cabinet and took out a pitcher.

"Hey, girlfriend, great, you brought the limes. I got more tequila at the store today. Cointreau or Grand Marnier?"

"Hmm, Grand Marnier. Feels so high class." Peri pulled a knife out of the drawer and began to slice and juice the limes. "I need it after today."

"I know the feeling. How'd the new client work out?"

Peri shook her head. "No sale. I felt bad, too. It was an older woman, very sweet, wanted to hire me to find her cat."

"A cat?" Blanche laughed.

"I know. It was kind of heartbreaking. She's flashing all these crumpled one-dollar bills at me, saying she'll pay me fifty dollars to find her lost kitty. I guess she hasn't seen the news reports about all the recent coyote sightings."

"Poor kitty."

"I just wish she'd told me what she wanted over the phone. We could have saved the meeting." She squeezed a lime half until it surrendered its juice to the bowl. "So how's the fam?"

"Paul started summer golf league tonight, so he'll be home after the nineteenth hole. Dani's probably at her job. She's waitressing at Panera Bread. And Nick... he's okay."

Peri heard Blanche's deep voice wobble when she mentioned Nick. "Everything okay with Sonny-Boy?"

"Yes. No. Mostly." Blanche pulled margarita glasses out of the display case and poured salt onto a plate. "Salt?"

"Please. What's up with Nick?"

"He's okay, it's just embarrassing. His grades last year looked like a drunken man's roadmap—up, down, here, there. He seemed to have good intentions. He'd sign up for advanced classes so he could get the weighted GPA, then get C's in them, when he could have taken the regular class, gotten a B and come out even. Then he dropped out of soccer, and almost got kicked out of band because he missed so many rehearsals."

"Why'd he miss rehearsals?"

"Because they're at night and he doesn't have his driver's license yet, and he didn't tell us he needed to get there." Blanche sighed. "Here Paul and I sit, thinking our job is almost done and didn't we do a good job as parents, and then our son acts like he's falling apart and taking us with him."

"I think you and Paul have been great parents. Not everyone is ready to grow up, just because society tells them they have to." Peri tossed the last wrung-out lime half in the wastebasket and rinsed her hands in the sink, giving them a quick wipe dry on her denim shorts.

"You don't have to use your clothes." Blanche pointed to the roll of paper towels, but Peri waved them off.

"It's denim, Beebs. That's like, synonymous with napkin, isn't it?"

"No. Neither is 't-shirt'."

"You're no fun."

Blanche combined the lime juice with a little margarita mix in a pitcher, added the alcohol, and then filled two iced, salted glasses. "Shall we go watch the sun set?"

They took their drinks, plus some chips and salsa, to the patio. The sky was ribboned in colors, gold and red and deep blue, announcing the evening's arrival. The two women sat down at a large iron table with smoky glass insets. Peri sipped her drink and pursed her lips.

"Wow, I think you got plenty of tequila in here," she told Blanche.

"Too much?"

She took another sip. "Never too much."

Blanche leaned back in her chair and tested her own drink. "You're right. Plenty, but still not too much."

They were silent for awhile, picking at the chips and chunky pico de gallo, watching the light dance on the freeform pool, its curves distorting the shadows from the flagstone.

"Nick will be fine," Blanche said at last. "I guess I'm still feeling a bit—offish about that kid in Benny's house."

"Don't suppose you'd like to spill any particulars? Benny wants me to find out who he was and what he was doing in there." Peri stirred the salsa with the edge of her tortilla chip. "It's been almost two days, and I haven't found out a thing. Benny's paying me and I feel like I'm just spinning my tires."

"Two whole days, huh? Wow, what a slacker." Blanche laughed, then grew somber. "I know the kid's name was Alex McHale. Same age as Nick. They've been classmates since middle school, although Nick says he hasn't seen much of him at Yorba Linda High School lately."

"Oh my god, is Nick okay?"

Blanche took a breath before answering. "As okay as he can be. Boys hide it pretty well. Dani would've been weeping, texting, weeping. Nick has these moments where he gets a hangdog expression on his face, then says something out of the blue, like, 'Life sure sucks sometimes'. I hate to admit it, but it's been almost nice to hear more than a single syllable a day."

"Any preliminary COD?"

"Well, his airways were completely swollen shut, lots of ash, so smoke inhalation is primary cause. I wondered why a healthy teenager wouldn't just get out of the house, so I did a tox screen. So far, it shows he had a blood alcohol of .29, which might have killed him if the fire didn't do the job. I'm also running it for the usual suspects. Cocaine, X, all the party drugs."

"Wow. Why was he drunk in Benny's?"

Blanche held her glass up toward Peri. "You're the private eye. I'm just the gal who figures out what killed 'em."

Peri returned the mock toast, and they both drank. "So young," she said. "Seventeen?"

"I know. His folks are kind of big deals in Yorba Linda. Dad's on the city council, Mom's a popular realtor. Nick and Alex were in the same group of friends for a long time, then Nick said Alex kind of 'phased out,' as he put it."

"Have they got other kids?"

"Yeah, twins in middle school. Girls." Blanche poured herself another helping of margarita. "Kids. You can't predict how they'll turn out, whether you raise them the same or treat each one different."

"You're a good mom. Nick is a great guy, he's just probably nervous about the future. I remember feeling a little lost myself at his age."

"You turned out okay, but I guess you haven't led the most conventional life."

"It's not what I'd wish on anyone else, but I'm content." She drained the last of the pitcher into her glass. "I'd be a lot more content if I knew who to talk to about the fire in Benny's house. So far, Chief Danes hasn't returned my calls. I think he might be dodging me."

"Or maybe he's really busy. Too bad you don't have a best bud in the coroner's office to help you."

Peri sat up. "Do tell."

"Chief Danes sent me instructions today. When I get the full report, I'm supposed to send a copy to Skip, and to the fire investigator, James Murray."

"James Murray. Where do I know that name?"

Blanche laughed, her full, throaty alto giving it a dash of naughty delight. "Because a hundred years ago, I set you up on a blind date with him."

"Oh. My. God. I completely forgot." She leaned back in her chair. "Was that after Husband Two or Husband Three?"

"Which one was Chuck?"

"Two."

"Definitely after him." Blanche smiled. "This should be interesting."

Peri fluffed her blonde hair away from her scalp. "James. James Murray. Tall and dark?"

"Blond. Define tall."

"Six-five?"

"Try five-eleven. Although he was slender, carried himself as if he was a bigger dog."

"Wait." Peri leaned over the table, pointing a chip at her friend. "Super Upright Guy. Upright, uptight, and cheap, too. Uber-athletic, did a lot of triathlons. Didn't drink because alcohol was 'expensive calories'." She used air quotes to frame the last two words.

Blanche nodded. "That'd be him. Wonder what he's been up to, besides getting his credentials as a fire whisperer."

"Guess we'll have to do a little catching up." She dug her chip into the salsa. "You know, we went out twice. He actually asked me on a third date."

"I remember. As I recall, you said, 'If I ever agree to go out with him again, hit me in the head with a rock'."

"Yeah, well this won't count as a date, but if I remember him correctly, I may need you to keep a boulder handy."

CHAPTER 6

"Well, I'll be damned." When Peri first looked up James Murray's business address, she was stunned. Newport Beach was one of the ritziest, most high-priced beach communities in Orange County, and possibly southern California. Granted, his office was on the inland side of Pacific Coast Highway, but it was still Newport Beach.

As she drove south on the 55 freeway, she wondered if perhaps he was sharing a small space with ten other businesses. Maybe it was some industrial warehouse on the wrong side of town. She knew people who would do anything for the right zip code.

When she arrived at the address, she didn't find a warehouse. The brick façade and white railings made her think of a country home, down to the ivy on the trellises and hanging flower baskets. Maintenance alone on such a high-end property had to be pricey.

She walked into the foyer and looked for the directory. A framed panel hung between the elevator and the open stairwell, listing both names and a map. James's office was in the back corner, on the second floor.

Peri walked up a set of open wood stairs, turned left, then left again, down an outdoor walkway, with an atrium in the middle of the building. She glanced down to see a well-manicured garden with stone walkways, benches, and bistro-style tables.

Finally she reached her destination. *James Murray Investigations*, engraved on a brass plate, was mounted in the middle of a red door. She pushed it open, and was surprised to see an expansive secretarial foyer. Either the offices in the building were extra large, or James had rented several and combined them.

A middle-aged woman sat behind a rich oak desk. She smiled and stood.

"Hello, I'm Emma. You must be Miss Minneopa. Mr. Murray is expecting you. Right this way." She walked around the desk, leading Peri toward a black lacquered door. Emma looked professional in a peach suit and upswept, dark brown hair. Her red nails clicked on the wood as she pulled on the handle and motioned for Peri to enter.

As she walked into James Murray's office, Peri nearly stepped back from sheer awe. It was as austere and clean as she had imagined, but she hadn't figured on the opulence. She observed the rich mahogany of the desk, the plush leather of the chairs, details like crown moldings, a beautiful chandelier and matching desk lamp. The wood floor, pale and unscarred, made her want to take off her shoes.

"Peri." The quiet voice behind her brought back an instant memory, asking for that third date in a disdainful, almost mocking tone.

She turned to face him. Blanche was right; he wasn't as tall as she had remembered. He was, however, as blond as her friend had described. Blond in an icy way, she always imagined he would be cool to the touch. He didn't look like he had gained weight. In fact, he had that gaunt quality of someone who runs a marathon every day, bicycles to and from work, and only eats a half cup of macrobiotic food for breakfast and dinner.

He wore a suit of charcoal pinstripe, with a white shirt and burgundy tie, shiny black wingtips on his feet. The slight scent of a clean, masculine fragrance played around her nose. Hating men's cologne, she at least appreciated the subtlety. She noted how straight he stood, and that, even in the privacy of his office, he had his jacket on, buttoned.

No man had ever made her feel underdressed, but she felt self-conscious in her beige slacks, red shell and striped jacket. Hot weather or not, next time she had to talk to him, she would break out the wool suit.

If I had ended up with this guy, I'd have killed myself.

"James, it's nice to see you." She offered her hand. His handshake was firm and quick. Efficient.

He directed her to a chair. "Why don't you have a seat?"

She took a quick glance around his desk as she sat down. A family photo was in view, of James with a stunning brunette. Their two small sons were carbon copies of their father, from their white-blond hair to their thin, drawn lips.

"Is this your family? The boys really look like you."

James walked around and eased into his large, dark chair. "What can I do for you?"

"Well, I heard you were the investigator on the fire at Angelina Drive in Placentia. I'm doing some work for the homeowner, so I thought I'd touch base and ask to be kept in the loop with your findings."

He smiled. "Why would I do that?"

"You don't have to. My client is rather nervous about what's going on in his house, and I'm always curious about anything that might be educational for me as a private investigator."

"I don't see any reason to train you on fire investigation."

She had met resistance before, but never so much brick and mortar refusal. "Well, no, I'm not really talking about training. Like I said, my client is nervous, and I'd like to do what I can to reassure him. I just thought, since we know each other, perhaps you'd consider it a courtesy."

"There's no need for courtesy. That we know each other is immaterial." His smile faded.

Peri frowned. "James. We dated twice. We weren't a good match that way, but I thought we ended on good terms. I'm just trying to help my client."

"This isn't about friendship, or a couple of dates. I'm not some jilted boyfriend. It is about protocol and process. You are a private investigator. I am a professional, hired by the city in an official capacity, to determine the cause of fires, whether they are arson, accident, or negligence. I am not obligated to give you any reports, or any insight."

She could have continued to be polite, but the way he said *professional* made the blood ring in her ears. "Okay, James, I get it. You're not obligated to give me the time of day. My client is concerned about the fire, the dead body, the whole shebang. I thought I'd see if I could at least let him know what was being done."

He stood up, stretching himself taller. "Perhaps you'll have better luck with the police, or the insurance company."

His vertical stance meant the meeting was over.

"I dare say I will, James," Peri told him, rising from her chair.

She wanted to stomp out of his office, but didn't want him to know he'd bested her, so she strolled to the door, swinging her pink snakeskin tote casually.

As she reached for the doorknob, she turned. "Thanks for the chat. It was a real slice."

It wasn't at all her fault when his big black door slammed shut behind her.

CHAPTER 7

Peri's next stop was the Placentia Police Department. The chief of police had tried to discourage her visits, but she found one trip every couple of weeks didn't seem to wear out her welcome. If she could disguise it as a lunch date with her boyfriend, she sometimes slipped in twice in one week.

Skip was in his office, staring at his computer screen, squinting through a pair of small, square reading glasses. He looked up at the sound of Peri shutting the door.

"Hey, Doll, is it lunchtime?"

She dropped herself into his hard, plastic visitor chair, remembering the velvety feel of Murray's office. "I just came from the fire investigator's," she said, and told him of their encounter. "Can you believe that horse's ass?"

Skip leaned back in his chair and smiled. "Finally met someone who was immune to your charms?"

"Most guys go out of their way to show off, tell you what they know about something. This guy likes to withhold what he knows—he's a hoarder. That's what he is, an information hoarder."

He laughed.

"And you're supposed to be supportive." She crossed her arms and muttered, "Horse's ass."

"I know he is but what am I?"

She grinned. "You're my horse's ass."

Skip glanced at his watch. "Eleven thirty. What sounds good for lunch?"

"I'd love to, Skipper, but I can't. Benny's case is the only one I've got at the moment, and I need to be doing something. You think if I stopped by the fire station, Chief Danes might talk to me?"

"How should I know? I don't know that much about Danes. But I know you. If he won't talk, I'll bet you find a firefighter who will."

"I'll bet you're right." Peri stood and walked around to him. "See you tonight?'

He reached up to give her a kiss. "I get off at six."

"Come over when you're done. We'll figure dinner out then." She opened the door. "Later."

* * *

The Valencia Street fire station was a one-story, brick crew-sized office attached to a large engine-sized garage. The roof was red tile, as fireproof as possible for the desert.

Peri walked in the front door and looked around. To her right was a metal desk with a couple of chairs. Behind it, a large room with a kitchen and dining table. A hallway was to the left with two doors she could see, both closed.

No one greeted her, but she was hesitant to go any further. If she needed information, she couldn't be seen as an interloper. Soon she heard the sound of heavy footsteps and a familiar face appeared from the direction of the garage.

"Tom Flores?"

He looked at her, recognition washing over his eyes at last. "Peri, isn't it? Peri Money—"

"Minneopa. Just call me Peri." She extended her hand. "I thought you were at the Bradford station." Tom had helped her on a previous case, as part of a team called to rescue an elderly woman who had been abducted.

The tall, trim man shrugged. "They offered to promote me to captain if I came here. It's less than five miles from my old job, so how could I refuse?" He sat down at the desk. "What can I do for you today?"

"Well I was hoping to discuss the recent fire on Angelina Drive with Chief Danes. I'm working with the homeowner and I'm trying to keep in the loop."

"Chief's in a meeting, but I might be able to help you. I was on the crew that put the fire out." He smiled, showing a row of straight, white teeth, startling against his cinnamon skin.

Peri sat down. "I've heard the initial thought is that paint cans in the house caught fire. An electrical short or something."

"That's our first theory, but the investigator should be able to determine the cause. There was a residue of turps, and we found two melted cans."

"Turps?"

"Mineral turpentine. It's a common paint thinner, and also used to clean brushes. Maybe someone left a can with brushes soaking near something flammable." Flores ran his hand across his wavy black hair. "I've never seen so much junk in one room."

Peri was glad Benny wasn't here to listen to Flores talk about his beloved memorabilia as junk. "I agree, Benny has too much stuff for his house. The thing is, he only hoards specific items. And I've never seen him do a lick of home improvement, unless you count changing a light bulb. He swears he never bought any paint, and I don't think he knows what turpentine is. I mean, you saw his house."

"Well, by the time we got there, it was mostly ash and charred wood. It's normal for a frayed cord to spark during an electrical spike, but any kind of dry material, like papers or old fabric can turn it into a fire. And paint or turpentine will accelerate it into flame."

She sat back, out of questions. It was Benny's word against reality that he had no paint cans in his house. What did she know about fire investigations, anyway? "James Murray's the investigator. When do you think you'll have his report?"

"Not before next week. He's a pretty thorough guy. He'll have pictures to put in the correct order and lab results written precisely. All that takes time."

"At least he'll give an accurate report on the cause."

Flores' smile stiffened in a way that made her suspicious.

"Won't he?"

He leaned back in his chair, rolling his neck as if to loosen his muscles. A large silence hugged the room. Finally, he spoke.

"I'm not the best judge. I worked a fire that seemed suspicious. I knew the homeowner, and knew their home was in perfect working order. They had been having problems with their son, who had joined a gang. He had a rival gang hunting him, plus his homeys were mad at the folks for trying to interfere and make him quit. Suddenly their house goes up in smoke."

"Sounds like a vendetta to me." Peri sat back.

"Except there was no trace of anything flammable. Murray writes great reports, but he's very one-dimensional, at least on that case. No obvious trace of arson, fire originated in the fireplace, papers stacked too close to the opening, case closed. The family had to take their case to arbitration because the insurance refused to pay for owner negligence."

"Did they get it resolved?"

He nodded. "Only when arbitration hired their own investigator, which the family paid for. Found the fireplace had been tampered with. A lot of time, money, and sleepless nights trying to get what was owed to them."

Peri wasn't surprised to hear that James Murray was about the cut-and-dried. If it walked like a duck and talked like a duck, he was not going to check under the feathers. She was now officially worried about Benny.

"Thanks for your time, Tom," she told him as she stood up. "Do you think you could give me a call when that report comes in? I'd like to see it."

"My pleasure." He rose and offered his hand. Peri shook it, and turned to the door.

As she got in her car, Peri realized how little she had to investigate. There was no link between Benny and the dead teenager, and no reason for him to be in Benny's house. And, unless James Murray's report said it was arson, the house fire would not be investigated further by the police.

She had come to rely on information from Skip and Blanche, and even Jason, to help her figure things out. Without them, this might be the true test of her sleuthing talents.

Seatbelt on and engine started, she reached down to put the car into gear when her cell phone rang.

"Miss Peri, they want my insurance company." Benny's voice was an octave higher than normal, indicating his distress.

"Who are they and what do you mean, they want your insurance company?" she asked.

"Someone named Murray wants to send something to my insurance company."

"Oh, right. James Murray is investigating the fire. He needs to know where to send the report."

"But I don't know who my insurance company is."

Peri frowned. "Well, who do you make the check out to?"

"What check?"

"The yearly check for your homeowner's insurance."

Benny was no help at all. "I don't make out a check. My mom's estate handles all that."

"Okay, who handles your mom's estate?"

"I don't know. Some bank."

"Benny." Her worn patience spat his name out. "Where do you get your money? Do you write checks? What's the name of the bank on the checks?"

The line went silent.

"You'd never talk to Dean Martin like this."

Peri sighed. "I'm sorry. We need to find your insurance company, though. You won't get any money until you contact them. Do you have any idea of where there might be legal papers, or documents?"

"Oh. I know my mom kept a bunch of papers in a metal file cabinet in her room."

"The room in the house that is sealed off due to fire damage? How am I supposed to get papers from there?"

"Well, that's where they are. I'll go to the house and—"

She interrupted. "No, Benny. It isn't safe yet." She looked back at the station, and turned off the engine. "Let me see what I can do."

None of this is going to be easy, she thought as she got out of the car and headed back inside.

Tom Flores wasn't at the front desk any longer, but she could see Chief Danes in the office beyond. She wished Tom was still there. Chief Danes looked rather imposing, and she needed a favor. Taking a big breath, she walked into the office.

"Chief Danes? Peri Minneopa. You can call me Peri. I'm trying to help my—" She hesitated.

The chief might have an opinion about her line of work. She decided to try a different spin. "Trying to help my friend, Benny, whose house burned a few days ago. I'm afraid he's not a very organized man, and he has no idea who his insurance company is or how to contact anyone. He knows all the papers are in his late mother's bedroom, which is unfortunately, in the burned house. I was thinking I could perhaps climb through the bedroom window, as long as you felt it was safe."

Chief Danes ran his index finger down the side of his mustache as if outlining it.

"Technically, we can't keep the homeowner out of his house," he said at last. "All I can really do is caution you, although in my opinion, you shouldn't be in the house until the beams are shored up in the living room and everything has dried."

"I suspected that, but I know Mrs. Needles' room was not burned, and he did give me permission to enter."

"I don't mean to eavesdrop." Tom appeared at the door. "But if Peri needs to get anything out of Benny's house, I'm on my lunch break. I'd be happy to help."

The chief shrugged. "What you do on your lunch break is up to you."

"Thank you so much," Peri said. "This will be a big help with my client."

And it might wrap this case up, she thought as she walked out of the station.

CHAPTER 8

The house still smelled strong, even from the outside, stabbing past Peri's nose and boring into her sinuses. Tom handed her a mask.

"This will help a little," he said. "At least keep the big chunks out of your lungs."

They walked around to the back of the house, Tom carrying a stepladder and Peri with her tote on her shoulder. He placed the ladder against the wall, under the window.

"Stay here. You can tell me what to look for when I'm inside." He stepped up the rungs.

Peri waited, her tennis shoes squishing in the still-moist ground around the house. The ladder beside her sank into the mud with each of Tom's steps. She thought about poor Benny losing his things, so precious to him, and hoped they'd be able to recover a few trinkets.

"Where did you say they were?" Tom asked.

"Benny said there was a file cabinet in the room."

She watched the beam from his flashlight sweep past the window.

"I see it. It's kind of a mess."

"Mess?" Her heart sank as she pictured the files melted or waterlogged.

"The drawers are open and there are papers everywhere."

"That doesn't sound right." Peri retrieved a pair of gloves and an empty bag from her tote, and started up the ladder.

The legs wobbled slightly and her gloves felt awkward on the metal. She was able to grab the window casing within two steps and was halfway through the window by three. There was no graceful way to step into the room, so she slid forward, catching herself on the floor with her hands and crawling until her legs were free.

The room wasn't blackened, but it was still damp, and the carpet sparkled with shards of colored glass. She felt a prick in her kneecap as her leg hit the floor.

"Ow." She brushed the glass from her leg and examined her slacks for holes.

"It's kind of a mess in here," Tom said as he helped her to her feet.

"I know but what you said—Benny doesn't go in these files. I don't know why papers would be out."

She looked around, following the glow from Tom's flashlight. It didn't take long to view the small, Fifties-style bedroom and locate a black metal cabinet. Both drawers were open and papers were half-stuffed in folders, like handkerchiefs in suit pockets. More papers covered the bed, and the floor.

The room smelled like mildew already, mixed with a heavy dose of floral cologne and the lingering odor of the body.

"Tom, were you in this room the day of the fire?"

He shook his head. "No, I was busy with the living room."

She removed one glove and dug her phone from her pocket. "Skip? I'm at Benny's house, trying to get some insurance papers for him. When you were in Mrs. Needles' bedroom, was the file cabinet open and papers everywhere?"

"Why are you at Benny's? Don't you know it's dangerous?" Skip's deep voice raised in alarm.

"Don't worry, I'm under supervision. Tom Flores from the fire department is helping me. Now what about the file cabinet?"

"I don't remember a file cabinet. Hold on." Peri heard a muffled conversation of more than a minute. "Jason looked at his photos to verify," he told her. "The cabinet was closed."

"Well it's open now and there are papers tossed everywhere."

"Leave it alone. We'll be right there."

Peri turned to Tom. "Have you got a few minutes to hang out? PPD's coming over to collect some more evidence. Seems like someone else has been in here after the fire."

She could see his eyes widen in the dim light. "How is that possible?"

"I don't know, but let's get out of here so we don't contaminate the room."

Tom nodded and backed out of the window, onto the ground. Peri left the empty bag on the floor and followed. After some awkward window-straddling and Tom's helpful guidance, her feet were both on the ladder and she was soon outside again. She looked around the base of the house.

"Whoever was here must've left some sign of entry, prints in the mud or something."

They began to walk around the house, looking for the telltale marks of a break-in. They stopped in front, where there were numerous prints in the mud.

"We were all over this area." Tom pointed to the deep boot marks.

Peri stared at the ground. "If I were trying to sneak into a burned building, would I want to walk through the part that's been destroyed and boarded up?"

Tom smiled at her. "Let's try the other side."

The tracks disappeared on the far side, except for some under the second, untouched window in Mrs. Needles' room. Four deep, rectangular furrows, surrounded by footprints. Tom reached up to the bars on the window. They were loose.

"That looks like a ladder," Peri said. "And those look like it was just one person. Of course, I'm no expert."

"You're not? I thought you were a P.I."

"Well, yeah." She laughed. "I guess I am the expert, then. But we'll still wait for Skip and Jason to collect the evidence."

"Good idea," Skip said as he walked up behind them. "What are we looking at?"

Peri showed him what they'd found. "Tom and I figure this is where the guy entered. You'll see what he did inside."

Jason joined them, bag over his shoulder, and a ball cap covering his dark blond hair. "What's first?"

As the CSU officer took pictures of the disturbed ground around the window, Peri informed Skip of what she and Tom had done.

"As soon as I realized you'd need to process the room, we left it," she said. "Like good and responsible professionals."

Skip rolled his eyes. "And because you wanted to search for where the guy might have entered."

"Well, that, too. But I didn't touch anything in the room, other than my hands and knees on the floor, getting in. Oh, and I left an empty bag inside."

"Why?"

"I was here to get some legal papers for Benny. Basically, he doesn't know anything about his insurance, his house, anything. I brought the bag to put the papers in. I thought, once Jason's done his thing, you could put everything from the file cabinet into the bag." She sighed. "Perhaps Mrs. Nickels wouldn't mind helping me sort through Benny's life."

Skip smiled. "He says he's your employee. Don't suppose you could pay him to go through his own papers?"

"I could try it, but I'm pretty sure if Dean Martin's name isn't on it, I won't get him to read it."

"You're probably right." He stepped over to the ladder. "Wait here."

He climbed the steps and swung his leg into the window with a minimum of effort. Peri stood and watched.

You may be in good shape, girl, she told herself, *but face it. You're a klutz.*

A minute later, Jason followed Skip into the room. Tom walked over to Peri.

"What do you think they were looking for?" he asked.

Peri shook her head. "I haven't a clue. As far as I know, the Needles were just another boring, middle-class family."

"Ain't no such thing." He laughed. "My family's boring and middle-class. Didn't stop my great-grandmother from killing her first husband with a butcher knife."

She considered his response and thought about what she knew of Benny and his family. She had started cleaning their house when Benny was fifteen, which was about twenty years ago. His mother, Beth, seemed old even then. A short, stocky woman who always wore cotton shifts in small, flowered patterns, covered by decorative aprons, Mrs. Needles was a wonderful cook who doted on her only child.

Peri never knew Benny's dad. It took her a few years to discover that Mr. Needles had left when Benny was ten. Neither Ben nor his mom liked to discuss it. She often wondered why. Was there another woman? Did he finally just succumb to the difficulties of raising someone like Benny?

After fifteen minutes, she heard Skip's voice.

"Heads up."

Her bag, stuffed with papers, dropped to the ground. Peri grabbed it and hefted the handle over her arm. She watched Skip and Jason descend.

"There was definitely someone inside, but I don't know what they took. Jason got some prints off the cabinet. We'll see how they check out." He gestured to the bag. "If Benny can't identify what was in the cabinet, how will he know what's missing?"

CHAPTER 9

How, indeed, would Benny know anything about anything, Peri thought as she sat on her living room floor, sorting through her client-employee's paperwork. It took her two hours to find a way to categorize what she was filing. Mrs. Needles had kept utility and mortgage statements for at least five years, and manuals for every appliance they'd ever bought, since the fifties.

There were personal items, too. Peri found Benny's report cards showing a student who excelled in science but drowned in literature. There were school pictures, of a young boy with perpetually untamed dark hair and confusion in his smile.

She pulled out a manila envelope and shook its contents onto the floor. More pictures fell out, along with a smaller white envelope. There was a wedding picture of Benny's parents.

Beth looked beautiful in a white satin dress with a lace bodice and full veil. Her groom appeared a head taller, leaning toward her in a standard tuxedo. It was the first time Peri had seen Benny's dad. She looked at the back of the picture. *Robert and Elizabeth Needles, June 8, 1967.*

A second picture was of Robert holding an infant. Peri verified, from the back, it was Benny and his dad. She could see Benny in his dad's eyes, and the fullness of his mouth. From Beth, he got his height and girth.

The last photo was of the three of them. Benny looked to be about ten, meaning this was probably the last picture they took as a family. Beth still wore a simple cotton dress, although she had removed her apron. They sat in their living room. Peri recognized the lean, Seventies-style gold couch. Robert sat upright, almost apart from Beth. Benny sat on the floor, between them. Beth smiled for the camera. Robert also smiled, but his mouth looked awkward, as if his jaw was clenched. Benny stared at the ground.

One small, happy family.

Picking up the smaller envelope, she turned it over. It was addressed to Benny. *In the event of my death, please open.* It was signed *Robert Benjamin Needles*.

Peri sat back on her haunches. Wow, a letter from Benny's dad. Bet it explained a lot of things. *Wonder if he knows about this? Wonder if I should give it to him? Who knows if his dad is alive or not?*

She put the pictures and letter back in the large envelope, set it aside, and kept filing papers. One hour, two iced teas and a bowl of popcorn later, the tote bag was empty and her floor was full. Unfortunately, none of the papers included any insurance or banking information.

"Great, Ben. Now what?" she said to herself. She had turned on the TV, to the classic movie channel. The Thin Man was playing. Nora Charles was ordering five martinis.

"Save one of those for me," Peri told her, and rose from the floor. She stretched out her back, then picked up the phone and called Benny.

"Miss Peri, when is the insurance company going to pay me? I don't want to stay with my aunt anymore. I want to be in a hotel."

"I don't know. Are you sure the insurance papers were in your mom's cabinet?" She didn't want to tell him about the break-in.

"Yes. My mom always said anything I needed would be in there."

"Well, it wasn't."

"You're wrong. It has to be there."

She realized she couldn't argue without telling him the truth. "I'm sure you're right, it probably was there. We had a little problem, though. Um, when I went to get the papers today, well... someone had been in your mom's room again."

"Why are people in my house?" His voice sounded like he'd been sucking helium. "No one is supposed to be in my house. They need to keep out. Keep out—"

"Benny, Benny, Benny." Peri tried to get his attention. "Calm down. We don't know why they were in your house, but we will figure this all out."

"I don't have anything." The voice had become a wail. "My stuff is all gone. I don't even have my music here at Auntie's. She doesn't have the right player for my tapes."

No one has an eight-track player except you, Peri thought. "Try to be a little patient. We'll get it all taken care of." She added, "I suppose, in the meantime, you can listen to your music in your car."

There was silence on the other end.

"Work with me, Benny. It will all get better. By the way, I know your dad left when you were young. Do you know whether he's still alive?" She knew a change of subject might be a bad idea, but curiosity overruled her sense of survival.

"We don't talk about my dad. I gotta go."

With those few words, the conversation was over.

Peri went to the kitchen and got another iced tea, then looked at her watch. It was four o'clock in the afternoon, so she put the tea back and got a beer. It seemed more appropriate for how she felt. She wandered back into the living room and gathered the paperwork, carefully putting it into the bag so it could be properly replaced in its original cabinet. She saved the manila envelope for last, and considered giving it to Benny. In the end, she decided to stay out of his family matters, and put it with the other papers.

Nick and Nora were still on TV, still drinking, joking, and solving murders. Peri lifted her beer to them in a salute.

"It's easy for you two," she told them. "You don't work with Benny."

The slam of the back door and sound of footsteps let her know Skip had arrived. The whoosh of the refrigerator said he needed a beer, too. She walked into the kitchen and greeted him with a kiss.

"Rough day?"

He nodded. "I was almost thinking it was an unfortunate chain of events. Autopsy is showing the McHale boy was so pumped with drugs and alcohol, he wouldn't have survived the night without medical intervention. I'm figuring he stumbles in, high as a kite, passes out in the bedroom and suddenly there's a fire. We're still waiting for the fire investigator's report, but it could have been accidental."

"Except for the paint cans, which don't belong, and the break-in today," Peri said. "That's got your Spidey senses all tingly."

They walked into the living room as they spoke.

"More or less. The kid still may be collateral damage. The fire is looking more suspicious." He looked down at the bag of papers. "Should I even ask if there was anything missing?"

"Depends. According to Benny, the insurance papers were in there, except now they're not. We do have five years' worth of mortgage statements, except the house has been paid off for three years, all the appliance manuals you could ask for, oh—and this." She picked up the manila envelope and showed Skip the contents. "Benny's dad. Cool, huh? And a letter. Wonder what it says."

"I'm surprised you didn't try to open it. Do you know if his dad is still alive?"

"I asked Benny about it. He hung up on me. I mean, I knew he and his mom didn't like to talk about his dad, but he's determined not to talk about him at all."

Skip looked at the pictures before replacing everything in the envelope. "What a family."

"Speaking of family, how's your daughter's wedding plans?"

He laughed and grabbed her by the waist, steering her to the sofa. "This morning I got a plaintive call from her. Her little wedding in Chicago with just family and dinner at a restaurant is becoming a Hollywood production with a cast of thousands, thanks to her mom."

"Oh, poor thing." Peri snuggled in beside him and put her head on his shoulder. "What did you tell her?"

"I offered to pay for her and her fiancé to go to Vegas and elope. Other than that, I reminded her I never could control her mom, even when we were married."

"At least Amanda sounds reasonable."

Skip chuckled. "Not really. She just likes to be contrary to her mom."

"What daughter doesn't? I mean, I got along great with Helen, but I still found myself pushing away from her, trying to carve my own life out. I think it's a matter of same-sex children. My brother wanted to be his own man, so he fought Eric all the time."

"You never talk much about your brother."

"Dev." She frowned. "Endeavor. Two years younger than me. We haven't spoken in years. Not since Helen's funeral."

"Bad blood?"

"Not really. I mean, no Battle Royale or anything. Dev just… hated us."

Skip winced. "That's pretty strong."

"But pretty true. Eric and Helen were free spirits, hippies, beatniks, whatever. They didn't impose their values on us, tried to let us grow up to 'be who we were destined to be.' I was okay with that, I mean, we had a big fight over my going to UCI instead of Berkeley, but I knew they still loved me. Dev hated the freedom. It was like a desire for structure was in his DNA. He hated them for not providing it. He left our farm when he was sixteen. I had to track him down when Helen died—he'd even changed his name. When Eric passed, I didn't bother."

"Same family, such different kids," Skip said. "It cracks me up to hear you call your parents by their first names."

"And it cracks me up that it cracks you up. It really wasn't a big deal." She took another sip of beer. "If I'd had kids, they'd have called me Peri."

"How would your husband have felt about that?"

"None of them would have gone for it, except the third one, but he was gay. Which is why I never had kids."

"It's not too late, is it?" Skip asked.

She laughed. "At fifty? Yes, sir. And why would you want to start all over, when your last one is almost married off?" She took his beer and set both bottles on the table. "But we can practice all you like."

He enfolded her in his arms as she caressed his face and they kissed, sliding further down the soft leather sofa. Before long, they were removing pieces of clothing until nothing remained between them and there was nothing left to do but whatever came naturally. After some time, they were tamed and quiet and lay in a tangle, listening to each other's breathing, another old movie providing background noise on TV.

"What do you want for dinner?" Peri's voice was muffled against Skip's chest.

"Don't know. Do we have to go out?"

"No, but it narrows your choices to ice cream or call for pizza."

"Had pizza for lunch."

"How do you feel about Ben and Jerry's for dinner?"

Skip sat up and tossed Peri her shirt. "I feel like putting my clothes back on and hitting Marie's for some chili and cornbread."

"I'm gonna need more than my shirt for that." She gathered her clothes and headed to the bathroom. "Marie's, huh? I'll try to have salad, but you know I'll want pie."

CHAPTER 10

The evening crowd was heavy at Marie Callender's in the Placentia Town Center, forcing Skip and Peri to park in the larger parking lot that served the discount stores. Several families shared the small entrance, with children trying to escape their parents' efforts to corral them.

Skip turned to Peri. "Care to eat in the bar?"

"Love to."

They found an open booth and sat down. Peri looked around. The bar itself had four patrons, men who were watching baseball on TV, but there were a few people in the booths. She spotted a familiar couple at one of the tables.

"Hey, it's Phil and Nancy," she told Skip, waving at them. "Get me a Sam Adams. I'm going to go say hello."

Peri went over to their table, reaching across to give each one a hug.

"We just came in for a bite before we go to the movies," Nancy told her.

"How's Benny's house doing?" Phil asked. "Is the insurance company working on it yet?"

"What insurance company?" Peri replied. "Benny doesn't know who his insurance company is, or even who his bank is. I can't find his accounts anywhere. I admit, I'm kind of frustrated right now."

Phil looked troubled. "That's too bad."

"You're such a good investigator." Nancy patted her arm and glanced at her husband. "I'm sure you'll figure it all out."

Peri saw Skip motioning to her. The server was trying to take their order. With another hug, she returned to her booth.

"I'll have the chicken fettucine," she told the young man, then turned to Skip. "I left my phone in your car. I forgot, I was going to call Beebs about our lunch date tomorrow."

He tossed her the keys. Peri excused her way through the people waiting to be seated and strode to the parking lot. The sun was making a last attempt at lighting the southern California sky before it disappeared behind the horizon. As she reached into the passenger seat of Skip's car, Peri heard a cacophony of young male voices. She glanced to her right and saw a forest green SUV, filled with the shadows of several occupants.

Several loud occupants, who were accompanied by a thumping bass line from their stereo. The driver's door was cracked open, allowing the sound to spill through the air.

Peri locked Skip's car and turned to walk back to the restaurant, when she caught a glimpse of the boys getting out. There were four of them, laughing and poking one another, jumping on each other's backs, and generally behaving like exuberant teenagers.

Peri could feel them coming closer as she returned to the restaurant. Within five steps, they had overtaken her. They parted, two by two, to pass. As they blew by, they left a cloud of beer and marijuana in her nostrils. She recognized a head of dark, curly hair.

"Nick?"

The boy slowed as his name was called, then stopped and turned.

"Hi, Aunt Peri."

As if throwing the weak one to the wolves, the rest of the herd continued toward the Baskin Robbins store on the corner. Blanche's son remained, caught, to talk to his mom's friend.

Peri wasn't certain how to start a conversation that had to end with *Gee, you smell funny*. "How have you been?"

"Good." Nick shifted back and forth, gazing past her, toward his buddies, who were disappearing into the distance.

She stared at him until he looked at her. Even in the dusk, his eyes were bloodshot. There was no way she could play nice. "So, Nick. How much have you had tonight?"

He smiled. "How much of what?"

"Beer and grass, buddy. I can smell both on you."

"Nah, it was just my friends, they were—"

Peri stopped him. "Don't screw with me, Nick. I'm your Aunt Peri, the one with the Super Sniffer."

He hung his head and said nothing.

"Here's the deal. Your business is your business, but your mom is my best friend and I love you kids. I can't let you drive anywhere else with your friends. It's not safe."

"What are you gonna do? Don't call my mom, Aunt Peri. Please."

Peri stood and considered their options. Her phone vibrated once. She saw a text from Skip. *WTH R U DOIN?*

"Right now, I think you should come to dinner with me and Skip," she said at last. "Sober up. Then we'll figure out what to do from there."

They both went into the restaurant. Skip's eyes widened when he saw Nick.

"I found Nick in the parking lot," Peri said. "He's going to have dinner with us."

Skip extended his hand. "Hey, Nick, how are you?"

The boy lowered his head, not meeting Skip's eyes and shook his hand quickly, then sat at the far edge of the booth, as if he was ready to bolt at any second.

Skip looked at Peri and nodded. She knew he'd seen plenty as a detective, and that he could tell when someone had indulged in both drugs and alcohol.

"Do you want a menu, Nick? Or would you just like a burger?"

"A burger would be fine, Detective Carlton." Nick's shoulders sagged.

Peri patted his arm. "Look, Nick, we all know what you've been doing, but we're not going to get on your case about it. We'll just have a nice dinner and get your head a little clearer."

"And you can call me Skip," the detective added.

Peri summoned the waiter and got Nick's food ordered, along with a soda.

"Are you gonna tell my folks?" he asked.

Skip and Peri looked at one another. Peri finally spoke. "Nick, I've never been able to keep a secret from your mom, but I'm willing to at least not tell her if you tell her first."

"Oh, I can't." His eyes appeared fearful and pleading.

"I know it's not going to be an easy discussion, but I've watched your parents raise you. You should be able to tell them anything."

"But Aunt Peri, we were just out messing around, partying. All the kids do it."

"I know a lot of kids do it." Skip's deep voice sounded like God issuing a commandment. "And more than once, I've had to clean them off the road where they've wrapped their car around a tree, or killed someone else. No one thinks it's going to happen to them. Everyone, including me, thinks alcohol doesn't affect them as much as it does."

He held up his glass. "See this beer? Do I think I could drink it down, then go get in my car and drive responsibly? Of course I do. But realistically, I can't. A little bit impaired is still impaired. Which is why I'm having one beer with dinner, and I plan to be here for an hour. I'm not going to risk my life, my career, or someone else's life because I think I can handle more than that."

"Are these guys your normal party crew?" Peri asked.

"Sort of. Not really. We kind of hung together a little before Alex..." He trailed off. "Now we're tighter."

"And you're partying more," she said.

Nick nodded.

Their food arrived, and they were silent. Peri watched Nick as he demolished his cheeseburger and fries, in the neatest, most efficient way possible.

"You have great table manners, Nick. Even when you're not—yourself."

He smiled. "I'm not that bad, Aunt Peri. I drank two beers and probably got three or four hits."

"Still too many," Skip told him. "What about your friends?"

"Oh, man, Detective, I mean—Skip, are you gonna bust them?" Nick looked horrified. "They'll think I did it."

"If your buddies are smart, they've taken off. If we leave and they're still there, I'm calling it in. Otherwise, unless you want to give me their license plate number, all I can do is hope they make it home." Skip sat back and glared at him. "Look, I know being a teenager means doing stupid things sometimes. What pisses me off is, I can't believe you guys thought you could come slumming over to Placentia to be stupid. Next time, keep your antics in your own neighborhood."

Nick hung his head. "I'm sorry. I know I shouldn't have, but getting high lets me forget for awhile."

"Forget what?" Peri asked.

His head jerked up. "Nothing. I mean..." He fumbled around for words. "Um, just the pressure, you know. Grades. College. Stuff."

They left the restaurant and saw an empty parking space where his friends used to be.

Nick sighed. "What now?"

Skip unlocked his SUV and opened the back door. "Now we take you home. We'll drop you off, and you can go inside and tell your parents what happened."

"I'm having lunch with your mom tomorrow," Peri said. "I suggest you tell her before then. I won't bring the subject up, but if she starts talking about it, I won't lie."

She leaned forward and hugged him. "I know it won't be easy, Sweetie. We're all in your corner, rooting for you to succeed. No matter what happens, know that."

They got into the car and headed toward Yorba Linda. The trip was quiet. Peri listened to the low roar of the tires on the road, and felt lulled by the steady rocking movement. She wanted to say more to her best friend's son, to tell him to stay away from those guys and find something worthwhile to do. Perhaps she could let him know these years were full of everything, a roller coaster of highs and lows, and he could survive them if he just focused on getting through school. God knows Skip could give him tales of teens on drugs and alcohol, tales that ended badly.

By the time they reached the Debussy home, she hadn't said a thing. Skip pulled over to the curb and Nick got out.

"Thanks. For the ride," he said.

Peri and Skip watched him walk up the steps. He dug in his pocket, fiddled at the lock, opened it and stepped in. When the door closed, Skip looked at Peri.

"We've done all we can, Doll."

"I know you've been down this road before."

"Yeah." He pulled away from the curb. "I managed to dodge a bullet with my two, but I've watched other officers' kids crash and burn."

"Poor Blanche and Paul. I feel like I want to jump in and help, somehow, but I know parents can circle the wagons pretty quickly, even when they are your friends."

They were silent for awhile as Skip drove out of the upscale Yorba Linda neighborhood, toward Esperanza Road.

"Ever tempted to check in on your brother?" His voice was soft.

Peri didn't say anything at first. She had been thinking of Dev and their last meeting years ago, how empty it had seemed. He wasn't happy to see her, or sad or angry or anything. The memorial service had been in the small Presbyterian church where Helen volunteered. Peri helped her dad pick out flowers and a song, but the service itself was more like a gathering of people who stood around and told stories. As freeform as her parents, the event had been just the way Helen would have wanted it.

Eric announced there'd be a picnic at the house, and Peri watched her brother slip out the door. That was the last time she saw him.

She came out of her reverie. "Sometimes. On the one hand, he and I were never close, not even as kids. I was the big sister, but he was the one always yelling about me being in his space, bugging him. I'd say we have nothing in common, except I don't even know enough about him to say that."

"On the other hand?"

"I get this weird urge to be connected to him. He's family. I know Eric and Helen were casual about our roles, but he's my brother. If he's dead, I wouldn't even know it."

"Don't feel too bad. My youngest brother's back in jail."

"When did that happen?"

"Renette, my older sister, called yesterday. Bobby's in Arizona, felony B and E. We all decided we have to let him take his lumps this time. It's hard to stand back and watch it happen."

"Families." Peri shook her head. "How do we survive them?"

CHAPTER 11

The next morning, Peri picked up her cell phone and wandered through her bungalow, trying to dial Blanche's number. It was the first time she had felt tentative about talking to her best friend. If Nick hadn't told his parents what happened and she let it slip, life could get awkward. She loved Blanche.

They had been friends since high school, good friends, without a lot of teenaged drama. Peri didn't want to start fighting now.

She finally pulled a bottle of cranberry juice out of her refrigerator and sat down at the small table in her kitchen. The hard seat and straight back lent some stiffness to her spine, so she pulled up Blanche's number and pressed SEND.

"Hey, Beebs, we up for lunch?" She tried to keep her voice normal.

To her surprise, it was Blanche who sounded cagey. "Um, yeah, can I get a rain check? I'm really swamped at the office here. I'm afraid I let my paperwork slide."

"Sure. Everything okay?"

"Oh, yeah." Blanche's deep voice would have sounded normal to anyone else's ears, but Peri heard the lie in those two words.

She decided to play along, but leave the light on. "Well, give me a call when you come up for air. If you need help with anything, I'm available."

Peri heard the beep of the call ending and felt a vague unrest. After convincing herself Nick would get through this phase without harm, she suddenly realized how hard it would be to watch him struggle.

Her phone rang, so she picked it up. It was Benny's number, although it seemed early for him to be conscious.

"Miss Peri, they want my money." He shrieked so loud that she had to hold the phone away from her ear.

"Calmer, Ben. Who wants your money?"

Calm was relative, but he managed to slow his words. "A man came to my door, woke me up, Woke. Me. Up. Gave me a paper. That boy's parents, the boy who died, that boy's parents are suing me. Suing. Me."

"The McHales? How could they be suing you already? We don't even have the investigator's report." Peri found his anger contagious. "You should be suing them for their son breaking into your house. How dare they?"

"What are we going to do?"

"What exactly does the paper say?"

Benny's voice lifted again. "I don't know, I can't read this stuff. I just know their names are under Plaintiff and my name is under Defendant and there's something about willful negligence and punitive damages—what does that mean?"

"It means you need an attorney. Do you have one?"

"Just the one who talked to the judge when I went to jail." Benny's brief life of crime consisted of paying a police officer to steal a ring from the evidence room, a deed which earned him a month behind bars and a hundred community service hours.

"He's a criminal lawyer. I don't know if he does lawsuits." She paused for a moment. "Let me talk to Skip. He may know of a lawyer who can help. I'll call you back."

Skip sounded just as surprised by Benny's news. "I still haven't seen the report, so I don't know what basis they've got to say he was negligent."

"Well, I gotta admit, Skip, he was pretty negligent when it came to taking care of his property. But I never thought the McHales would sue him because their son broke into his house on the one night it caught fire."

"People grieve in different ways, Doll."

"I just wish I knew something, anything. I'm supposed to be helping Benny and I've never felt so tied up, like there's nowhere to turn to get information."

"I'm finally getting an appointment with the McHale family today. Maybe I can get a feel for why they filed so soon. It's not unusual for people to file a suit like this, figuring the insurance companies will hash it all out and no one has to pay actual money."

"Wow, I'd love to hear what they have to say. Any way you could—"

Skip interrupted her. "No, I'm not taking you with me. It's against department protocol."

"You've done it before."

"And I think I've learned my lesson."

"I promise to behave."

She heard him chuckle. "Yeah, that'll happen."

"Come on, Skipper." Peri knew how desperate she sounded. "I need the information."

"Absolutely not." She heard the dip in his voice that signaled finality. There'd be no trip as his sidekick.

She said the only thing she could think of. "You're mean."

"Tell you what. Go get those legal papers Benny received and read through them, see if you can figure out what the McHales want. Then call David Campbell. He was great when Benny got busted for receiving stolen goods. If he doesn't handle personal injury, he might know someone who does."

"And you'll tell me what the McHales say."

She heard him sigh. "If it's helpful to Benny. But that's all."

"Well, thanks for that much, I guess. Want to go to lunch?"

Skip didn't answer at first, but Peri could hear his quiet mumbling while he tried to make a decision. "Can't. I'm meeting the McHales at two, and I've got a stack of reports to go through before that. Dinner?"

"That'll work. See you tonight."

Peri ended the call and leaned back into her chair. She should get dressed and go see Benny at his aunt's house. If she could read the lawsuit, it might help her figure out why the McHales filed it so quickly. Of course, asking them would get her an answer a lot faster. She looked at her watch. It was almost nine-thirty. Skip wouldn't be able to give her anything until late afternoon.

Peri got up and went into the bedroom. She picked out a pair of white slacks and a bright turquoise top. In fifteen minutes, she was dressed and primped for the day.

I'm going to see Benny, she told herself. *Going to Aunt Esmy's house.*

She grabbed her tote, her cell phone, and keys, and headed out the door. Easing her blue Honda sedan out of the drive, she angled it right and drove toward Bradford Avenue. Her intention was to turn right and go to Aunt Esmy's, which was off Chapman, near Central. Instead, she turned left, toward Yorba Linda Boulevard and the McHale residence.

Maybe I'll just drive by the house, check it all out.

The McHales did not live far from the Debussys, but their homes only resembled each other in their sense of luxury. This was a long, low ranch-style, painted in pale yellow with stone façade. The front lawn stretched out in perfect green to the sidewalk, buffered from the house by bright flower gardens.

Peri pulled over to the curb and stopped. She sat and admired the home's lean lines, the way the stones had been fitted together to make a planter around the two large windows. There was a small courtyard in front, fenced by two squat stone columns and a wrought iron gate.

A slight figure moved inside the yard, kneeling, bending, then rising. Peri got out of the car. Whoever was working in the courtyard, she would see what kind of information they could give her.

The woman did not appear to notice her walking up. Peri stopped at the gate and watched her. She was tall, dressed in pale blue capris and a sleeveless top. Her arms were tanned and sculpted, her short, dark hair tucked behind her ears. As Peri stood behind her, she plucked the faded blooms from one of the rose bushes, placing them in the basket hanging on her arm.

"Some of these I won't prune," she said. "That way I'll have some rose hips to cook with."

Peri wasn't sure if the woman was talking to her but answered her anyway. "That's a good idea."

"Ordinarily it's best to prune your roses. It encourages them to bloom."

"Yes, ma'am."

"You must be disciplined if you want beautiful roses. But if you have beautiful roses, you won't have the hips, and they're so good for cooking."

"Mrs. McHale?"

The woman turned to Peri. Her face was pale and lined, and her brown eyes were sunken in dark circles, rimmed in crimson from crying. "Discipline is key for beautiful roses."

"Mrs. McHale, my name is Peri Minneopa and I'm a friend of Benny Needles."

"Who?"

"The man who owned the house your son—" She couldn't finish. "I stopped by to tell you how sorry I am for your loss."

"Children need discipline, too. I didn't understand with Alex. I thought love and understanding was enough."

"I'm sure you did your best."

71

"My girls are easy." Mrs. McHale gazed at the pavement. "I saw so much of my brother in him, I thought that's the way boys are." She lifted her head, as if hearing a sudden noise. "Needles? Was that his name?"

"Yes. I was hoping you could help me understand why you filed a lawsuit so soon. We don't even have the fire investigator's report."

"What lawsuit?"

They were interrupted by the slam of a door. A tall, broad man stomped out and put his hand on Mrs. McHale's shoulder. Peri recognized him from a recent article in the *Placentia News-Times*. He looked larger in person, dark haired, with a swath of gray at the temples, and brown eyes.

"Excuse me, but who are you?"

"I'm Peri Minneopa and I'm a friend of Benny Needles, Mr. McHale. I just came by to offer my condolences and perhaps ask why—"

Mrs. McHale turned to her husband. "She asked me about a lawsuit. What lawsuit, Matt?"

Peri saw his jaw clench.

"I think you should be talking to our attorney," he said.

"Sir, all I'm trying to understand is why you would file so quickly. Benny is devastated and I told him I'd help if I could."

"We all know Mr. Needles kept a messy home." He had a patronizing tone that made Peri want to punch him. Still, she was there to get information and that meant playing nice.

"Mr. McHale, Benny hasn't even contacted his insurance company. Shouldn't you wait—"

He cut her off with a hand wave. "It doesn't matter. Benny Needles has two million dollars in the bank and a corner lot that's worth something. I don't need the insurance company. The report says it was negligence, anyway."

Peri felt her blood pressure rise. "Maybe his house is disorganized, but I know it was locked when your son broke in."

Mrs. McHale burst into tears and ran inside.

"Get off my property." His jaw was now locked, his cheeks purple and his neck a roadmap of veins.

Peri turned to go then stopped and faced him. "By the way, Mr. McHale, how do you know how much money Benny has in the bank? That kind of information is usually confidential."

He pointed to the road. "Get. Out."

But she wasn't finished yet. "And how is it you know what the fire investigator's report says, when no one else has received a copy?"

"Get the hell off my property or I'm getting my gun." His voice had the solemnity of pure rage, so she retreated to her car.

That went well, she thought as she drove off. *Maybe now I should go to Benny's.*

As she maneuvered out of the neighborhood, Peri considered calling Skip. Grieving or not, McHale should not have access to Benny's finances. And why did he have a copy of James Murray's report? Skip had told her earlier, he didn't even have one yet. At the stop sign on Esperanza Road, she picked up her cell phone and pressed Skip's number. He was going to interview the McHales at two, so he should know that—

She stopped. *He should know what? That I got there before he did and started a fight? I may not have started it, but I certainly threw gasoline on it.*

It was possible McHale had already called the police, although he wouldn't call Placentia for something that happened in Yorba Linda. Either way, Skip was going to be furious with her, and there was little to no chance of him not finding out.

I might as well get ahead of this and try to explain it. He'll be twice as mad if he's ambushed. She pressed SEND.

"Hey, Doll."

At the sound of his voice, Peri fought her urge to press END. "Skip, I'm glad I caught you. I need to tell you something before you go to the McHales'."

A few seconds of silence ticked by, until Skip said, "I'm waiting."

"I drove past their house awhile ago. I wasn't going to talk to them, but Mrs. McHale was outside and I thought it was a karmic opportunity to pay my respects and see why they were suing Benny."

"Peri." She could hear his disapproval in those two syllables.

"Honest to Pete, I was polite, I was sincere, I was not rude or pushy in the least." She paused. "Okay, here's what you need to know: One, Mrs. McHale did not know anything about the lawsuit; it was all Mr. McHale's doing. Two, McHale has already at least seen the fire investigator's report, if he doesn't have a copy. Three, he has intimate knowledge of Benny's finances. That can't be legal.

"Oh, and four, he chased me off his property and threatened to get his gun."

"Peri." His words were brusque. "Why do you make my job so hard?"

"I didn't know I was always such a burden."

"Well, not always, I just meant that, I hate interviewing parents who've lost a child and I'd rather visit when they're not as raw, emotionally. I can usually get them to help me. Sounds like I'm going to be walking into a hornet's nest. All thanks to you."

"Skip, I had no intention of stirring things."

"You never do."

"Seriously, I didn't provoke anyone." She told him about the conversation with Mrs. McHale and Mr. McHale's subsequent interruption. "So you see? He started it."

"But you finished it, which doesn't help me."

"Could you call and postpone your interview? Give them a chance to cool down?"

"Suppose I could, but either way, it sounds like McHale has enough connections to know you're not just Benny's 'friend' and you are more than a 'friend' to me."

"Look, I'm sorry. But I have to do my job."

"I know. When it comes to your job, this is not my first rodeo."

"Yee haw, Cowboy." A car horn behind her told Peri she had been stopped at the sign a little too long. "I gotta go, but call me if you still want dinner tonight. Love you, Skipper."

"You, too."

There was no preceding growl of resignation to his "you, too," which Peri took as a good sign that he was not as angry as he could have been. She turned right and headed toward Chapman Avenue, to Benny's aunt's house.

Fifteen minutes later, she had pulled up to the curb in front of a standard, single-story southern California home, Seventies style. The beige stucco exterior gave the edges a soft look, and the arch over the entryway was reminiscent of the Spanish heritage of the area. A glossy black Cadillac sat in the short driveway, fins gleaming in the morning sun.

Peri steeled herself for entrance into Esmy's house. Her first visit to Benny's aunt had revealed a somewhat obsessive hobby—taxidermy. Esmy had filled her home with creatures she had personally stuffed and mounted.

Just as Benny had his collection of Dino memorabilia, Esmy had her compilation of roadkill.

Peri rang the doorbell and waited. In addition to the muffled strains of music, she heard shuffling footsteps, then an impatient fumbling at the locks. Finally, the door opened, revealing a very nervous Benny.

"Miss Menopause, I'm so happy to see you." He spoke at full volume, to be heard over Dean Martin's crooning.

She felt her jaw spasm in annoyance. "Peri, Benny. Call me Peri. Call me Miss Peri. Call me anything but that."

"I forgot I forgot come in come in." His jumble of words matched his energy. "Aunt Esmy's at church right now."

Peri entered and looked around the room, her mouth open. There were no more owls perched on doorways or cats staring at her through glass eyes. The plethora of wildlife had been replaced.

Now there were flowers. Roses, lilacs, daisies, and more, on every table and shelf. Boughs over the doorways. Garlands hung across windows.

But it didn't smell like flowers. There was a spiciness to the air, cinnamon and nutmeg. At a loss for words, she gawked at the room. "Ben... what... how... what the hell happened?"

"Aunt Esmy figured she got too involved in stuffing dead things. Lost her perspective, you know? So she decided to mount flowers instead."

He took a rose from its vase and thumped it on the table. "Preserves them, see? They never die. They just get dusty."

"Wow. She's been busy."

Benny shoved a document into Peri's hands, before picking up his ashtray. "Yeah, some people are too obsessive."

She watched him rub the smooth glass, the only Dean Martin remnant he had been allowed since the fire. "It's better to be just obsessive enough, I guess."

Taking a seat at the round oak table in the kitchen, she read through the lawsuit. As far as she could tell, it accused Benny of not properly maintaining his home, resulting in a fire that caused loss of life. There was, of course, no mention of the fact that the life lost was in his house illegally.

"Benny," she said at last. "I understand most of this, but I'm no lawyer. Skip recommends we call the guy who helped you last time, David Campbell. Do you have his number?"

He stood upright, chin lifted and shoulders back, as if in a recitative trance. "David Campbell. Five-five-five, three-nine-eight-six."

Peri regarded his intense focus. "I'm going to give him a call and see if we can offload the legal crap onto him." She dug her cell phone from her tote. "What was his number again?"

As before, Benny snapped to attention and rattled off the numbers while she entered them in her phone. A secretary answered.

To her relief, the secretary put her through to the attorney. David Campbell remembered both of them ("Benny's not a guy you forget"), and after she had explained the lawsuit, said he would be happy to help.

"I'm free today at two, if that works," he told her.

"Great, we'll be there." Peri ended the call and turned to Benny, who was now shuffling through his aunt's CD collection.

"It's a good thing I got her that CD last Christmas," he said. "She wouldn't have any Dean Martin in the house at all if I hadn't."

"Yeah, good thing. Listen, we're going to meet David at two today." Peri glanced at her watch. It was barely breaking twelve. "Why don't we go grab something to eat first? I need to make some notes."

"Antonia's?"

She felt her hand flutter across her hips and winced. The Italian restaurant by the post office was definitely good, but nothing on the menu was under twelve hundred calories and she was trying to fit into last year's shorts.

"I was thinking more Panera today," she told him. "Can we do Antonia's for dinner later? I just want a quick sandwich, or salad."

He pouted for a moment. "Ah, Miss Peri, I never get to—"

Dean Martin's baritone interrupted him. "Grab your coat, oh get your hat, leave your worries on the doorstep…"

Benny stared at the ground, shaking his head, then looked up at Peri. "Let's go to Panera's. Life can be sweet on the sunny side of the street."

"I'll keep that in mind, Ben." Picking up her keys, she added, "Let's go."

"Not yet, Miss Peri. I have to change."

She looked at him. He wore a pair of light gray slacks and a striped, short-sleeved shirt. In many ways, he was better dressed than she was.

"You look fine," she told him.

"I can't go to a lawyer looking like this. You wear a suit to see the lawyer."

"Well, I'm not going home to put on my pantyhose."

"Oh, Miss Peri, it doesn't matter what you wear. You're not the client."

While he went back to change clothes, she tried to decide whether he had insulted or complimented her.

79

CHAPTER 12

Skip stood at the front door of the McHale residence with his partner, Craig Daniels. They were there to interview the couple, and Skip readied himself for a lukewarm reception, if not an outright hostile exchange.

A young person's death was always tragic, but he would need to know the truth about Alex, while his parents would need to preserve a more saintly memory of their son.

"Do you think they know about you and Peri?" Craig asked. Skip had told him of her run-in, to keep his partner from being caught off-guard.

He heard footsteps inside the house. "We'll find out."

Matt McHale opened the door and looked both men up and down, as if deciding whether to slam it or not.

"Mr. McHale? I'm Detective Carlton, we spoke on the phone." He held up his badge, and waited for the screaming to start, or the punch to be thrown. To his surprise, he watched McHale's body relax.

"Detective, yes, I almost forgot about our appointment." McHale held the door open. "Come in."

Skip and Craig entered the large foyer and were ushered down a step, into an expansive great room. One end was a cozy gathering of sofas and chairs in soft, knobby fabric, clustered around a fireplace. At the other end was the game room, complete with pool table and mini-bar. Everything was in subdued tones of caramel, cream, and sky blue. The back wall of the room was floor-to-ceiling windows, revealing a natural rock pool and spa, an outdoor kitchen and dining area, and a magnificent view of the city below.

Two young dark-haired girls were outside, one draped across a chair, reading a book, and the other pacing beside the pool with a cell phone in her hand.

McHale pointed toward them. "Our daughters, Lisa and Erin." He turned back toward the detectives. "Make yourselves comfortable. I'll go get Christine."

Skip pulled out his pad and pen, looked around the room, and scribbled a few notes.

A few moments later, the couple came in. Matt McHale held his wife's arm with a light touch of his fingers. Christine McHale floated across the room, as if in a dream. She was a study in angles, from the precise cut of her straight, dark hair, to the sharp lines of her body. As she eased herself into one of the couches, Skip thought her knees might tear holes in her rust-colored slacks.

"Mr. and Mrs. McHale, we are very sorry for your loss." It was a cliché but Skip wanted them to know the PPD cared about their feelings. "We realize this will be difficult for you, but if we want to find the truth behind your son's death, we must ask you questions you might not want to answer."

Mrs. McHale nodded, slowly lowering her head, until she finally took a deep breath and sat up. "I'm ready, Detective."

"First of all, can you tell us about Alex's life at home? How had he been acting lately?"

"Same as always," his father said. "Typical teenager."

Skip saw Mrs. McHale flinch, so he asked her, "Is that correct?"

Her voice was so soft, Skip had to lean in to hear her. "His father says he was a typical teenager."

Skip and Craig exchanged glances. There was something to be found here, if they could get this couple to be honest.

"How was his school going?" Craig asked. "It looks like he'd missed a few days."

"His junior year had been difficult." Mrs. McHale dabbed at her eyes, but not before Skip saw her look up at her husband. "Allergies," she added.

"He was a good boy." Mr. McHale said it as if he were spouting a scientific truth. "A hard worker. Genius IQ. High school classes bored him. He was finishing his junior year and planning to apply to several East Coast schools in the fall. I'm a Duke man, myself, and was going to put in a good word for him at my alma mater."

Mrs. McHale shrank further into the sofa as her husband expounded on their son's virtues.

I suppose he volunteers at a homeless shelter and feeds stray kittens, too, Skip thought. He looked at Craig and raised his eyebrows, to see if his partner would like to be the bad cop. Craig stared at his notepad, indicating his disinclination to start the rumble.

Skip turned back to the couple. "Mr. and Mrs. McHale, I don't wish to be harsh, but this is not going to get us anywhere. We've been to Yorba Linda High School. We know Alex failed four of his six classes this year, and had been absent enough days to warrant a phone call from the superintendent. Even if he had made the classes up in summer school, you'd have to kiss Duke good-bye."

He paused to let them digest his knowledge of their son's activities. "The coroner's report shows he had a blood alcohol level of point-two-nine and enough OxyContin in his system to kill someone twice his size. If the smoke had not asphyxiated him, the combination of drugs and alcohol would have been lethal without immediate medical intervention."

At each statement, Skip watched Matt's face turn a deeper shade of red as his shoulders slumped forward. Christine wept harder with each fact.

"No," Matt said. "It's not true—"

His wife cut him off. "Stop lying, Matthew. It's true. All of it." She cried a little more, then spoke again. "Of course, my husband thinks Alex was a typical teenager. He was always at the office, while I was the one trying to get Alex to school, trying to get him to do homework, wondering where he was and when he'd be home.

"Christine—"

She pushed away from him, stood, and began pacing. "I kept telling myself he's always been independent. Always had to figure things out for himself, could never take my word for it the stove is hot or the pavement's hard or drinking too much will make you sick. My brother was a rebel, like him, and he turned out fine. I thought I understood him. I thought we had a common bond."

"Mrs. McHale." Skip stood and put his hand on her arm. "Would it be possible to see his room?"

She paused for a moment, staring at Skip's hand. Without a word, she nodded and walked toward the hallway. Skip and Craig followed her.

Sun lightened the hall from three open doors, two on the right and one on the left. The last door to the left was closed. Mrs. McHale stopped and turned the knob. Skip entered, Craig close behind.

The room was dark, so Skip felt along the wall for a switch while Craig went to the back of the room to open the curtains. A small lamp on the desk turned on first, revealing in the dimness a rumpled bed to the left and a wall of shelves to the right. Once the blackout curtains were pulled aside, the room gave up its secrets.

The rumpled bed was actually a tidy one with a stack of folded clothes on top. The black shelves were stocked with video games, controllers, and gaming systems. The rest of the room was fairly clean. A hamper stood in the corner, full of clothes. The newest iMac sat on the desk, surrounded by headphones, open game cases, and empty energy drink bottles. Walls were adorned with posters of solitary figures in shadows, with names like *Call of Duty* and *Halo* in scrawling video game font.

Craig inspected the shelves, moving things around, looking underneath and behind the games, while Skip sat down at the desk and opened the drawers. At some point, Skip looked up to see Mrs. McHale behind Craig, watching him go through things.

"Mrs. McHale," he said, causing her to jump back. "Can you tell us about Alex's friends?"

"Alex has had the same friends since grade school," Mrs. McHale told them. "I know their families."

Craig turned to him and they exchanged glances. After a few years as partners, it was all they needed. Craig put his hand lightly at her back, steering her in a quiet and gentle way toward the door. "Could you get me the names and addresses of those kids and their families?"

Her head lifted a little, as if pleased to be useful. "Yes, Detective. They're in my book in the kitchen."

While they went hunting for names, Skip completed his search of the room without interruption. He looked down at the bottom drawer he had opened. A stack of papers lay at odd angles, so he picked them up. Underneath was a bottle.

Whiskey, cheap and half-empty. Skip put it back in its place. He had a brief memory of his own teenage years, and a bottle being found in his room.

"Charles David, what is this?" his mom had demanded.

"Nothing, Mom. All the guys are doing it." He tried to sound nonchalant, but his mom's wrath had frightened him, even at sixteen.

He chuckled. His mom was ninety-three now and he still didn't want to get her mad.

Nothing in the other drawers gave him any clues as to Alex McHale. The top drawer had several scraps of paper with phone numbers, so he bagged those to look up later. He then turned on the computer. It asked him for a password. He'd ask the McHales but he'd probably have to take it back to Jason for processing.

Skip returned to the great room, where Mrs. McHale sat next to Craig on the couch, showing him a photo album. "Mrs. McHale, do you know your son's password for his computer?"

"No. We used to, but he changed it." She looked back at the pictures. "He changed a lot of things."

"We'd like to take his computer to our lab, if that's all right."

Craig reassured her. "We promise to return it."

She agreed, so Skip retrieved the iMac and loaded it into his SUV. Craig joined him, getting in the passenger seat while his partner took the wheel. They drove back to the station.

"What's your take?" Craig asked as he looked over his notes.

"I'm thinking it was the boy's rotten luck to OD in a house on fire. McHale didn't mention his encounter with Peri at our meeting. I confess, I'd like to know how he got all his information."

"Do you think he didn't mention it because he hadn't figured out who Peri is, or do you think he's got an agenda?"

"Not sure. He acted like the stereotypical workaholic dad who doesn't realize how bad it is at home."

"Maybe too stereotypical."

Skip nodded. "Maybe. I'd like to do a little checking on these friends of Alex before we talk to the McHales again."

"I don't know how much you'll enjoy checking on one of Alex's friends."

Skip grimaced. "Nick Debussy?"

Craig seemed surprised. "You talk to Blanche?"

"Actually, I saw Nick the other night. He and his buddies were in Placentia, drowning their troubles, with beer and weed. Gave him the talk, took him home, now Peri's hoping he told his folks what he's been up to. She doesn't want to be the one to tell Blanche."

"I wouldn't want to, either. Who'd want to deliver that kind of news?"

They pulled into the parking lot and walked into the station, Craig carrying the CPU. Jason met them at the door, smiling and bouncing.

"Good timing, Jason," Skip told him. "We were just going to hand this over to you for processing."

"Timing, nothing. Dispatch said you were coming in. I got something to show you. I found it on YouTube."

CHAPTER 13

Peri stood behind Benny at the counter of Panera Bread, waiting for him to stop grilling the perky young girl at the register about the source and quality of their ingredients. It had been an irritating ride to the restaurant, between Benny's curb-hugging, his insistence on playing Dean Martin songs at full volume, and his obsessive concern over the ashtray. The keepsake never left him now, and Peri often saw him rubbing it, as if to calm his nerves.

"Sir, you can't smoke in here," the girl behind the counter said.

"It's okay." Peri spoke up before Benny had a chance to argue about what Dean Martin would do if he were here. "It's a souvenir. He doesn't actually use it."

The smoking issue settled, Benny returned to his questions about the menu. Once he had moved past the Ciabatta bread and was asking what spices they used in their salami, she had to step in.

In his sharkskin suit, he might be the best dressed man in the restaurant, but he was also the most annoying.

"Benny, either order the sandwich or don't. You're holding up the line."

"This is why I don't like fast food. Everyone's in a hurry. No one has time to answer my questions."

"I understand, but we've got to be at David's office at two. All their sandwiches are tasty. Pick one."

At last he ordered the Italian club. Peri ordered a turkey on rye, and steered him toward the tables. The place was full of women with strollers and young people with laptops, but they managed to find a small table in the corner with two chairs.

Benny held up his empty cup. "Why did they give me this?"

"So you could get your drink." She motioned to the right. "There's a drink station around the corner."

"I don't know how."

"It's not rocket science, Ben. You press the buttons and stuff comes out."

He looked down at his sleek gray suit, tailored specifically to his short legs and round girth. "What if I splash on my clothes? This is my favorite suit. It's just like Dino wore in *Ocean's Eleven*."

"For Pete's sake—" She stopped. Arguing was a waste of time. "Give me your cup. What do you want?"

Peri took the cups to the station and filled both with ice and tea. She was digging out the appropriate lids and straws when she heard a familiar voice behind her.

"Hey, Aunt Peri." Blanche's daughter, Danielle, stood there with a tray in hand.

"Dani, hi, I forgot you work here. How are you doing?"

"Great but busy." The petite brunette had her hair pulled back into a long braid, showing her delicate features and large, dark eyes.

Peri looked down at the tray Dani was holding. "That looks like our meal."

"Yeah, I saw you guys order so I wanted to bring your food to you."

They maneuvered around the room until they arrived at the table.

"Benny, I don't know if you ever met Blanche's daughter, Danielle. Dani, this is Benny Needles."

Dani's eyes widened, along with her smile. "Mr. Needles, it's a pleasure to meet you." She picked the sandwiches from the tray and sat them on the table.

Peri handed him his drink and sat down. He held up his sandwich and began the slow process of evaluation by sight, smell and nibble. Finally he took a full bite, signaling his approval.

"I haven't seen much of your mom lately," Peri told her. "She says she's been busy."

Dani rolled her eyes. "That's one way to put it."

"Is there another way?"

"Mom's been having awful problems with Nick." Dani paused to look around the restaurant, then lowered her voice. "Ever since Alex died, he's been staying out all night, coming in smelling like alcohol and grass, and refusing to talk to Mom or Dad. He won't even say anything to me, except to, well, you-know-what off."

Peri felt a shadow pass across her heart. "Oh, Dani, I'm so sorry. Your mom said he knew Alex, but it didn't sound like they were that close."

"She might not have known how close they were, but they hung in the same pack."

"I'll give your mom a call."

Dani smiled. "Could you? I know she acts like she's all uber-strong, but if I was her, I'd want a friend around to listen. She holds it in, you know?"

"I know. Thanks, Dani. I'll bug her until she talks to me."

The young girl nodded, and turned to wait on another customer.

Peri looked over at Benny. "And what are we going to do about finding your insurance policy?" She took a bite of her sandwich and savored the tang of mustard, balanced by the soft, silky texture of mozzarella.

"I swear Momma always kept all the papers in the file cabinet."

"Well, they weren't in there. I suspect whoever broke in took them. But why?"

Benny stuffed the last corner of sandwich into his mouth and smacked it down. "They were probably trying to steal all my stuff. Are you sure they didn't take any of it?"

"I don't think so. The things in the living room are pretty destroyed—" She saw his face contort into an expression of horror, so she tried to spin the information. "Well, maybe not destroyed. I didn't exactly see the living room. I'm sure there are things that survived. Most of the kitchen is okay, I think, and the fire didn't get to your bedroom. I'll bet you didn't lose very much, and the rest can be cleaned to get the smoke smell out."

He perked up. "Can we go see?"

"Oh, I don't think so. It's still pretty dangerous in there."

"But Miss Peri, you've done dangerous stuff before. Remember when we broke into—"

She cut him off. "Shh, yes, I remember. But I was working a case."

Benny stretched tall in his chair. "Well, you're on a case now. My case."

"I know, but..." She looked at her watch. "We need to get to the attorney's. We can talk about this later."

Peri took her drink with her as they walked outside to Benny's Cadillac. She stopped at the passenger side door.

"What are you doing, Miss Peri?"

"I'm waiting for you to unlock the door."

He stood and stared at her. "You can't drink in my car."

"But I'm not done."

"You can't drink in my car."

She realized he wasn't giving her an order. He was reciting a physical law. Pouting, she found a trash can and tossed her iced tea, then returned to the open passenger door.

"And don't sit on my ashtray."

Peri lowered herself into the passenger side, taking care not to brush against the heavy glass security blanket, clicked her seatbelt and counted the minutes until they were at their destination.

Attorney David Campbell had an office on Birch Street, about half a mile from the Brea Plaza Shopping Center. It should take them a maximum of ten minutes to reach it, unless Benny drove. It was hard to get anywhere quickly when traveling five miles below the speed limit, much less with half the car in the gutter. That's why Peri made certain they left twenty minutes before their appointment.

They barely made it on time.

Benny led Peri into the five-story glass and steel building, around the corner to the right and onto the elevator. At the third floor, they exited and walked to the last door. The brass plate read, *David Campbell, Attorney at Law*. They stood there for a moment, until Peri reached for the door. Benny walked in ahead of her.

I guess this is equal opportunity, she thought.

A tall black woman sat at the receptionist's desk. She looked up and smiled. "Why, Mr. Needles, how nice to see you. I'll tell Mr. Campbell you're here."

She walked around her desk to the door, rapped twice, then cracked it open. A muffled voice answered, causing her to turn to them. "He'll see you now."

Peri hadn't seen David Campbell since Benny's court appearance for receiving stolen goods. She always expected criminal lawyers to look like Perry Mason. They never did. Campbell looked more like he should be in law enforcement. His close-cropped hair, mink brown eyes, and muscular physique seemed more appropriate to fighting crime than defending criminals. He held out his hand.

Benny stood and looked at the man's hand as if it were a foreign object, so Peri reached forward instead. "How are you, David?"

"Good. Have a seat and tell me about this lawsuit."

His office was neat, with a lack of extraneous décor. A large cherry wood desk separated him from his clients, who sat in smaller versions of his captain's chair, with black leather and high backs. Peri resisted the urge to swivel back and forth like an impatient adolescent, but Benny spun his seat around a few times.

She handed the lawsuit papers to the lawyer. "Benny was served these this morning."

Campbell skimmed them. "Unless these people are ready to take you the whole way, it looks like a nuisance suit. They're hoping the insurance company settles."

"I don't think so. Mr. McHale told me today that he's going for Benny's entire estate."

"My entire what?"

"David, McHale has knowledge of things that should be private, like Benny's exact worth. He also seems to have gotten hold of the fire investigator's report ahead of anyone else. I'm actually worried."

Campbell nodded. "I understand. Losing a child makes parents grieve differently. Some set up a scholarship fund, some lobby for a new law, some try to sue anyone they think might have contributed to what is usually a tragic accident." He smiled at his client. "But don't worry, Benny. I'll do my best to get this dismissed."

"Thanks, David," Peri said. "We've got our plate full right now with the insurance stuff."

"Thanks, David," Benny repeated.

She rose and walked toward the door. "Let me know if there's anything you need. Benny? You ready to go?"

"Oh, yes, Miss Peri." Benny took one more twirl in the chair before getting up and joining her.

They left the office and returned to the car. Peri took out her notes and read them while Benny drove. At the corner of Kraemer and Yorba Linda boulevards, she looked up to see they were in the left turn lane.

"Benny, why are we turning? Aunt Esmy's house is straight ahead, off Chapman."

"We aren't going to Aunt Esmy's house."

"Where are we going?"

The light turned green and he drove the car onto Yorba Linda. "We're going to my house to get my stuff out."

"I don't think we should, Benny. It's still pretty wet and unstable in there."

He was hushed, continuing to drive toward his home, turning right from Yorba Linda to Angelina Drive.

She tried to name a specific risk. "The roof could fall on top of us."

"I want my stuff." He pulled up to the curb. "You promised me I could go into my house in two days. That was two days ago."

She tried to reason with him. "Sometimes things take a little longer than we think they will. And how are you going to get your stuff into the Caddy? There's no room for it."

He didn't say anything for a moment. "I guess I don't have to move all my stuff. Maybe I can move some of it."

"Are you sure you're ready to see it? Some of it didn't survive. This might be hard for you."

Benny frowned. "I know. But I gotta see it." His last sentence sounded like he was fighting back tears.

"Okay, Ben. I understand." She got out of the car and looked down at her white slacks, then looked at the dried rivers of dirt streaking the yard. She hoped she'd be able to get the stains out.

They stepped under the yellow police tape and walked up the sidewalk toward the porch.

"Wait a minute." Peri stopped and held her arm out to halt Benny. Getting her keys out of her tote, she took a small flashlight off the ring. She pointed toward the boards over the windows. "It might be dark inside."

Benny unlocked the scorched door and they entered. While not truly dark, the interior was gray and hazy. Peri clicked the flashlight and swept the beam around the room. The smoke and chemical smells were still strong here, and burned her eyes and nose. To the right, there were stacks of tables, blistered by the heat.

"My end tables from *Some Came Running*." Benny's voice sounded like a howl.

Peri tried to lift his spirits. "Maybe you can save the tops or something. Get them refinished."

The couch next to them looked flattened. By focusing the flashlight, Peri saw the fabric had melted into the frame. She heard Benny's soft moans, so she redirected the light to the left. This side of the room had the most damage. Nothing but molten black shapes could be seen. The walls were burned to the point of destroying the drywall and exposing charred studs.

"My albums." Benny nearly sunk to his knees, but Peri held him up. "My albums were there. And my movies. Gone. They're gone."

They kept walking further into the house, Peri lighting the way and Benny moaning. When they came to the staircase, it looked as if the flames had just licked the railing. She took the first step, testing its strength. It felt firm, so she nodded to Benny and picked her way to the top landing.

"Be very careful up here, Ben. These floors may be weakened by the fire." She walked forward, leaving her weight on her standing leg while she tested with the stepping one. Within a few minutes, she was in Benny's room.

As packed as the first floor rooms were, Benny's room was immaculate. The space was large, dominated by a round bed in the middle. On the walls were Dean Martin posters, so many it looked like wallpaper.

"My bed." Benny ran over and jumped on the mattress.

"Benny, don't—" Peri gasped, but the floor held and the bed didn't fall through to the kitchen. "What did I just say about the floorboards and the fire? Be careful."

"Oh, right, Miss Peri. I forgot." He curled his nose and got up, backing toward her. "My bed stinks."

"Probably the smoke. I think there are companies that get the smell out of furniture. I know dry cleaners can get the smell out of clothes." She swung the light around the room. "Your insurance company should know. If only we knew who your insurance company was."

"I don't know. Stop asking me because I just don't know." Benny's face burned red in the low light, his arms waving and eyes filling with tears. "I shouldn't have to know this stuff. Somebody burned my house down and it's not my fault."

Peri patted his shoulder. "Of course it's not your fault. We'll get the answers. It'll be okay."

He wept for awhile. At last he stopped, pulled out a monogrammed handkerchief, and dabbed at his eyes and nose.

"Is there anything in this room you want to take with you?"

He shook his head. "It all smells bad."

"Okay. Now that you know what it looks like, can we go?"

"Yes, Miss Peri."

They returned down the stairs, taking care to step lightly until they reached the bottom. Peri turned the light toward the front door, then stopped.

"Stay here. I want to look in your mom's room one more time."

She walked back into the small bedroom. It used to be the guest room, but as Mrs. Needles got older, climbing the stairs became more difficult for her. Peri remembered the day she helped move Benny's mom downstairs. The older woman supervised where to put everything, clearly uncomfortable that she could not do any of the heavy lifting. Her son arranged and coordinated it all so that the clothes were hung in order of item and color. Even the glass bottles on the dresser were lined up by size. Peri was just the muscle.

The room now smelled of perfume and smoke and death. This time she detected a whiff of whiskey as well. It must have been Alex's.

Creeping around the bed, she leaned over and lifted the bedspread, shining the light underneath. She wanted to see further, but didn't want to get her slacks filthy. Toward the headboard, something glowed white, so she reached for it. Just another mortgage statement.

But it was relatively clean, so she placed it on the ground and put her knees on it. She could now see completely under the bed. There was nothing else there, apart from waterlogged dust bunnies.

Standing, she picked up the paper and moved back toward the door. She was almost out when she heard a thump in the closet. Her flashlight swung around. The noise stopped.

Peri knew someone or something was in there. She could feel a presence, however, she wasn't certain how to proceed. It would be easy enough to pull the door open and expose whoever was there. The problem would be if it was someone armed with a weapon. Peri had her pocket flashlight and a pink snakeskin tote. They weren't the best means of self defense for a private investigator.

I really need to get a gun.

She looked around the room, trying to find a stick or pipe or anything she could swing at the intruder. Suddenly, she felt two hands on her back, pushing her forward. She fell to her knees, hard, breaking her fall with her hands. The glass embedded in the carpet dug into her palms as her left wrist twisted, and her forehead hit the bed's footboard.

"Ouch." Peri tried not to scream, but it all hurt. She turned to see who had pushed her, but they were gone. Maybe Benny saw them run out. She yelled out to him. "Benny—someone's in the house!"

There was no answer, which worried her. She felt around the floor until her fingers located her flashlight, then pushed to her feet and ran back into the living room. Benny wasn't there. She raced through the house, calling for Benny and shining the flashlight into every corner. He was gone.

Peri's stomach lurched. She looked at her hands and saw how bloody they were from the glass. Her left wrist was already getting larger than the right.

Oh my god, they took him. We weren't supposed to be here, and now he's gone.

She ran out of the house, slamming the door, and then reached for her cell phone. That's when she saw Benny, sitting behind the wheel of his Caddy. He was rocking out to Dino singing "Mambo Italiano." She nearly cried in relief.

Reaching into her tote, trying not to get blood on it, she pulled out her cell phone. She should call Skip and report the newest break-in. Her hand poised on the SEND key, the scene flashed across her mind. The hands, the breath, something made her sick to her stomach.

She put away the phone and hobbled to the passenger side of Benny's car.

"Miss Peri, you're so messy. What happened?"

"I fell down." She glanced at her stained and blacked slacks. The knees had little glass shards poking out of them, which she brushed off. Might as well toss them in the trash now.

She started to ask Benny if he'd seen the intruder, then stopped. If he had, he would still be screaming about it. If he hadn't, it would be better if he didn't know. She reached for the passenger door, but he interrupted her.

"You can't ride in my car."

"What?"

"Miss Peri, you're dirty. You can't ride in my car."

"Well, how do you expect me to get home?" Her wrist was beginning to ache.

"You can't ride in my car."

"Benny, my hands hurt, I've twisted my wrist, I need to clean my wounds and see if I need an X-ray. Now open the damned door or you can forget about me working for you."

Scowling, he got out and went to the trunk. He retrieved a plastic bag and placed it on the passenger seat.

"Sit on this and don't touch anything."

She got in and reached for the seatbelt.

"No seatbelt." No negotiation, either. "You can ride in the seat, but you can't touch anything."

"Fine, just take me back to Esmy's and I'll get my car."

It took them ten excruciating minutes to drive the two miles to his aunt's house. Every time Peri tried to put her hands anywhere but her lap, she got a lecture. At last, he pulled into the drive and Peri reached for the door handle.

"Don't touch that." Benny's voice was stern. "I'll open the door."

Peri waited as she was told and managed to climb out of Benny's car without touching the car or Benny, who was as reluctant to offer his hand as he was to offer a ride. She wondered, if she wrapped her hands around his neck, would he be more upset about the dirt or the strangling?

"Let's keep working on the insurance, Benny. I'll call you when I've got anything."

"Okay, Miss Peri." She watched him walk to the front door, then turn and give her a stilted wave.

Peri limped to her car and got in. Only two days on the case and she was hurting. Sometimes she thought Benny Needles would be the death of her.

CHAPTER 14

Back at home, Peri struggled through a shower to rinse the dirt and smell from her. The water stung her hands and knees, which had also gotten pierced, and her wrist did not move without protest. She put on a pair of shorts and t-shirt, then pulled a bag of frozen peas from the freezer to wrap around the swelling.

Sitting on the couch, she picked up the old mortgage statement she had clung to when the stranger pushed her. She tried to remember the scene, tried to replay it in slow motion. The hands were big, or were they hands? Something sharp, like an elbow, was involved. Peri remembered the person's breath at her ear, which would make them taller than her. It smelled like whiskey.

She suddenly got a sour feeling in her stomach again. Her intuition was telling her something she didn't want to believe.

The mortgage statement caught her attention. Escrow information included the breakdown for taxes and insurance. It was ten years old, but the company still might have some records. She reached for the phone and dialed their customer service number.

It took six transfers and a half-hour of listening to pre-recorded ads and soft music to finally reach someone who had a clue. The woman on the other end of the phone had a magnificent Southern drawl that Peri could have listened to for days, and she was eager to help. One more round of soft music and she came back on the line with the answer: Bennett and Smith Independent Insurance Company.

Peri thanked her in joyful tones, and hung up. Who the hell was Bennett and Smith Insurance?

Typing the name into the computer yielded an address in Placentia, with a phone number. She called it.

The voice was male and impatient. "Bennett and Smith."

"Hi, I'm trying to verify a homeowner's insurance policy for a Mr. Benjamin Needles. It might be under his mother's or father's name, Elizabeth or Robert Needles."

There was silence, to the point she wondered if the line was dead. "Hello?"

"What name did you say?"

"Needles. Benjamin, Elizabeth, or Robert. I have Benjamin's social security number, if that helps."

"No, no that doesn't help. We don't have a policy on them."

"Could you at least check your records?"

In the middle of her question, she heard a click. Now the line was dead.

Okay, it's possible they have a small client base and know everyone. It sounds like a small company. She got up and went to the kitchen, where she retrieved a beer and tried to unscrew the cap with her mangled hands and useless wrist.

"Screw this," she told the bottle and reached for the opener and a dishtowel to cushion her palms. A bag of salt and vinegar chips was on the counter. She grabbed that, too, and returned to the living room.

The man's voice bothered her. It was gruff and rude, and the silence when she told him the names, he sounded startled. Something was wrong here.

Her phone rang, so she picked it up. It was Skip. She wondered how upset he would be when he found out where she was today. Better to say nothing now and wait until she saw him.

"You get on YouTube a lot?" he asked.

"A little. Why?"

"Go to the site and look up *posse on fire*. Jason discovered it on YouTube."

She did as he directed. There was a two-minute clip that began with dim images swinging flashlights around, laughing. They were pointing the camera at things she recognized in Benny's house. Suddenly, out of frame to the left, there was a red glow and smoke. The laughter turned to yelling, and coughing.

"Dude let's bail," one voice said.

There was a confusion of mumbles, then she heard, "Alex is probably already out."

The next thing was a gruff voice, saying, "I'm out," and the video ended.

"Oh my god." Peri sat back into the couch and rubbed her eyes. "Do you recognize any of the voices?"

"No, but in between searching Alex's files on his computer, I've got Jason working on finding the person who uploaded the video to the internet, and I've asked the Brea police if they know anyone on the tape."

"Do you think the boys set the fire?"

"There's no evidence, but there are those paint cans that are unaccounted for. It's possible they were huffing, and they set the fire accidentally."

"They ditched that boy. Do you think they did that on purpose?"

"I think if they didn't do it on purpose, we're looking at a lot of guilt on their minds."

Peri's stomach turned again. "I've got a bad feeling, Skip."

"Want to share?"

"Not yet. Let me verify a few things before I make you sick, too."

"Still want dinner? I can stop at Brian's and pick up some chicken and ribs."

"Hell, yes. I'll keep the beer cold."

She hung up and turned back to the computer, where she replayed the video five more times. Each time, she watched the flashlight sweep across the boys' shoes, she listened to their voices. Each time, she tried not to recognize the green Converse low-tops.

Nick Debussy was there.

Now Peri could admit what she suspected earlier, that Nick might have been the one to push past her in Benny's house. She couldn't prove it, of course, unless the police lab examined his clothes. But something felt familiar about the intruder, something she couldn't name. Perhaps his breath, or the way he moved.

If he was there the night Alex died, it would make sense. No matter what kind of growing pains he was having, Nick was a good kid. He'd be consumed with guilt over Alex. He'd be seeking a way to both forget and remember.

She thought about another good kid, and did a quick search on her brother. The last time she hunted him down, he had changed his name to Devlin Young. She entered the name into her people finder. There were two hundred Devlin Youngs in the database. She narrowed her search by age and race, which cut the two hundred down to fifty. Although she had a poor memory for his birth date, she knew he was born in August. That gave her two names, one in Chicago and one in Las Vegas.

Peri couldn't imagine Dev in Vegas. She clicked through the Chicago link and saw he was on a few social media sites. His profile on Facebook was public, so she looked him up. Dev was an attorney, specializing in corporate law.

He was also dead.

It took her a moment to understand what she was reading, but there were multiple posts on his wall, saying how much they missed him and what a great guy he was. She looked for a picture to prove it was her brother, Endeavor, but all he had up was his company's logo. His profile information was of no help. He had no birthplace listed, only his college. Peri had no idea what he'd done after he left.

It was just like him to keep his online presence ambiguous.

She sat back and put her hand to her face, staring at the computer. Her brother was gone, without so much as a word. According to the posts, it had been cancer. He'd fought a long battle with it. Did he care so little for her, he couldn't even contact her to say goodbye?

The crying came to her slowly as she realized what had happened. Her entire family was now gone. She had always functioned well as a bit of a loner, and often preferred her own company to a crowd, but the feeling of isolation hit her with an intensity she'd never experienced.

The only thing she could think of was calling Skip. She knew he was busy, but she needed to hear his voice.

"Now, Doll." His voice was like a balm to her nerves. "You said there were two Dev Youngs. Why don't you verify that the one in Chicago was actually your brother?"

"I can't imagine my brother in Vegas." Her voice still quivered, although her tears had dried.

"I know, but make certain. Sometimes your work relocates you to places you'd rather not be. I've got about an hour's worth of work to do, then I'll pick up dinner and be over."

"You're right. I need to do a little more research to know for sure. I'll see you later." She hung up, feeling a tiny ray of hope in her leaden heart.

Before she could hunt for the Vegas Dev, she had a more immediate errand. Going into her bedroom, she threw on some lipstick and a pair of flip flops. She needed to go to Blanche's, to talk to her, and possibly Nick. The police weren't stupid. They'd figure out he was involved and come with lots of questions. It would look better if he volunteered the information first.

She grabbed her tote on the way to the front door. As she stepped out, she tripped over something on the top step. Catching her balance, she turned and picked up a small box. It was a simple cardboard rectangle, no more than six inches long and a couple inches wide. There was no return address, or even any address at all. It was simply marked *Perry the P.I.*

Peri began to open it, then remembered horror stories of bombs and gifts that shot acid and white powder with plague viruses. On her way to see Blanche, she'd drop this by the police department. They could open it safely.

She hopped in her Honda and drove to the Placentia Civic Center. In the courtyard, centered by an arched fountain with blue tiles, the library, City Hall, and police department all shared a common space. As she walked across the paved stone, she looked at her reflection in the smoky glass doorway of the police station. It was like a funhouse mirror, stretching her tall frame up, then squishing it down.

Skip was in his office, when she knocked and entered. He glanced up from his typing. "Hey, what's up? How are you doing?"

She shrugged. "I'm okay. I'm going to do more research on Dev, but I just need your lab to look at something for me."

He sighed and pushed his glasses up on his nose. "Peri, we are not your personal lab service. If this has something to do with one of our cases, we'd be happy to process it, but it's then our evidence, and it's shaky at best because—"

She cut him off. "I don't know what it is, Mister Procedure Follower." She put the box on his desk. "This was on my doorstep. I didn't know whether to open it or not. It's what you might call suspicious."

He took out a tissue and turned the box over, examining it. "It is a little unusual. We could at least X-ray it, I guess."

Peri was trying to keep her wrist from attracting attention, but it was soon aching again. She nestled it in her right hand to try to elevate it.

"Hurt your wrist?"

"Took a fall, landed on it wrong."

They walked down the hall toward Jason's office.

"Where'd you fall?" Damn that Skip, he always wanted just a little more information.

She took a breath and dove in. "At Benny's house. I took him in to see his stuff. Actually, he took me, so in a way, this wasn't my fault. While I was in his mom's room, someone else had broken into the house, yet again, and pushed me down to escape. No, I didn't see his face. Yes, I'm pretty sure it was a he. Taller than me, big hands, sharp elbows, smelled like whiskey. Now then, go ahead and yell."

He stared at her a moment before shaking his head. "Would it do me any good?"

"Not really. It's a done deal."

"Did you learn anything from it?"

"Possibly. I may need to carry a gun."

"What?"

"I knew someone was in the closet, but I didn't have a thing to hit him with. With a gun, I could've made him come out."

"Or accidentally shot him. Or yourself."

"Well, I wouldn't use it until I was fully trained."

They had been standing outside Jason's office long enough for him to open the door. "You guys want to take it somewhere else? You're bugging me."

"Sorry," Skip told him, then held the box out. "Peri found this on her doorstep. Knowing her, it's a cyanide canister, all set to go off when she opens it. Can you just make sure it's safe?"

"You bet. Hey, Miss Peri." He took the box and disappeared into his office, closing the door.

"I've got one more errand to run, then I'll be home," she said.

"I'll meet you around seven with dinner."

She rushed out of the station, across the court, to her car. As she started the engine and wrapped her seatbelt across her, she wondered why she was in such a hurry to get to the Debussy house. It's not like she wanted to go.

CHAPTER 15

Peri pulled into the Debussy driveway, her heart beating like a paddle ball against the wood. She had always been able to tell Blanche anything, and she believed her friend held her in the same loving regard. Nothing was off-limits to them. But she'd never told her such difficult news about her son, especially when she could feel her friend's hesitance to talk about it. Part of her hoped no one was home.

The rest of her saw Blanche's white SUV in the driveway.

As usual, she rang the doorbell, then opened the door, or at least tried. It was locked. Maybe no one was home. She heard the sound of the lock turning and the door opened. Blanche stood there, looking like a deer staring down the barrel of a shotgun. Her shorts and t-shirt had wet patches on them, and she held a sponge in her gloved hands.

"Oh, Peri. Come in. I was, I was so busy cleaning, I guess I got a little focused."

They walked around the corner to the kitchen.

"Drink?" Blanche asked.

"Maybe in awhile." Peri watched her friend putter around the kitchen, so she sat at the breakfast bar, and took a deep breath. "Beebs, we need to talk."

Blanche stopped wiping the counter and put the sponge down. "I know. I'm having a problem and I know we talk about everything, but I can't get the words out of my mouth."

"I saw Dani at Panera today. She told me you were having some problems with Nick. Said I was supposed to hold you down and force you to drink cheap tequila 'til you talk to me."

"Really?"

"Not exactly, but close. I have something to show you and I don't think you'll like it."

"Is this like when you tell me you think the milk is bad so I should taste it to be sure?"

Peri smiled. "I wish it were only spoiled milk."

She reached for Blanche's tablet and brought up the YouTube video. Handing it to her friend, she watched her face as it played. Blanche kept her expression steady, but Peri could see the color disappear from her cheeks.

"Recognize anyone?" Peri asked. "Because I know who it looks like and sounds like."

Blanche went to the cabinet and brought out two glasses. "I think I need that drink now."

They sat down on the couch, wine glasses half-filled with garnet-colored liquid.

"Tell me what's been happening, Beebs."

"This is so hard." The brunette removed her glasses and rubbed the bridge of her nose. Then she took a long sip of cabernet. "Nick's been staying out late with his friends, really late. School's out, he turned eighteen in May, so it's hard to order him to stay home. We limit the use of the car, but he just gets a ride with his friends.

"The night of the fire, he was out all night. I don't even know when he came home because Paul and I had already gone to work. But a few days later, I went into his room to see if it was tidy enough for the cleaning lady to vacuum and I noticed a smell. It was on his clothes in the hamper. It was the same smell as at Benny's house." She smiled at Peri. "You'd have been proud—for a moment, I had your Super Sniffer.

"I couldn't stand it anymore. We've got the GPS locator activated on his cell phone, so I tracked him down at his friend Dylan's house, woke him up and dragged him home. We had an awful fight. He denied everything. I threatened to test him for drugs." Blanche slumped back into the peach-and-teal-striped sofa. "It was a lot of screaming with no one winning. Now he avoids me completely."

"Oh, Beebs, I'm so sorry. You and Nick had such a great relationship." Peri took her friend's hand. "Here's the thing. I didn't stumble onto the video by accident. Skip told me about it. So far, they don't know who the boys in the video are, but they're getting the identity of the poster right now. If that doesn't lead them to Nick, then when Jason starts processing the video…"

Blanche nodded. "I know. It would be better if Nick volunteered his information, instead of waiting for the police to hunt him down."

"I'm beginning to think the fire was intentional, but the boys' presence was coincidental. Benny's house doesn't look so good. They might have believed it was abandoned. It was their bad luck that someone wanted it to burn down."

"Who would want to burn Benny's house?"

Peri smiled. "The neighbors probably want to, but I doubt they would, just in case the flames crossed onto their property. Other than that, I'm still trying to find out who Benny's insurance company is."

"Doesn't he know?"

"He knows nothing." She laughed. "And he expects me to find out everything."

"Well, of course you will. You always do."

Peri shook her head. "I don't know. I've been stonewalled from every angle." Tipping the glass, she finished her wine.

"Wouldn't it be weird if the insurance company set the fire?"

"Why would they do that?"

"I don't know. You're the detective." Blanche rose and took her glass, as well as Peri's, into the kitchen.

Peri glanced at her phone, then leaped from the couch. "Holy crap, I told Skip I'd meet him at my house at seven. Beebs, I gotta go." She ran over and gave her friend a hug. "I won't mention Nick to Skip, as long as you can get him to come in."

"If not?" Blanche looked at Peri, who shrugged a little. She nodded. "If not, you have to tell him what you know. It's okay. Maybe Nick will finally get his head on straight."

They hugged one more time and Peri rushed out the door to her car. After sending a quick *On my way running late* text to Skip, she pulled away from the curb and drove toward Esperanza Road.

She had wanted to tell Blanche about Dev, wanted to share her fears and be bolstered by her friend's steady attitude. This was not the time, however. Blanche had bigger problems and didn't need one more weight on her shoulder, even if it wasn't her family. Devlin's possible death would have to wait until Nick was out of danger.

Skip's car was in the driveway when she got there, so she pulled in behind him and walked in through the back door. The smell of barbecue hit her as she entered. He was at the counter, pulling paper plates, covered in tin foil, out of a large paper bag.

"Oh man, that smells good," Peri told him. "I'm starving." She gave him a kiss on her way to the refrigerator, where she got out the iced tea.

"Did you have a glass of wine?"

"Yeah, I was at Blanche's."

"And you drove home?"

She put the pitcher on the counter and looked at him. "A half of a glass, no I'm not buzzed, and if I was, I certainly wouldn't drive home, Officer."

"Just checking." He pulled the foil off one plate, to expose a full rack of ribs, along with two small containers of beans and potato salad. "We've been looking at that video today. The more we watch, the more out of control those boys seem."

"Have you identified anyone?" She tried to keep her voice casual while she got glasses out of the cupboard and filled them with ice.

"Not from the video, although one of the voices sounds familiar." Skip stared at her. "Did you recognize anyone?"

She met his eyes. "Can you ask me that tomorrow?"

"I understand, you're protective, but—"

"Please, Skip." The lump in her throat surprised her, as much as the tears building in her eyes.

He smiled and kissed her forehead. "Okay. Just so you know, Jason's got a name and address for our camera man. Max Pilsner. Lives in Yorba Linda, attends Yorba Linda High School, yadda yadda. We're going to talk to him tomorrow, after we get the warrant for his original file."

"I love you." She leaned into him, thankful for his understanding and his warning.

Nick didn't have much time.

They sat down at the table and began eating. Peri found the taste of her chicken as delicious as the smell, and she was soon tearing pieces away with her fingers and dipping them into the sauce. She looked up to see Skip grinning at her.

"How's the chicken?"

She wiped the sauce from her mouth. "Good."

He laughed. "I can tell. You remind me of that scene in *Tom Jones*."

"I'm hungry."

"I guess." He cleaned his fingers on his napkin and reached into his pocket. "By the way, this is what was in the box you gave me. No poisons or explosives."

"Already? What'd I get?" She started to reach for the object, but looked at her messy fingers and nodded for him to put it on the table.

It was a long, flat key, with a business card from Citibank on Kraemer Boulevard tied to it. Peri wiped her hands and turned the card over. In neat print on the back it said *Box 216. Bring Benny.*

"A safety deposit box." She looked at Skip, her eyes wide. "Did you get any prints or trace?"

"Some prints. We're running them now."

"This is so cool. I wonder who sent it to me." Peri sat back, picking at her coleslaw. "Too bad the bank is closed. I'll call Benny and we'll go down there first thing tomorrow morning."

Skip threw an empty rib bone onto his plate. "Say, didn't that scene in *Tom Jones* end with a roll in the hay?"

"I believe it did. I don't have any hay, but I'm happy to improvise."

She reached across to wipe barbecue sauce from his chin. He caught her hand and licked her fingers. Soon their meal was abandoned in favor of other delights.

An hour later, they lay entwined in bed, sheets twisted around them. Skip leaned across her to find the remote, and turned on the small TV. The local news was blasting the latest scoop, but he flipped through the channels until he settled on a baseball game. The Angels were fending off a run from Boston.

Peri got up and threw a shirt on. "I forgot to call Benny," she said as she walked to the living room. She sat on the couch, rubbing her wrist, and called her client.

Benny didn't seem to understand the significance of the key, but agreed to meet her at the bank at ten o'clock, after he complained about the early hour.

After ending the call to Benny, she decided to send a text to Blanche. *They know who filmed*, she wrote. *Nick has 12 hours, max.*

If Skip knew, he'd probably hit the roof, but she couldn't help it. She told herself she'd do the same for him if it was his daughter in a jam. Loyalty wasn't just a word in the dictionary.

While she was near her laptop, she did a quick search for the Devlin Young in Las Vegas. There were no photos, or even a Facebook status. She found an address, nothing else. She rose and went to her office for a piece of paper, then sat back down and began to write.

Dear Mr. Young,

I am looking for my brother, who changed his name from Endeavor Minneopa to Devlin Young. I have traced the name to two locations, yours and a Devlin Young in Chicago. If you are my brother, please let me know by contacting me at 714-555-2929.

Thank you,

Peri Minneopa

It was a dry communication, but she didn't know what else to say, without degrading into a mewling, desperate *please just tell me you're alive* plea. An envelope and a stamp sealed the inquiry. Tomorrow, she would stick the letter in her mailbox.

It was going to be a long night.

CHAPTER 16

Peri was sitting in the Citibank parking lot at nine-forty-five, waiting for Benny to show up. She had untied the card from the key and was rubbing it with her fingers, checking the clock every thirty seconds and messing with the brace on her wrist in between. What could be in the box?

If I was a cat, I'd be dead by now.

At thirty seconds until ten, she saw the black Coupe de Ville sail into the parking lot and try three spaces before settling on one as far away from the building as possible, straddling a white line. Benny had arrived.

She got out of her car and stood, watching him. He opened his driver's side door and stepped out, wearing a dark blue suit, white shirt, and dark tie. Apparently still carting his ashtray around, she saw him lean inside, pick up something, put it back, take it out, and finally slide it under the seat before locking the door and shutting it. At long last, he strolled over to her.

"Why do we have to be here so early?"

"Because they open at ten and I want to know why someone sent me a key to a safety deposit box that belongs to you."

He shrugged. "I guess."

She handed him the key and the card. "These are, technically, yours. We're going to go into the bank and you're going to ask to see your safety deposit box, number two-sixteen. They're going to ask to see your ID. and then you'll unlock the box and we'll see what's inside."

Benny stared at the key and the card. "Two-sixteen," he repeated.

They were the first customers in the small branch. A young man sat at the receptionist's desk. He was junior executive material, with his gray suit, slick hair and metro-grooming. According to his pewter-colored badge, his name was Chad.

"May I help you?"

Benny straightened his posture, as if reciting. "My name is Benjamin Needles and I need to see my safety deposit box, number two-sixteen."

Chad nodded. "May I see some ID?"

He took the driver's license Benny gave to him, glanced at it, then returned it, and escorted them to a back room with a table and two chairs, and a wall of metal doors, all with numbers and keyholes. Chad pointed to Benny's box. Benny inserted the key, and Chad pulled the box out, placing it on the table.

"Take your time," he said, and left the room.

Peri reached over to the box to lift the lid, but was surprised when Benny took it from her. "It's my box, Miss Peri. I get to open it."

She sat back in the chair. "Of course you do."

He put it on the table and looked at it, until she lost her patience. "If you want to open it, do it."

"Chad said I could take my time."

"Chad's not sitting in here, wondering what's so important about this box. Open the damned thing."

He pouted, but slid the lid open. A thick stack of papers, rolled and folded, were inside. Peri started to reach for them, then stopped and looked at Benny. He smiled and pulled the papers out.

"These are papers about my house." He handed them to Peri. "Here, I don't understand."

She scanned the various groupings. There was a set of papers outlining the original purchase of the house, and another set of homeowner's insurance premiums and policies. The company listed at the top was Bennett and Smith Independent Insurance Agency. Peri read through the package.

"So they are your insurer," she said. "Why did they try to deny it?"

She read the terms of the policy and whistled. "Geepers, Ben, your house is insured for a million bucks. There's no way your house has ever been worth that much."

"Wow, I could buy a lot of Dean Martin albums with that."

Peri looked at him. "You do know the company will require you to spend the money fixing your house, right?"

"But Miss Peri, my things, my Dino things, don't they have to replace them?"

"Yes, but first you need a place to live." She continued to read. "This policy will only pay out if the damage is not a result of homeowner negligence, whether intentional, accidental, or the result of non-upkeep. That might be kind of weird. I know insurance won't pay if you set your own house on fire, but it sounds like if you accidentally leave the iron on or don't update the wiring, they won't pay out."

Benny looked in the box again. "Hey, I missed something." He held out a single piece of paper to her.

She skimmed it. "Okay, here's the information on your money. Your account is in this bank. How did you not know your money is in this bank?"

"I have a card." He dug into his pocket and produced his wallet, then opened it toward her. "I use the card."

She took the wallet and removed the debit card from its holder. In the upper left corner, it said *Citibank Check Card*. She sighed and replaced it, handing the wallet back to him. "And you never looked at the name of the bank?"

Benny shrugged. "Is it important?"

"Yes. It is." She got up and looked around. "We need a copier."

"What for?"

"I want to make copies of the insurance policy and the bank account info."

Benny held up the papers. "Why don't we just take these?"

"Because I think I want these papers to stay in safekeeping. Someone broke into your house and all they took, according to you, was this information. They might try again. You stay here."

122

Opening the door, she saw a copier to her right, so she quickly removed the staple from the documents and ran them through the machine. She returned the originals to the metal box and closed it, then opened the door again and looked around.

Chad was standing by the counter, chatting up a pretty teller, possibly Korean, by Peri's guess. "Chad?" She tried to call out just enough to get his attention, but the girl had his complete focus. "Chad." Her second call could have roused a dead man.

Safety box locked back in its place, Peri and Benny were on their way out the front door, when she stopped.

"Benny, we need a copy of your bank statements for the previous year. I want to make certain your insurance is paid up before I go see this company."

The pretty Korean girl was happy to help them get copies of Benny's statements. Armed with his financial information, they finally left the bank.

"What shall we do now, Miss Peri?"

She was sifting through his papers. "Here it is—a check made out to Bennett and Smith, back in February. This should prove your insurance is still active. Why don't you go home and I'll visit the insurance company? I'll make certain they know where to get the investigator's report, and all about the lawsuit."

He looked at his watch. "Ah, geez, we've only been here a half hour? Why couldn't we have done this at a civilized time, like noon?"

"For Pete-freakin' sake, I am trying to unravel this mess of a life you've got and you're pissy with me about getting up early? Get over it."

She saw the hurt in his puppy eyes and regretted her outburst. "Sorry, Benny. I've just been very frustrated trying to help you, and this is the first break I've had. I know it's early for you, but the sooner we get the insurance involved, the faster your house will be repaired and the better I'll feel."

He smiled. "When will I get the money?"

"I don't know, but I'll try to find out."

She got in her car and used her phone to find the office of Bennett and Smith. As she mapped the route to Crowther Avenue with her navigator, she saw the black Caddy drive away.

Ah, Benny, I hope this all works out.

The stretch of Crowther between Kraemer Boulevard and Placentia Avenue always looked less like a street and more like an alley to Peri. On the north side was Placita Santa Fe, the old part of Placentia with a charming array of Mexican restaurants, shops, and apartments. To the south were stodgy rows of beige and gray businesses and warehouses, blockish and windowless. A tall pedestrian bridge, built to match the style of the historic old town, spanned the railroad tracks that separated Crowther from the Placita. The city leaders tried to keep people safe, although there were always individuals willing to play chicken with oncoming trains. They usually lost.

Peri's GPS navigator led her to a general driveway on the blockish side of the street. The actual address was a number plus a letter, indicating a suite somewhere in the compound, so she crept her car up and down the aisles, looking for a "K".

At last, squeezed between a warehouse and a window tinting business, she saw a dark glass door with a "K" over it. On the door, it said *Jinx Hi-Photography* and in smaller letters below, *Bennett and Smith Insurance*.

"Classy," she said as she pulled into a space. Gathering her tote, she got out and walked to the door. She had a bad feeling about this.

She entered a small reception area with a counter jutting from the wall to her left and two folding chairs to her right. The walls were white, but looked in need of paint. There were a couple of posters tacked up, advertising quality printing at reasonable prices. Two doors led back into other spaces, one behind the counter and one to the right. Both were closed. There was no indication of which one led to Bennett and Smith.

Peri wondered what to do. No one had come out to see her, although the door didn't seem to have any kind of bell on it, and no one else had entered. She supposed she could try both doors and see which one had the lady and which one had the tiger...

Taking out her cell phone, she dialed Bennett and Smith. She began to hear a ringing from the door to her right. The same gruff voice answered as before.

"Hi, what are your office hours today?"

"I don't see anyone without an appointment." She could hear the man's voice in her phone and beyond the door. It was like having a grouch in stereo.

"Then I'd like to make an appointment."

"What about?"

"I need to talk to you about an insurance policy."

"You buying?"

"I'm at least pricing my options."

"Call me when you want to buy." The phone went dead.

Wonder what he'll do with a drop-in client, Peri thought as she knocked twice on his door, then turned the knob.

The room was drowning in chaos. Two tall bookcases held nothing but binders, stacked at odd angles, papers exploding from every corner. Boxes sat against the far wall, making the small room feel miniscule. The smell was of mold and book glue, with a hint of body odor. A metal desk faced her, olive green with a dark top. Behind it sat an old, angry man.

"Who the hell are you?" He was hawkish-looking, with a long, pointed nose and overgrown eyebrows that perched over his glasses. His voice was no happier in person than it had been on the phone.

Figuring she couldn't make it any worse, she snapped back at him. "Peri Minneopa. Who the hell are you?"

"Burton Smith. Get out of my office."

"Mr. Smith, we spoke yesterday on the phone. According to you, Benny Needles does not have a policy with your company."

"You came down here to tell me that?"

"I came down here to show you, you do have a policy with the Needles family." She handed him the copied papers. "Mr. Needles' house sustained some fire damage last week, so he needs to file a claim. In addition—" She didn't get to finish.

"Yes, the Needleses did have a policy, but they let it lapse."

Peri handed him the bank statement. "I don't think so. You can see this automatic withdrawal, made out to Bennett and Smith. Unless you can show me proof their policy was cancelled, they need you to fulfill the terms of the insurance."

She watched his face flash red, then fade. "Let me find his paperwork. Perhaps I'm thinking of another client."

He went to one of the bookcases and ran a knobby index finger down two shelves, then across four binders before he picked one out and leafed through it. Peri waited as patiently as she could manage without screaming he was a charlatan and Benny's family had been pouring their money into a scam all these years.

At last he put the binder on the desk, opened the rings, and pulled out a group of papers. "Here it is. Yes, we do still carry their policy. What we'll need is a copy of the fire investigator's report."

"Before you interrupted me, I was also going to mention a lawsuit has already been filed against Mr. Needles. A teenager broke into his house and died as a result of the fire."

Smith sat back and looked in her direction, although Peri felt she was being looked through. His mouth twitched a little and his left eyebrow lifted. "Get me a copy of that report and the suit."

She handed him a copy of the lawsuit. "James Murray is doing the investigation, and David Campbell is Mr. Needles' attorney, working on the suit. I'll make certain they know to coordinate with your company."

He started leafing through Benny's policy again, while she stood in the middle of the room. After a minute, he looked up. "Well? What else did you want?"

"I'm curious, Mr. Smith. This looks like a one-man company. Where's Mr. Bennett?"

His eyes narrowed. "Dead."

She took one more long look around the office before walking out the door.

"I guess you're too mean to die," she muttered as she got back in her car.

Her cell phone rang. It was Skip.

"Hey, Doll, thought I'd give you a heads-up. We got the report from Murray today. He called it homeowner negligence."

"What?" Peri slammed her fist on the steering wheel, then winced at the pain. "Look, I know Benny had crap stacked everywhere, but none of it was a fire hazard. Getting out of the house was the hazard."

"Can't help it, he called it differently. Says a frayed cord was near a can of turpentine and that was the source."

"Tom Flores told me about some cans, but Benny says there weren't any. I mean, can you imagine Benny painting?"

"I know, but—"

"But nothing. This is wrong. I've got to try to fix it."

"Don't do anything stupid, Peri." She heard the worry in his voice.

"I won't. I at least need to talk to James to see how he came to his conclusion. It's not right, Skip. Could I get a copy of the report? I got a funny feeling about this insurance company. I don't think Burton Smith is going to actually do anything unless I spoon-feed him the information."

"Sure. I have to go out, but I'll leave it at the front desk and tell them to make a copy for you."

"Two, please? I want to keep one to share with my buddy, James."

"Make good choices," he said, then laughed.

"What's so funny?"

"I used to tell my daughters that when they were teenagers. Didn't work on them, either."

Peri laughed, too. "Dinner tonight?"

She heard him hesitate. "Um, not tonight. I may not get done until late. Tomorrow?"

"Sure. See you then." She put her phone back in her tote and pulled out of the parking lot. Turning right onto Crowther, she made her way to Kraemer Boulevard, to pick up the report from the station. James Murray had some explaining to do.

CHAPTER 17

As Skip hung up the phone, Craig opened the office door. "You ready to go?"

"Yeah." He stood up and hesitated, checking his pockets for keys, picking up his cell phone and his notepad. "Let's get it done."

"You sure you're okay?"

Skip ran his hand across his hair, thinking perhaps he shouldn't be on this interview. Nick Debussy had called him that morning, and in a trembling voice said he needed to talk. He asked the teenager if it was official or just a request for advice and waited through a long, hard silence for him to say, "Official."

Now he and his partner were on their way to the Debussy home to do an interview, and he had to keep his sympathy for his friend's son in check.

"I'm okay with it," he told Craig.

They got into his SUV and drove east on Chapman Avenue, toward Orangethorpe Avenue, Esperanza Road, and Nick Debussy.

Fifteen minutes later, they pulled into the driveway. As they approached the door, Skip looked over at Craig. "Maybe you should take the lead."

Craig reached over and rang the bell. "You got it."

It took a few minutes for the door to open a crack, swinging in slow motion to reveal a tall, dark-haired youth in plaid shorts and a black Skrillex t-shirt. It was almost noon, and he looked as though he'd just rolled out of bed.

He didn't speak, but opened the door and let the two detectives inside. Once in the foyer, Skip turned to Nick. "Why don't we go in the kitchen and talk at the table?"

Nick nodded, so Skip led the way. Sunshine lit the large space that stretched out to include the family room. They sat at the mahogany table, decorated with rattan placemats, and a napkin holder in the center. Skip eased back in his chair and took out his notepad, while Craig leaned forward.

"So, Nick, I understand you called Detective Carlton and told him you needed to talk."

For a brief moment, Nick looked at the detective with large, tear-pooled eyes. Then he lowered his gaze, ran his hand across his nose and sniffled. Skip noted how hard the boy's hands were shaking when he started to speak.

"Me and my friends, we kinda been partying, okay? Maybe we let it all get out of hand, I don't know. But a few nights ago, everyone's folks are home and the cops keep cruising the park so we need a place to just hang out, you know? Nothing hardcore, a little drink, a little smoke."

Skip kept writing. Nick was not owning his behavior, but maybe it would come.

"So where did you go looking?" Craig asked. He knew the answer, but didn't want to lead the boy.

"We tried to get high behind the church, but there was a dog in the next yard, kept barking. So my friend says—"

Craig interrupted. "Your friend who?"

Nick turned to Skip. "Do I have to say?"

The detective nodded. His stomach rolled a little, but he couldn't show it. "This is a homicide investigation, Nick."

The boy was quiet for a few moments, running his fingers through his hair, massaging his scalp. Finally, he spit it out. "My friend, Dylan, said there was an old house next door."

"Dylan?"

"Biehl." Nick choked on the name. "The place is real run-down, no car, no lights. So we go over there, but the doors are locked."

He waved his hands and looked at Craig. "Okay, I thought it was a bad idea. But when you're with your bros—"

"It's easier to go along."

Nick nodded. "Then, Dylan feels around and finds a key over the door. He unlocks it and says, 'Come on, ya wusses.' So we go in. Max has his phone up, recording everything." He stopped and gave Craig a hangdog look. "Max Pilsner. The house is all messed up. We go through the rooms and end up in the kitchen. Everyone's passing a bottle of whiskey around, we're all drinking, but Alex and Max are getting more wasted than me and Dylan."

"Were they used to whiskey?" Craig asked.

"Yeah, I found out later Dylan had given them a pill to take with their first drink. Told 'em it was a cocktail. Alex thought that was funny. Cock tail." He wiped his eyes.

Skip kept writing. He looked over and saw Nick's hands were steadier, so he interrupted. "By the way, were you guys huffing paint or turpentine?"

"What? No. That's for losers."

Damn, thought Skip, *we can scratch that idea for how the cans got in Benny's house.*

Craig continued his interrogation. "Did you all stay in the kitchen?"

Nick shook his head. "Alex went exploring. He was mumbling about stars or something. Then it happened."

"And then what happened?"

"I heard a pop and saw a light. I pointed. 'Dude', I said, or something. We went toward the living room and saw the fire. It happened so fast. There was smoke, it was hot, I was calling for Alex, Dylan was yelling at me, Max hung back 'til the last minute. Then Dylan said, 'Alex is probably out' and he left. I went toward the living room again and heard someone talking by the front door."

He started crying. "I thought it was Alex. Who else could it be? I thought he was on his way out. So I left, I left, and he died." Nick collapsed onto the table, shaking.

Skip stopped writing and put his hand on the boy's shoulder. "You thought he was safe, Nick. You were the only one who stayed to make sure he was okay."

"But he wasn't, he wasn't, how do I keep living when he died?" Nick sat up and grabbed a napkin, then wiped his eyes and nose. "All because we wanted to party. Stupid, freakin' party."

"Teenagers make mistakes all the time," Craig told him. "Sometimes they are brutal, tragic mistakes. All we can do is learn and go forward. You did participate, but you didn't unlock the door. You didn't send Alex into a back room where he could get caught. And you certainly didn't set the fire."

"I think you'd feel better if you talked to a counselor," Skip added. "I know it sounds corny, but there are people who are trained to help you deal with your feelings, instead of medicating them away."

Nick stared at Skip. The way he looked at him made the detective think about Peri's story of the intruder, the large hands and sharp elbows, and the smell of whiskey.

"It was you yesterday in the house, wasn't it?" he asked.

"I needed to see it." His voice was a raw whisper. "I needed to be where Alex was. Aunt Peri wasn't hurt, was she? I didn't mean to hurt her, I just panicked."

"No, she's okay. Twisted her wrist a little, and you owe her a pair of slacks."

"I'm sorry."

"She'll live." Skip patted his shoulder. "And so will you. The pain will never be gone, but you'll learn how to keep it from ruling your life. You got lucky, Nick. You could've been trapped in that fire, along with the rest of your friends."

Nick nodded, although he didn't look convinced.

"You said Max was recording everything?" Craig asked. "The only video we've seen is the one on YouTube."

"He was recording lots of stuff on his phone. Most of it was boring, just us goofing off, but the fire was pretty intense." Nick scratched his head. "I guess he wanted everyone to see it."

Skip exchanged glances with Craig. They planned to talk to Max, but now they needed a warrant for all of the videos.

"We're going to be reviewing all of Max's videos," Craig told Nick. "We may ask for your help in studying the scene. Could you do that?"

"Yes, sir."

"In the meantime, I don't think you should be alone." Skip dialed Blanche's number and stepped out to the yard. "Could you come home? Craig and I have been here talking to Nick… no, he's not in trouble right now, but he had a lot of information to give us, and I think he needs, well, I think maybe he needs his mom."

He walked back inside. "Nick, you said someone was talking in the living room. Could you hear what they were saying?"

"Sounded like 'I'm out'. I thought…" He propped his elbows on the table and cradled his face in his hands.

"You thought what any of us would think," Skip said. "It had to be Alex, telling you he was okay."

"Mind if we hang out with you," Craig asked, "until your mom gets here?"

Nick shrugged.

For forty minutes, the men sat around the table, taking notes and saying little. Discussing the case would not be appropriate, and small talk might seem insensitive. Nick remained between them, his head on his outstretched arm, rubbing the placemat with his other hand. After an eternity of ticking silence, they heard the garage door open and the sound of an engine roaring to a stop.

At last, Blanche appeared from the hallway.

"Nick, is everything all right?"

"He's fine," Skip said. "We had a long talk about where he was the night of the fire. He's not in trouble right now, although he may have a breaking-and-entering if Benny presses charges. Even if that happens, he's given us a lot of information and promised to help us with the video. Cooperation goes a long way."

Blanche walked over to her son and hugged him. "Thanks, Skip, Craig."

"Call us, Nick, if you think of anything else," Craig said. "Otherwise, we'll contact you when we have the video footage."

The two detectives walked to the front door. As Skip reached for the knob, he felt a hand on his shoulder.

"How bad is it?" Blanche asked.

"Basically, he was in the house, tried to save Alex. It's traumatic. I recommended therapy, but your words might have more weight."

"Did you tell him about the drugs? Alex would have probably died anyway, whether he was rescued or not."

Skip shook his head. "You may want to tell him. It was a judgment call on my part—he seemed to be taking everything so hard."

"Okay. Thanks, both of you."

They left the house and got in the SUV to return to the station. Craig looked around at the million dollar homes on large, rolling fields of green. "Welcome to the land of gracious living."

"Yep," Skip replied. "Different income bracket, same problems."

CHAPTER 18

Peri picked up two thick packets from the desk at the police station and thanked the woman who made the copies. She took them back to her car, got behind the wheel, and read through one of the reports before starting the engine.

Even to her untrained eye, the fire investigator's work looked shoddy. The report blamed the fire on a frayed lamp cord resting across a can of turpentine, but none of the supporting photographs showed any evidence. The photos were blurry, of black, shapeless blobs and exposed wooden beams, charred. Some of the views didn't look like Benny's house. Then there were the typographical errors. Even Benny's name was misspelled.

The lack of precision and quality in Murray's work surprised her. He seemed more meticulous than the report indicated.

Tossing it in the passenger seat, Peri pulled out of the lot and onto Chapman Avenue, toward the freeway. She had planned to run a copy over to Burton Smith, but that could wait. First, she had some questions for her old buddy James.

Traffic moved in fits and starts, clogging at each freeway interchange. Peri tried to relax and not let the snarls get to her, but it was difficult. She wanted to be in Murray's office now. Where was a Star Trek transporter when you needed one?

It took her forty-five minutes, but she reached Bristol Street and drove east, back to his office. On her last visit, she saw a set of stairs near his corner, and was tempted to take them, but decided to slow down and get control of her anger. She parked the car near the foyer, marched into the building, and forced her legs to walk and not run to the second floor. With each step, she coached herself.

Okay, don't get up in his face right away. It'll only make him defensive. You need him to tell you why he wrote that report. He won't respond to nice, but he might respond to logic. Keep your cool and don't swing your tote at him.

By the time her hand was on the red door, her pulse was lower and she felt more in control. Emma was at her desk, staring at her computer monitor and tapping her red nails on the mouse.

"Miss Minneopa, how can I help you?"

"I need to talk to James—Mr. Murray." She started to add "if that's okay", but she didn't really care if it was okay or not.

"Well, his wife just went in, but I can interrupt that." She picked up the phone. "Mr. Murray? Miss Minneopa is here to see you… all right."

Emma put down the phone and turned to Peri. "Give him five minutes."

"Thanks, Emma." Peri wandered around the room, looking at the artwork.

Photographic prints were on the walls, of familiar California scenery, like the Mojave Desert, the Sierra Nevada Mountains, and northern Californian beaches. After one lap around the room, she was bored.

"How long have you worked for Mr. Murray?" she asked.

"Only about a year. He had just moved into this office." Emma smiled. "It was perfect timing."

"You like working here?"

Her smile faded a little. "Puts food on the table."

As they chatted, the door opened and a woman walked out. Peri recognized her from the picture on James's desk. The photo made her seem taller, but in person she was still bigger than life. At only five-five, Mrs. Murray was sheer elegance. Peri didn't know much about couture design, but she could tell a St. John suit when she saw one. This one fit Mrs. Murray's Barbie figure as if tailor-made, in a royal blue that complimented the woman's long mahogany waves and alabaster skin.

"Mrs. Murray? Hi, I'm Peri Minneopa." Peri held out her hand.

The brunette ignored her at first, digging a pair of blonde leather driving gloves from her purse and putting them on her well-manicured hands. At last, she looked up, her jade eyes scrutinizing Peri, and offered a quick set of covered fingertips to her palm. A delicate wave of perfume drifted past Peri's nose, subtle and clearly expensive.

"Babette Bennett Murray." She turned to the secretary. "Emma, would you get Mr. Murray his chamomile tea? He told me you forgot and you know how important it is to him."

Peri glanced at Emma, who kept staring at her monitor, and pointed to the cabinet behind her. "It's brewing right now, Mrs. Murray."

The tonal iciness was obvious to Peri, but Emma didn't seem to care if her boss's wife heard it, and Mrs. Murray didn't seem to care what a mere secretary might think of her. Her demeanor suggested she didn't care what Peri thought of her, either.

The outer door opened, and a large man blustered into the space. He was dark and thuggish, with a round face and slick hair. Navy work pants and a long-sleeved shirt made him look like a delivery man. As he entered, he looked around at Emma, then at Babette.

He pointed to the inner door. "Is he?"

"Not now, Ronnie," Babette told him.

Peri absorbed the scene. James's wife and Ronnie stood apart, giving each other cautious glances as if longing for conversation. Emma had turned her back to both of them, in either indifference or disgust.

"I'll catch him later," Ronnie said at last, with an awkward nod.

Babette looked over at Peri, her green eyes narrow and lips tight. Not much frightened Peri, but a cold numbness rippled down her spine. She imagined Mrs. Murray probably had enough force in that little body to pick her up by the nape of the neck and hurl her like a stray cat.

Emma came to her rescue. "This way, Miss Minneopa." She walked to James's door and held it open for Peri, following her inside. "Mr. Murray, I just wanted you to know your tea is brewing and I'll have it for you shortly."

"Tea?" James was sitting at his desk, looking over papers. He glimpsed at the secretary. "Sure, thanks."

It seemed to Peri he wasn't as excited about chamomile as his wife believed. She approached his desk.

"What do you think you need, Peri?" He did not look up.

Peri's pep talk jumped out the window and landed on the parking lot. She threw the report in the middle of his view. "I need to know who wrote this piece of crap because it doesn't look like anything you'd do."

He flinched a little, then rolled his eyes at her. "Really? Do you have to be so dramatic?"

"Do you have to be so sloppy?"

"What are you talking about?"

"This report." She stabbed at the package with her index finger. "Okay, so I've never read one of your reports, but when I look at you and your office, I expect your work to be thorough and perfect. This is anything but."

He picked up the papers and skimmed them, stopping to squint at a few of the pictures.

"How did you get this?"

"It was delivered to the Placentia police today."

James got up and walked to a file cabinet, where he opened the top drawer and fingered the tabs. He then walked back to his desk, sat down and started typing on his computer. For several moments, he alternated between staring at the monitor and flipping through the pages of the report.

Peri took a seat and watched, waiting. The silence ate at her.

"For Pete's sake, James, what is going on here?"

They both looked up at the sound of the door. Emma walked in with a tray, holding a teapot with two cups. "Your tea, Mr. Murray, just as your wife ordered." She lifted each cup and saucer and set it on a coaster, in front of Peri first, then her boss.

"Mrs. Murray thought you might like one, too, Miss Minneopa," she said as she poured.

"Thank you, Emma." Peri watched her close the door, then turned back to James. "So, what is it about that report?"

He took a sip of tea. "You should try it. Emma makes the best chamomile tea."

Peri held up her cup. "Yeah, yeah, delish. What about the report?"

"The report... well, it isn't mine. I mean, it looks like mine, but it's different."

"How?" Peri sipped her drink.

"I would never have so many typographical errors in mine. And did you notice the commas? Definitely not following Oxford comma guidelines."

"But the substance. Do you really think it was Benny's negligence?"

"I'm still a long way from that verdict." He sat back and took another long sip, prompting Peri to do the same. "My report is still very preliminary. Yes, the fire seems to have started with a frayed lamp cord and a can of turpentine, but there are some puzzling elements to the case, so I can't release a final version. This report is also missing the extensive labels for the photographs, as well as a copy of the initial report from the fire crew..."

He was still talking, but Peri was having a hard time listening. She felt relaxed, and snuggled into the chair. His words began to run together and didn't make sense. Her eyelids were heavy. She blinked a few times, keeping her eyes closed a little longer with each blink. At some point, James stopped talking. She looked up at him to see his eyes closed.

I might as well join my host. She closed her eyes and settled back in the soft leather. There was a slight pressure on her wrist and a warm embrace of her hand around coldness. Nothing followed except sleep.

* * *

She awoke to darkness. At first, she didn't know where she was supposed to be, didn't know what day it was. She was draped across a chair, her feet sideways on the floor while her head rested on the arm. There was a sliver of moon through the window that outlined the desk in front of her, so she leaned forward, feeling around for a light.

Her fingers touched a cold hard object that turned out to be the base of a lamp. Running her hands over it, she found the switch. Nothing happened when she pressed it. She pressed it over and over until she discovered the correct position and a soft light appeared. While she fumbled with the lamp, she tried to remember.

I'm in an office. The fire guy's. She was having trouble focusing her thoughts. *Fire guy. James something. I'm Peri something and I'm in James something's office.*

Murray. James Murray. She kicked at a lump by her feet. It was her tote. She fumbled around until she found her cell phone. *Three o'clock in the morning—what am I doing here at three o'clock in the morning? Where'd James go?*

There was enough light to get a glimpse of her surroundings, so she went over to the wall and flipped the overhead light switch. The glow from the chandelier popped the room into focus. Turning back around, she found James. He was face down on the right side of his desk. She moved forward to wake him.

Then saw the letter opener in his back.

Peri backed away and shook her head, in an attempt to get some clarity. At last a logical idea pierced the fog. Call Skip.

His voice was deep and sleepy. "What, Doll?"

"Skip, something happened. I'm at James Murray's office... I don't know... I was talking to him and then I wasn't talking to him and then I woke up and it was three a.m. and he's dead now, he's stabbed." She was trying not to cry, but she couldn't stop shaking.

"Where's his office?"

"Um, that, um, beach, um, Back Bay place."

"Newport Beach?"

"Yes. That's the name. I don't know what's wrong with me, I can hardly think."

"I'm on my way, Peri. Call 911, no, wait, I'll call them. Listen carefully. I want you to find a clean cup and pee in it."

"What?"

"Find a clean cup and pee in it. You sound like you've been drugged. It's probably still in your system, but I don't want it to metabolize before you can be tested. Can you do that for me?"

"Okay."

Skip's voice got stern. "Tell me what you're going to do."

"What? Oh, yeah, I'm going to hang up and find a clean cup."

"And?"

"Pee in it?"

"Yes, Peri. Be there as soon as I can."

She hung up and looked around the office. There was a credenza on the wall to her right, so she rifled though the drawers and found a mug that had James's family picture on one side and *World's Best Dad* on the other.

"Sorry, James," she said to him as she took the mug to his private restroom. "Police orders."

In the bathroom, she looked at her reflection. There were dark circles under her eyes, worry lines in her forehead, and her hair was smashed against one side of her head, a tangled mess on the other. There was also a large bloodstain on her coral polo shirt. She lifted the shirt and checked herself. No wounds.

She stared into her own, dilated pupils. "What the hell happened?"

CHAPTER 19

"I'm a little surprised none of you look like, um, that guy," Peri told Officer Lewis, a tall, broad gentleman with gray eyes and a dark hair in a regulation cut. He stood by her while another crew of police officers, CSU agents, and the night shift coroner huddled around James Murray's body.

"What guy, ma'am?"

"You know... the TV show, the people on the beach, running, big boobs..." Her brain continued to search for words."Hassle. David Hasselhoff."

"Who is that, ma'am?"

"Actor. You're probably too young."

He nodded, but his face looked blank, so she added, "I'm sure it was before your time."

"Maybe not, ma'am. I never watched much TV. I was homeschooled."

Now Peri nodded. "It's okay. You should look like a normal cop. It's better."

"I'm glad, ma'am."

"And if you weren't a cop, I'd hit you with my walker every time you called me ma'am."

He flushed. "Sorry, M-Miss..." He held up her driver's license and attempted to read it. "Miss Minnepooha."

"Minn-ee-OH-pa. But you can call me Peri. Was anything stolen?"

"I don't know. Were you familiar with this office?"

"Not really. I was just here to talk about, hmm, something." She still felt fuzzy-headed.

"I'll take over, Officer Lewis." A commanding voice interrupted them. Peri tilted her head to see a figure come from behind, walking around to her left. She followed his movement until he faced her.

"Miss Minneopa, I'm Detective Thompson of the NBPD. I'd like to ask you about last night." He was a square-jawed man, not much younger than her, with a shaved head and a bristle of a mustache. She thought perhaps he belonged on the A-Team, chewing on a stogie.

"Of course you do." Peri sat up a little while the detective pulled a chair in front of her and took out a notepad. "Some of it is a little blurry. Maybe more than some of it. Pretty sure I was drugged. I should probably be, um, what word... tested as soon as possible. Oh, Skip told me to pee in a cup. It's in the bathroom." She waved toward the door.

"Yes, Detective Carlton told me when I spoke with him. Just tell me as much as you know. Don't try to assume anything. If you don't remember, it's okay."

"I came here around four o'clock," she began, and stepped the detective through her conversation with Murray, the chamomile tea, and the foggy awakening. Her words began to flow easier the more she spoke, although she still wasn't certain of the exact chain of events.

"I know I'm the first person on your list of suspects. I mean, here I am, the only person in the room with the victim, with blood all over me. Okay, truly, I'm assuming it's his blood. But I didn't do it. I'll do whatever it takes to prove I didn't kill him."

Detective Thompson smiled. "We are going to have you tested, and we'll process your clothes. If you're lying, we'll figure that out."

"I know you will."

"Were you attacked or assaulted in any way?"

She rubbed her arms. "Like I said, I really don't remember any of it, but I don't feel sore or have any cuts or scrapes. I was fully dressed when I woke up, so I don't think I was raped." She looked at the detective. "If you want me to be tested, I have no problem with that."

He glanced from his notebook. "Under normal circumstances, we would ask for it. However, I'm going to leave it up to you. If you don't think you were assaulted, you don't have to be tested."

"Well, I certainly don't feel like I was." She considered the options. "No, no, I don't think I need it."

"All right. Do you know anyone who might have wanted Mr. Murray dead?"

"No, I didn't know him well. I was here on behalf of a client. I mean, I had dated him, sort of, fifteen or twenty years ago, two dates, but I didn't even know him well back then."

The previous afternoon's conversation with Murray was coming back to her, so Peri stood and looked over at the desk. The report she brought was still there. Everything looked the way she remembered. She sat down again.

"Is everything okay?" Detective Thompson asked.

"Yes. No. Everything on the desk is just how I remember it." She looked at the detective and ran her hand through her hair. "My gut is telling me this has something to do with his report on my friend's—my client's—house."

"Maybe. We're still in the collection mode."

A young woman with light brown hair in a pixie cut approached. She wore a shirt that said CSU and carried a kit much like Jason's. The detective acknowledged her and turned to Peri.

"Officer Mills will process you. Rita, Peri provided a urine sample earlier, in the bathroom. Take another one for comparison."

The young woman nodded and knelt in front of Peri. "I'm going to scrape the undersides of your nails. I'll try to be gentle, but I do need to get any evidence."

"Sure." Peri held out her right hand. "I'm not sure what you'll find under there. I don't remember struggling with anyone."

"It's standard, ma'am," she said as Peri winced from her collection. "Sorry, ma'am."

"Could you please call me Peri? It's almost dawn, I've had a helluva night, and I already feel old enough."

"Sure, sorry."

Scrapings completed, Officer Mills handed Peri a cup and escorted her to the bathroom. "Let me store and mark what you've already provided, then you'll need to go again in the cup I've given you."

"If I've got anything to give," Peri said, as the officer went into the room and put the contents of Murray's Best Dad mug into an evidence container. She exited and allowed Peri to enter, then closed the door.

It took a few moments for her body to surrender its meager offerings. In the meantime, Peri heard a familiar voice outside. Skip had arrived, and her heart lightened at the sound.

Someone knocked.

"Peri?" It was Officer Mills. "When you've finished, I've got clothes for you to change into."

Peri hurried and completed her task, then opened the door. Officer Mills stepped inside.

"I'm afraid I have to be in here while you change. It's important that I collect your clothes with the least amount of disturbance to them, so we don't cross contaminate."

"Of course." Peri stepped back and gave the officer some space. "Good thing it's so roomy in here. Executive privilege and all."

"I guess."

Peri removed her shirt and gave it to the officer, who wrapped it in paper then rolled it and placed it in a paper bag and wrote on the label before taping it shut. When that was completed, Peri removed her slacks and Officer Mills repeated the process. Only when all her clothes were bagged, she was handed a set of sweats to put on. She shivered, although it didn't seem cold in the room.

The sweatshirt had 'PPD' on the front and both the shirt and pants were miles too large, which meant they had to be Skip's. Their effect was immediately comforting. She didn't think she had ever loved him more than when she stepped into his clothes.

"I feel better now," she told Officer Mills as she pulled the pants' drawstring tight enough to keep them on her waist, and rolled the hems so she wouldn't trip.

The officer opened the door and Peri stepped out to find Skip. He was talking to Detective Thompson. Trying not to unroll the sweatpants, she shuffled to him. He held his arm out and she wrapped her shoulders in it.

"Sorry the outfit's a little big," he said. "I was in a hurry and forgot you might need a change of clothes."

"Are you kidding? It's my new favorite outfit." She couldn't resist leaning into him. "Detective Thompson, do you need me for anything else, or can I go?"

He looked at his notebook. "I think we've got enough to start with. If I have more questions, you'll be available?"

"Yes, sir." Peri offered her hand to the detective. "I'm happy to help out."

She went through the open door into the front office, Skip following behind. Her foot got caught in the sweatpants, so she stopped and rolled the hems up again. As she stood, she caught sight of a tray on Emma's desk, containing the teapot and its matching cups and saucers. Peri elbowed Skip.

"Wait, that's not right. That tray with all the stuff... it was with us." She rubbed her head. "Or was it?"

"You want to tell the detective about it?"

"Yes. No. What if I tell him and I didn't remember it right?"

"Tell him anyway, but make sure he knows you're not absolutely sure."

Peri turned back to the interior office and motioned Thompson over. She pointed to the tray. "I think that was on James's desk when I closed my eyes. I'm pretty sure, but it's still real fuzzy. I know we were drinking that tea."

The detective wrote in his notepad, then called over his shoulder. "Rita, make sure you process the tray with the teapot and cups in here."

"Like I said, it's still real fuzzy," Peri told him.

He smiled. "It's okay. We'll process this room as well as the inner office and figure it all out. Thanks."

She returned to Skip, who steered her toward the door and out of the building.

"I bet dollars to donuts someone spiked our tea," she said.

"Dollars to donuts?"

"Isn't that the phrase?"

He chuckled. "Yes, but I've never heard you use it."

"Must be the drugs." She leaned against him, feeling the weight of the day. "I don't know if I can drive home."

"I didn't expect you to." His deep voice against her ear felt reassuring. "I'll drive you home, then bring you back after you've slept."

"You know how I usually kick up a fuss and demand to take care of myself?" She reached up and kissed his cheek. "Let's pretend I did and you won."

On the way home, she dozed, waking in starts to talk about the meeting with Murray.

"James said he didn't write the report you received... The letter opener was in his back."

Skip pulled into her driveway, reached over, and kissed her. She awoke with a frown.

"Where could my brother be? I could have died."

CHAPTER 20

The constant chipper sound of "Rikki, Don't Lose That Number" kept creeping into Peri's dreams, until her mind began its journey toward consciousness. She opened one eye, just enough to see her cell phone on the nightstand. It played the tune and buzzed, all indicating a phone call.

She picked it up and looked at it. Nine a.m. and Benny was calling. She wanted to put it on ignore, catch the voicemail when she had gotten more than four hours of sleep. But it was Benny. She answered it.

"Miss Peri, they won't give me my money." His voice was indignant.

"Who won't give you what money? Explain slowly, please."

"The insurance man called me, Mr. Smith." She could hear him puffing and sighing, trying to slow his words. "He said the report said the fire was my fault. They don't pay if it's my fault. It wasn't my fault."

"I know it wasn't, Benny." Her brain ached from lack of sleep, but she tried not to sound cranky. "I'm afraid something bad happened last night. James—the man who wrote the report was murdered. Please stay calm. We're going to work it all out and you'll get your money, okay? Trust me."

"But what should I do?"

What he needed to do was start getting estimates for the cleanup and repairs on his house, but Peri didn't think he'd be up for that. "Can you pick me up at one o'clock? I need someone to take me to my car."

"Where's your car?"

"It's a really long story. I'll tell you when you get here, okay?"

She ended the call and snuggled down against her pillow. If she was lucky, she could get three more hours of sleep. Her body had just relaxed again in near-slumber, when the doorbell rang.

"Salesmen," she mumbled.

It rang again.

She rolled over. "Go away."

Someone began knocking, hard and relentless.

Peri pulled herself from her warm sheets and stumbled out to see who it was, vowing to look them in the eyes as she strangled the life from them. When she opened the door, she saw a young Hispanic boy, about ten years old. He looked frightened, but resolved, as if he needed to accomplish some task.

"Miss Peri? I was told to give you this." He held out a large envelope in his shaking hand.

"Who told you?"

"A lady."

Well, that clears up everything. "What lady?"

"I don't know. I was playing in my front yard with my brother." He pointed to the right. "She drove up and gave me this, and told me what to do."

"Did she give you anything else?"

His eyes widened. "Maybe a little money."

Peri smiled. "Don't worry, I'm not going to take it. How did she know you'd do as she asked?"

"She watched me."

"Is she still there?" Peri looked past him, up the street. There were no cars parked as far as she could see.

"No, she left. I saw her drive past when you opened the door."

"Dang. Hold on a minute." She ran into the kitchen and came back with a pencil. Opening the screen door, she reached for the envelope. "Can you give me your name and address? You're not in trouble. As a matter of fact, you can help me, maybe, by identifying the woman who gave you this."

She watched his internal struggle as it played on his face.

"I tell you what," she said. "Give me your mother's name and telephone number. I will call her and speak with her first, so you know I'm okay."

He agreed. "Selina Gomez."

"No kidding."

The young boy rolled his eyes. "Not the famous one."

"Of course not." She wrote the name and phone number. "And your name? So your mother knows I spoke with you."

"Ozzie."

"Great name, Ozzie. I may be in touch with you. Thank you." She closed the door and went back to her bedroom. If this was just a marketing ploy, she could read it from the comfort of her pillow. She got back in bed and undid the clasp on the envelope. As she stuck her hand inside, a brief thought of sabotage, white powder and plague crossed her mind.

Screw it, I'm tired and curious. She poured the contents onto her quilt. Several newspaper clippings spilled out, floating briefly before settling. She gathered them all, and saw one of them was actually a handwritten note.

Keep digging. It's time someone stopped them.

"Stopped who from what?" She glanced through the articles. They all had to do with Benny's insurance company. There were dates on all the snippets, so she arranged them with oldest first and began to read. The quiet house and her lack of sleep made it difficult to stay focused, so she got up and put on a pot of coffee, turned on some music and brought everything to the kitchen table.

Nothing like a hard chair to keep you from dozing off.

The first article was a paragraph about the opening of a new insurance company, Bennett and Smith. Two men stood in front of a door with their name on it, polyester suits and slick hair. They were smiling. Peri reached over and dug a magnifying glass from the junk drawer. The small print identified them as Burton Smith and Leland Bennett.

This wasn't the office she had visited, but she recognized Smith. Even as a young man in the photo, he had the same hard lines around his mouth and piercing stare to his eyes.

You were a coldhearted snake even then, Burton.

The next article was a small town report of the insurance company reaching the one-million-dollar mark in policies. It included a picture of three men and three women, holding champagne glasses, smiling at the camera. Peri took the magnifying glass to that picture, too. It was grainy, and didn't have a caption to identify anyone.

She recognized Smith and Bennett from the previous article. The women beside them were probably their wives. Smith's wife looked familiar to Peri. She tried to imagine her as older, but came up blank. As she moved the glass across the photo, she recognized the couple in the back. The arms of the wives partly obscured them, but she knew the faces.

They were Robert and Elizabeth Needles, Benny's parents.

She read the article again. Perhaps they were the clients that pushed them over the million-dollar mark. There was no mention of them. She got up and retrieved her notepad, poured another cup of coffee, and started writing.

Mrs. Smith's obituary was next, followed by Leland Bennett's. Peri created a mini-family tree for each man. Smith had three children, Vincent, Emily, and Burton Junior. Bennett had two, George and Hester. She wondered where these kids were now.

A fleeting image of her brother crossed her mind, along with the Facebook condolences. She pushed them aside to continue reading.

The last items were a series of articles about Bennett and Smith, claiming the insurance company had never paid out a claim larger than five thousand dollars. According to the reporter, Sam Todd, people who had been insured by the company all complained their claims were either substantially reduced or denied due to clerical errors, or incomprehensible clauses in their policies. Many of these people were non-English speaking. The reporter reasoned, given the large Hispanic population in the area, they were the easiest targets for a scam.

Amid the newspaper's allegations were letters to the editor, containing rebuttals from the insurance company and threats to sue. If anything came of these printed fisticuffs, it wasn't included here. She looked at the dates of these articles. The last one was in 1992. It's possible there were still people around the newspaper to ask.

Peri glanced at the clock. It was a little past noon, so she stopped and went to the bedroom to clean up and get dressed. A shower made her feel more refreshed, if not more awake. Throwing on some denim capris and a burgundy v-neck shirt, she was ready to get her car and do some more investigation.

At one o'clock, the black Cadillac pulled into her drive, Benny behind the wheel. She grabbed her pink tote and ran out the door to meet him. Dean Martin was singing something Italian at the top of his lungs from the open windows. Peri sat down in the passenger seat, avoiding the ever-present ashtray, pulled the seatbelt across her lap and dug around her tote until she found pain relievers and a bottle of water.

Benny gasped. "What are you doing?"

"Taking an aspirin. I have a headache."

"You can't drink in my car."

She held up the bottle. "It's water."

"You can't drink in my car."

"Are you serious?" She looked at him. He stared at the bottle. "Aaarrgh, I can't believe—" She stopped in mid-sentence. It was no use. She opened the door and got out, took her aspirin, put the bottle back in her tote, then got back in. "Okay?"

"Okay." He backed out of the driveway, then stopped. "Where am I going?"

"Oh, yeah, head toward the 91. My car's in Newport Beach."

She would have told him why, but there was no talking while he drove, unless it was to give directions. Benny's rules were strictly enforced. The traffic was light, so it only took them an hour to drive twenty-five miles. Benny never drove over fifty miles an hour, even on the freeway. Usually, this drove Peri to madness, but today it gave her an excuse for a nap.

At last, they reached the parking lot of James Murray's office building. *The late James Murray,* she thought. Benny pulled into and backed out of four spots until he found one that afforded his car the most safety. He turned off the engine.

"Now what, Miss Peri?"

"I'm going to drive my car home and do some more investigating on your case." She turned to him. "I know you don't like to talk about your father, Benny, but I need information. Someone sent me a bunch of newspaper clippings. One of them shows your mom and dad with the owners of the insurance company, the one that's denying your claim. Would you know how they knew the owners?"

"We don't talk about my dad." It was another rule. Immutable.

"I know you don't, but I need you to, if you know anything. I found an envelope in your mom's stuff. It said *In the event of my death* and was signed *Robert Needles*. Should you open it?"

"No. We don't open it. We don't talk about my dad. I don't know the insurance people and I don't know why my parents knew them." He turned on the engine, cranked up Dino and stared straight ahead.

"Okay, I get it. I'm on my own. All that talk about you helping me was just talk." She looked over at him. A rash of crimson painted his cheeks.

"I. Am. Helping." His words were clipped, his voice rising. "I told you where the papers were. I drove you here. My house is burned. My stuff is gone. The rest of it smells bad. I can't sleep in my own bed. Aunt Esmy won't let me listen to my music. My albums are gone—"

"Okay, okay, okay. I feel badly about it, I do. I want you back in your house as much as you want to be there."

She started to put her hand on his shoulder, then remembered his aversion to touch. "Take some breaths, Benny. We're going to fix all this, I promise. It will just take time. If you don't want to talk about your dad, or open that envelope, I understand, I get it. I'm just trying to get answers here. I'm sorry."

He relaxed after a few moments. "I'm so sad, Miss Peri. Thinking about my dad makes me sadder." He picked up one of his eight-track tapes and looked at the label: *This is Dean Martin.* "I used to wish Dean Martin was my dad. I lost my real dad. I don't want to lose Dino, too."

"You won't. We'll get your stuff cleaned or re-finished, or whatever it takes." She smiled at him, waiting for him to turn and smile back. Eventually, he did manage a small grin, one that looked almost like a wince. "Do you trust me?"

He nodded.

"Okay, then I'll call you if I learn anything. Thanks for the ride." She got out of his car and walked toward her own. As she unlocked the door, she looked up at the building. *What was in your real report, James?*

She drove out of the parking lot, onto the street, thinking about why someone would falsify a report and forge Murray's signature. Claiming homeowner negligence got the insurance company off the hook. It also set the stage for the McHale family's lawsuit. Two different factions could have done it. They had the same motive.

Who was the culprit?

Peri pulled over to the side of Jamboree Road. She typed *Newport Beach Police Department* into her navigation system and saw it was east of the road she was on. It had to be karma, being so close when she had a question or two for Detective Thompson.

CHAPTER 21

The Newport Beach Police Department was in a large, square building with a tall staircase up the front and rows of windows that reminded Peri of the story about the monster Argus and his many eyes. She imagined trying to slip anything into or out of the building under his watchfulness.

Wow, what kind of mayhem were they expecting in Newport when they built this?

She walked up the steps into the foyer, where a young, ruddy-faced officer sat at the reception desk.

"Hi, I was wondering if Detective Thompson is in. My name is Peri Minneopa. I'd like to speak with him."

The officer looked up from his work. "Um, the receptionist is on her lunch break, but let me see if I can get his number." He typed the name into the computer, then picked up the phone and dialed.

Peri tried not to listen. She instead walked to the opposite side of the foyer and pretended to look at pictures of all the past police chiefs. After a few moments, she heard the officer's voice drop with a final sound, and the click of the phone being put back in its stand. She returned to the desk.

"Detective Thompson is on his way down," the officer said.

For a brief moment, she wondered if she'd recognize the detective. Drugs and murder tend to make a gal forgetful. Fortunately, the solid frame and bald head of the man walking toward her looked familiar. She extended her hand.

"Detective, thank you for seeing me."

"I confess I'm a little surprised to see you here." He pointed her toward a couple of chairs in the public area, where they both sat down.

"I'm a little surprised myself," she told him. "I kind of thought I'd still be asleep."

"How can I help you?"

"Well, first of all, I hope I can help you. I don't quite recall much of last night, and I want to make sure I gave you all the information you need. I'm guessing I was at least coherent."

He pulled out his notebook and flipped through the pages. "I don't have your statement typed up yet, but if you want to go over it again, I'm happy to hear what you've got to add."

"Did I tell you I'm a private investigator?"

Thompson sat back and smiled. "No. But when we dug your wallet out to get your ID, we did see your license."

Peri sighed. "I know, we're not always a welcome sight. I have a client whose house caught fire. He's fighting the insurance company for his money, a couple is suing him for the death of their son in the house, even though he was there illegally, and I'm at my wit's end trying to help him. Did I tell you about my meeting with James?"

"You told me it was to discuss his report on the fire." He skimmed his notes. "Did you discuss anything else?"

"No, there was no opportunity." Peri sat back as a flash of memory popped in and out of her mind. "I keep having a weird—snapshot in my head that I can't quite focus on."

"Well, the tests aren't completed yet, but that's pretty normal for people who've been given GHB or Rohypnol, which would explain your symptoms. Can you describe any of it?"

She closed her eyes and shook her head. "My right hand feels warm and cold at the same time." Looking up at the detective, she said, "Sorry. It's kind of a sensation instead of a picture."

"That's all right." He wrote another note in his book.

"Detective, I know I'm asking a lot, but I would like to know what I was drugged with."

"Of course."

"And maybe one more thing? I need to know if you found more than one report on the Needles house fire."

He cleared his throat. "Peri, I don't mind letting you know about the drugs. You have a right to that information. But the report is a little murkier. I'm not fond of gray areas, especially when they might give you a motive for the killing."

"Killing? Why would I kill James? I needed that report."

"Well, theoretically speaking, if the report wasn't to your liking, you could have killed him and inserted your own."

"Well, that's a stupid idea. I date a detective, for Pete's sake. Do you think I think I won't get caught?" Last night, Peri thought the detective was sympathetic, but under today's scrutiny, he didn't seem so cuddly. "Criminals are stupid. They get caught. I'm not stupid, or a criminal."

His mustache flicked once. "According to you, I have a stupid idea. What does that make me?"

She tried to ignore the heat rising in her face. "A smart detective who's wasting time on a bad theory."

"It's my job to look in every stupid corner of the room."

Peri stood. "I'm guessing you'll let me know when I need to hire an attorney."

"We'll be in touch." He rose from his chair in slow motion. She appreciated the way his gesture both told her she had not ruffled him and impressed her with his sheer size. "Thank you for coming in."

She left the station feeling frustrated. It was too soon to have processed any of the evidence, but she was hoping to make friends with the detective now, in order to get information later. He was not going to cooperate.

Why should he? From his point of view, I might be the killer.

After getting in her car, Peri considered returning home and going over her notes, but the false investigation report nagged at her. The police and their CSI team had probably processed the entire scene by now. She wondered what they had found. Even more, she wondered what they had looked for.

Without hesitation, she turned her car back toward Murray's building. This time, she parked on the corner near his office and took the closest stairs. As she had guessed, there was yellow *Crime Scene* tape across the red door

She walked past his door toward the corner. The building looked like it ended at the outer railing, but there was a small alcove to the right, with another door. It was beige, like all the others on the floor, with an industrial-looking doorknob. Peri turned it. It was unlocked.

Inside, there was a door to the building to the right, with more police tape across it. To the left was an enclosed stairwell. It was an emergency exit.

Peri wanted into the office again. She kept kicking herself for not gathering more data the night James was killed, even if she was in no condition to figure out what to collect. She ran her fingers over the taped door. Skip would kill her if she broke into the office, especially if she got caught. Detective Thompson would never speak to her again, unless it was to accuse her of possibly planting evidence, or convincing himself that she killed James. But still...

She looked up at the corners. There were no security cameras in the alcove. Then she went back outside and checked the eaves. No cameras on any kind on these offices. She was returning to James's front door when she saw a familiar figure standing in front of it.

Emma, his secretary, stood with her keys in hand, looking at the door with a confused expression.

"Emma—"

She jumped at her name. "Miss Minneopa, you startled me. Why is this door taped?"

"The police haven't been to see you?"

"See me for what? Did someone break in? I keep telling Mr. Murray we need a security system, but he always says we don't keep cash in the office, so why do we need it. Sometimes that man is a little too cheap."

Peri had delivered bad news before, but each time was as difficult as the last. "Emma, I hate to tell you, but Mr. Murray is dead. He was found here last night."

The tall brunette swayed, as if her knees might buckle. Peri stepped in to support her.

"I know," she told the secretary. "It's a shock."

"He was in such fine health." Emma stood and brushed at her pale peach suit. "He rode his bicycle every day."

"I'm afraid he was murdered."

Emma's eyes widened. "Murder? Oh my goodness, who would murder him?"

"We don't know yet. The police are investigating. I must say, I'm surprised they haven't interviewed you yet, or that Mrs. Murray didn't call and tell you."

"That woman? No offense, she just lost her husband and her boys' daddy and all, but she wouldn't go out of her way to tell me good news, much less bad." She looked down at the key still in her hand. "Guess I don't need to come to work today. I was supposed to get some files entered into our database. Better go home and brush up the resume instead."

"Emma, I do have one question to ask you. Did you personally make the tea you served us yesterday?"

"Why, yes. Mrs. Murray taught me to make it just the way her husband likes it. Loose tea, no bags. A special mixture she buys from some fancy-schmancy store and brings in."

"Were Mrs. Murray and that man, Ronnie, still in the office when you were pouring it?"

"Yes, both of them. Mrs. Murray sent me to adjust the thermostat while the tea was brewing. That woman is always running cold. She's got no blood."

"So you were away from your desk?"

She nodded.

An idea began to swirl in Peri's mind. "You might want to give the Newport Beach police a call and tell them who you are and what you were doing last night. The detective's name is Thompson."

Tears appeared in Emma's eyes, and began to run down her face. Peri dug in her tote for a tissue and handed it to the weeping woman. They both turned and went back down the stairs to their cars. Emma got in and drove away. Peri watched her leave, noticing how she held the tissue up to her face as she eased out of the parking lot. Getting into her own car, Peri sat and took some deep breaths.

She still wanted in that office. She still knew it was illegal. But Emma had told her there was no security to record her actions. She pulled onto the street, thinking about what she would do if no one was around to watch her.

Peri had managed to turn onto Bristol Street toward Jamboree Road before her will to do what's right cried uncle to her curiosity. After pulling her Bluetooth earpiece out of a cup holder, she turned it on and managed to attach it to her ear using one hand.

"Call Benny," she ordered as she drove around the block, back toward Birch.

He answered after the second ring.

"Are you home, Ben?"

"No I'm not home, Miss Peri." There was a bit of huffiness in his voice. "I can't go home, remember? My home is burnt—"

"Sorry, I didn't mean home, I guess. Are you back at Aunt Esmy's?"

"Of course. I never answer the phone while I'm driving."

"Would you like to go out for a good Italian dinner? My treat." She knew she was being manipulative, but even her faux-employee might balk at what she was going to ask him to do.

Benny was more than agreeable. "Where?"

"Meet me at the office where you dropped me off earlier and—"

"All the way back to Newport Beach? Why so far away?"

"Because I still need to do a little work here, and I need your help. I thought afterwards, I'd take you to Amelia's on the island. Can you be here around seven-thirty?"

Amelia's on Balboa Island was a small family-owned restaurant featuring seafood and pasta. It was also Benny's favorite place for lasagna. He could not resist.

"Yes, Miss Peri."

Peri ended the call and continued driving back to Murray's office building, where she parked, reclined her seat, and closed her eyes. She thought about doing more work until Benny arrived, but decided a nap was what she needed.

After that, she needed it to be dark outside.

CHAPTER 22

The sun had nearly disappeared when she heard the growl of a large engine pull into the parking lot. She sat up and saw the brake lights of Benny's 1960 black Cadillac Coupe de Ville brighten as it came to a stop. The car then backed up and pulled out, as he took one more trip around the parking lot to find a better spot. She returned her seat to driving position and waited.

Ultimately, he found a space that pleased him and stopped. Peri grabbed her tote, got out of her car and waited for him in the shadows, away from the streetlight that stretched across the pavement. Benny, ever dapper in tan slacks and a diamond-patterned shirt under his silk bomber jacket, bounced up the curb to her.

"What are we doing?" he asked.

"We're breaking into James Murray's office. I need you to pick the locks." Peri had experienced his skill firsthand, when he helped her investigate a cheating spouse.

Benny backed away from her. "Oh, no, Miss Peri. That's against the law."

She considered spinning a story that would make it sound legal, then abandoned the idea. "Yes it is. If we get caught, it'll mean trouble."

"I'm not going back to jail." He put his left hand in his jacket pocket and seemed to be wiggling it. Peri assumed he had brought the ashtray and was rubbing it.

"That's fair. Here's the deal. That fire investigation report the insurance company has is a fake. Murray told me so. I think the real report is somewhere in his office. The report may clear you from negligence, in which case we can show it to the insurance company so they'll give you your money. There's also the chance it won't clear you, so we'd be back at square one."

Benny stared at the ground, weaving from one foot to the other.

"I don't want either of us to go to jail," Peri added. "You can unlock the door, then go to Amelia's and wait for me. You don't have to be a part of it. But if we get caught, I will tell them you didn't want to do this, that I forced you to unlock the doors."

"The report could clear me?"

"I think so, but I haven't actually read it."

"The fire was not my fault." He wrenched his left hand from his pocket to entwine his fingers. "Where's the lock?"

"This way." She led him to the bottom of the enclosed stairs and tried the metal door. It opened, so they went in. She dug in her tote and retrieved her flashlight to light their way up the flight to the second story.

"It's dark in here." Benny's voice echoed in the concrete walls.

"Shh, Ben. We stand a better chance of doing this if you're quiet."

"Oh, right." He lowered to a whisper.

At the top of the stairs was the door with police tape. Peri shone the flashlight on it and stood aside, waiting for her assistant to work his magic. She could smell his Aqua Velva in the small space. Looking back over her shoulder, she saw his face in the backlight, shadowed like a jack-o-lantern. He was looking at her.

"Well?" she said, swinging the flashlight's glow toward him.

"Oh. You want me to unlock this door?"

"Please. Then you can leave."

Peri pointed the light back at the door knob and waited. She heard the sound of change and keys jingling and could vaguely see him digging in his pocket. At last, he pulled something small and metal out and slipped it into the door's lock. A few seconds later, a click signaled his success.

"Thanks, Ben. I should be no more than ten, fifteen minutes in here, then I'll join you at the restaurant."

She pointed the light toward the stairs so he could get to the exit without falling, and watched him totter downward, his heels hitting each step in an arrhythmic manner. A slip of moonlight let her know he was out and on his way. She turned back to the open door.

The crime scene tape crossed the door, secured on the jamb. Peri put on a pair of gloves, then carefully lifted the tape from the right side and looped it back. She hoped she could press it down again and it would not look like anyone tampered with it. Once she had the door open enough to slide underneath the tape, she slipped in.

The back door led past the bathroom and into the office. Inside, it was dark, but there was a small shaft of light from the streetlights outside, peeking through the curtains. She stopped for a moment and let her eyes get as accustomed as possible, then walked to the file cabinet. Murray had opened the top drawer when he looked inside, so that was the first place she tried. The files were alphabetized, neat, and color-coded. She fingered her way through the tabs, until she found Benny's file.

It was empty, just as she feared it would be.

Either the Newport Beach police had taken it, or the killer had. Peri looked in the bottom drawer, just to be certain, but found nothing. She turned off her flashlight and thought.

Whoever killed James tried to set me up for the crime. My only link to him is this investigation. I'm betting they knew the real report was in that cabinet.

She turned on the light again and pointed it toward his desk. The report would have been on his computer, which she saw the police take last night. *Or was it this morning?* The drugs, trauma, and lack of sleep were catching up with her.

James was such a neatnik, she thought as she surveyed his desk. Everything was so pristine, so organized. His computer had been to his left. To his right, there was a phone, a desk organizer with exactly one pen, one pencil and two folders, and the picture of his family.

She tried the drawers. They all opened, except for the bottom left. *Why would he have a locked drawer?* It's not like people were traipsing through his office without his knowledge. She shone the light on the lock. There were scratches around the wood. Someone had tried to get into this.

Surely the police must have opened and searched this drawer, but she doubted they would have picked the lock. Maybe Babette gave them the keys to the office. Or maybe they didn't think a locked drawer was relevant, especially when they had a suspect in the room with him, with his blood all over her shirt.

"I could sure use Benny right now," she whispered.

Maybe James left the key somewhere. Lots of people hide their desk keys in their offices. She moved the organizer, looking inside the pen holder, shaking out the folders. No key. The family picture was next. She picked it up and regarded the photo again. Mrs. Murray was amazingly beautiful. Peri wondered about their marriage. When she'd met Babette, the woman seemed a little on the exacting side.

Peri ran her hand down the back of the picture and felt a lump. She turned the frame over and slid the backing off, expecting a key. She was wrong.

Taped to the inside of the back was a USB flash drive. She stuck it in her pocket, then put the frame back together and set it on the desk. It would still be nice to get into that drawer, but the flash drive may have information she could use. Or it could have pornographic photos. She didn't think James was that kind of guy, but people could be surprising.

A sound from the back door caught her attention. Someone else was coming in. Peri sank down under the desk, turned off the flashlight, and kept her breath shallow. She listened to the footsteps, slow and unsure in the darkness. Whoever it was, they did not have a light, and were bumping into things. She could hear jostling furniture and faint "oomphs" as each piece was hit.

Why this person didn't stop and get used to the dark, she didn't know. All she knew was that the desk suddenly lurched as they ran into it, forcing it against her shins. She stifled a yelp and heard another, stronger, "oomph."

In a voice she recognized.

"Benny?"

"Miss Peri, where are you?"

Peri crawled from under the desk, rubbing her legs. "What the hell are you doing here? You were supposed to go to Amelia's." She turned on her flashlight and pointed it at him.

Benny squinted against the glare. "I'm supposed to be helping you."

"You did help. Then I told you to go to the restaurant."

"You're paying me to help you."

"You're paying me to pay you." She stared at him in the glow, wondering how she got herself this particular sidekick. "Never mind, come over here and unlock the bottom drawer."

"Isn't that illegal?"

She gestured around the room. "I think we've already crossed that turnpike."

He nodded and came around the desk. She could see his eyebrows wrinkling in worry, but he took out his instruments and knelt down.

"Someone else has been trying to get in here. Amateurs. Gordo told me only slobs leave marks like that. Gordo was the guy I shared a cell with. He was a pretty nice guy. They said he broke into houses and robbed them, but he says he was innocent. I think—"

"Benny, could you talk a little less and pick a little more?"

"Jeesh, you don't need to be so cranky." With a couple of quick pokes, the drawer opened, and Benny stood up.

Peri pointed the light into the drawer, looked inside, and chuckled. It was filled with a cornucopia of junk food, from candy bars to Twinkies. Mr. Fitness was a junk food junkie. She thought about emptying the drawer to keep his widow from discovering his secret.

*If that's the worst Babette discovers, she's better off than most wives. S*he closed the drawer. "Let's go, Ben."

She lighted their way to the exit. Just as they reached it, she heard the interior door to the office open. She shoved Benny out the door and followed him, quietly latching it behind her. Benny started to walk down the steps, but she grabbed his arm.

"No noise," she mouthed, then put her finger to her lips.

They stood on the upper landing, waiting. Peri saw the light come on under the door. Whoever was in the room wasn't concerned about being caught. She pushed the crime scene tape back to its original position and pressed it down, then turned to Benny, leaning to whisper in his ear.

"Go down the stairs as slowly and quietly as you can. Get in your car and go. I'll follow."

He nodded and grabbed the stair rail. Peri could hear the unsteady shush-shush of feet as her unusual partner made his way in the darkness. It wasn't perfectly quiet, but it wasn't an echo of stomping at least. It took a few minutes, but she finally saw the sliver of light showing Benny's exit from the building. She sighed in relief.

Then he slammed the door.

The ring of the metal echoed around the stairwell. Peri stepped to the left side of the door and cursed silently at her assistant. *If I get out of this, you can kiss that promotion goodbye.*

The doorknob turned and she held her breath. The door pushed out against the tape. She could see light from the room.

"This door has tape on it, too," a familiar male voice said.

"Leave it. It was probably nothing." Peri thought it sounded like Babette Murray.

The door shut again. She waited for a few minutes, then began her own descent in the dark. Leaning much of her weight on the railing, she tiptoed onto each step. After what seemed like an eternity, she reached the bottom, carefully opened the door, then latched it again.

She hustled to her car, got in and locked the doors. Benny's Cadillac was nowhere to be seen, so he had obeyed her instructions. Two new cars were parked in the lot, a golden Toyota truck and a dark Lexus SUV. She knew she should leave, but she wanted to know who had broken into Murray's office. Slinking down in her seat, she reached into her tote and grabbed her camera. All that was left to do was wait.

Fifteen minutes later, she saw two people slip around the corner, both looking around, as if for witnesses. Peri lifted her camera and pressed the button. She got several shots of Babette Murray and the single-named Ronnie making their way toward the two cars. They moved apart from one another and didn't pause to speak before leaving.

Not lovers, thought Peri, *maybe business partners.* She took a few more pictures of their respective cars, making certain to include the license plates.

A few minutes after they left, she drove out of the parking lot, toward Jamboree Road. Her adrenaline kicked in and she began to shake, but managed to keep her foot on the accelerator and calmed down at some point. Along the way, she began to wonder why Mrs. Murray had broken into her husband's office.

As she approached the Pacific Coast Highway, her phone rang. It was Benny.

"Miss Peri, I've been waiting for you, where are you?"

"I'm on my way, Benny. I'll be there in about five minutes." She sailed across the bridge and found a parking place she could squeeze her little car into. Benny may have jeopardized her with that slamming door, but his lock-picking skills were worth an expensive lasagna dinner.

CHAPTER 23

Dinner with Benny was always an adventure, no matter what the venue. By the time Peri got to the restaurant, they were the last customers of the night. She tried to hurry her client along. He had been looking at the menu for an easy thirty minutes before she got there, and still had not made a selection.

"You know you love the lasagna, Ben. Why even try anything else?"

"But they have different kinds." He squinted at the selections. "Maybe I should try the verde, or the pollo."

The server, a young man, was glancing about at his fellow waiters, who were cleaning their stations. Peri felt badly for this poor kid who got stuck with them.

"You like the meat sauce," she told him, then turned to the waiter. "I'll have the angel hair pasta with tomatoes and basil."

Benny agreed to the meat sauce and then was forced to choose immediately between the soup and salad. Dinners ordered, the server disappeared and reappeared with a glass of red for Peri. Her insides were still a little gooey from the evening's activities. The deep, earthy bouquet of the wine mingled perfectly with the smells of garlic, onions, and other spices from the room.

"Miss Peri, can I get my money now?"

"Lower your voice a little." She looked at his innocent expression. "I don't know. I did find something, but I need my computer to read it."

"Why are you here then? Go home and read it."

"I'm buying you dinner, remember? To thank you for your help." She decided not to mention the slamming door.

"Wonder who was in the office after us."

"Shh, Benny, please."

"Oh." The light bulb popped on. "Oh, yeah."

Their food delivered, conversation stopped while he kept his mouth filled, first with pasta fagioli soup, then with the creamy, meaty layers of lasagna. Peri watched him as she ate her salad, then her lighter fare. She wondered, if it took him an hour to choose dinner, how was he going to get his home rebuilt?

"Benny, don't you know anything about who handles your finances? I mean, someone's got to be releasing money from your trust fund and making sure your bills are paid."

He shook his head. "The money's just there. Momma said I'd be taken care of."

"It might be time for you to get a little more involved in, well, your own life. Once you do get your insurance money, you'll have to fix your house so you can live in it again."

"But what about my Dino collection?"

She smiled. "Yes, you need to replace those, but you can't do that until you've got someplace to put them, right?"

He looked at her, then soaked up the remaining sauce with his garlic bread. "I guess."

"It's going to mean making some decisions. You may have to take charge."

"Phil and Nancy can help me. Or I can pay you."

Peri sipped the last of her wine. "I guess, but I just don't understand why you don't want to be in control of your own life."

"Because I'm not the dad." He half-stood, spitting his words in staccato rhythm. Scowling, he looked around at the servers, who were staring at him, and sat down. "I'm not the dad. My dad was supposed to be with me and teach me how to do things, how to take care of everything. When he left I was ten and he told me to take care of Mom. How could I take care of her? I didn't know anything."

He huffed for a few minutes, catching his breath. "My mom was the greatest. She handled it all."

Peri noticed his left hand in his coat pocket. She assumed he was rubbing on the ashtray again to calm him. Beth was a good mother, in that she took good care of her son, but she might have protected him too much. At least Benny appreciated what she did for him. Unlike Peri's brother, who railed against every attempt by his family to love him.

"I'm sorry, Ben. I know it's been hard."

The server interrupted their conversation with the check, so Peri took her wallet out and retrieved a card.

"I know you don't talk about your dad," she said. "But don't you want to know what's in that letter?"

She watched his body stiffen. "No."

"Okay." Collecting her credit card, she stood and gathered her tote. There was no moving him on this subject. "Thanks again. Drive safe."

* * *

Once at home, Peri checked the mailbox for a letter, but there were only advertisements. Disappointed, she entered her house, poured a glass of iced tea and opened her laptop. She dug the flash drive from her pocket and stuck it in the port. The folders popped up in the window. They were all audio files, with names and numbers. She looked down the list and found one titled *Needles061210*. The folder contained several files, all labeled by timestamp. Praying that her anti-virus software would protect her, she clicked on the first file and listened.

"This is James Murray, on site at 1400 Angelina Drive, investigating a fire at the home of..." He trailed off, then returned. *"Benjamin Needles. Preliminary analysis is a home in extreme disrepair."*

The first file was an in-depth description of the front of the house, including the yard, and the damage as seen from the outside. The next file was an equally boring description of the living room, detailing each black smudge, each melted piece of plastic, each pile of ashes.

His voice was measured, precise, and monotonous, and she found herself nodding off every few minutes, then jerking awake.

By the fourth file, listening and remaining conscious seemed to be two opposing forces. She had almost decided to stop the file and go to bed when Murray's words got her attention.

"The turpentine can was open, and there is a melted paint can nearby, but there is no evidence of brushes or indication of a reason for either can's presence— Ronnie."

"How's the investigating going?" She now recognized his voice. The ubiquitous Ronnie had been at Benny's burned house.

"It would go better if you weren't here."

"Ah, Jimmy, I'm just making sure you don't need help."

"Don't call me Jimmy." Murray's voice was so cold, Peri was surprised she didn't see icicles on the screen. "I do not need anything from you."

"Honestly, Jim—James, I don't even know why you're still here. Everyone knows Needles was negligent."

"I certainly do not know it. Now please leave and let me do my job."

"And my job is to make sure you understand." Ronnie's voice sounded low, menacing. "This is homeowner negligence. We don't care how you write it up, as long as that's what it says."

"I'm not your stooge, Ronnie, nor your boss's. For God's sake, a kid died here."

A chuffing sound was heard, then Ronnie said, "Collateral."

"I'm reporting the facts, Ronnie." James was firm.

Ronnie's voice got further away, but still threatened. "He won't like it."

There was a pause, then Murray began again. "Where was I? Oh, yes, the turpentine and paint. There's no evidence that any home improvement has been performed on this house. Although Mr. Needles has been negligent in all other areas, I cannot explain why there was a can of turpentine and a can of paint in the living room. I cannot say unequivocally it was homeowner negligence without further investigation. I would recommend the homeowner be asked to explain the paint and turpentine, and that perhaps this should be investigated as arson."

She quickly downloaded the files to her computer, then ran her backup program to store everything on her internet account. After removing the flash drive, she put it in a side pocket of her tote bag and checked the time. It was already midnight. Skip had caught a late shift, followed by an extension class at Fullerton College. She couldn't do anything with the drive until morning.

It was going to be hard to sleep tonight, with all this information burning a hole in her brain.

* * *

Nine a.m. couldn't come too soon, and Peri was walking into the police station at the top of the hour. She slipped into Skip's office and closed the door.

"Guess what I have?" She pulled the flash drive from her tote and put it on his desk. "It was in James Murray's office and it's got all his audio notes from all his cases, plus a big argument with that Ronnie guy who I met the day he was murdered."

Skip frowned. "And where did you find this?"

"In Murray's office."

"Peri—"

"What? Don't 'Peri' me. The Newport police weren't going to tell me whether they found Murray's real report and I need to know what he really thought about the fire."

"Please don't tell me you broke into Murray's office."

"Okay, I won't tell you."

Skip picked up the drive and shook it at her. "I don't care if this has photos of the killer in the act and an entire movie of the fire. We can't use it. It was gotten illegally."

"By me." Peri tapped her own chest. "You didn't know I was getting it, did you? No. I got it, I turned it into the police. You can say it was anonymous. Hell, you can say one of the officers found it. They have a damned warrant for the office, for Pete's sake."

"Was it in a marked bag?"

"Well, no."

"How about photographs? Any police photographs showing where this was located?"

"No." She looked at the ground. "I didn't take any photos, either. I didn't want to risk the light."

"Because you were breaking and entering."

"It was hidden within the frame of his family's picture, on his desk. I didn't exactly see it, I felt it when I picked up the picture. I was looking for the key to his locked drawer."

"I suppose you broke into that, too."

"Maybe, sort of. But someone else had been trying to get into that drawer as well. There were scratch marks all over the lock." Peri shrugged. "Turns out he was hiding a stash of junk food. No big deal."

Skip looked at her, squinting. "How did you get into a locked building, let alone a locked drawer?"

"Maybe I pick locks now."

"Or maybe you don't."

"It doesn't matter." She wasn't about to give up poor Benny. She had made a promise. "I got in. I got information. Would it be better if I asked you to meet me in an alley and offered to sell it to you?"

Skip sighed. "I don't like it." He looked at the drive in his hand. "I'll have Jason look at it, but I'm not happy."

"You're never happy with my job."

"I really don't like that you broke into a crime scene."

"Well I wasn't the only one. Mrs. Murray and Ronnie were there, too. They had the balls to turn on the office lights."

He sat forward. "Who is this Ronnie person?"

"I don't know who he is, but I saw him in James's office just before I went in to yell at him." She shrugged. "Of course, that didn't go as planned."

"And how do you know it was them?"

"After I left the building, I sat in my car and waited for them to come out. I do have pictures of that."

"An affair?"

She shook her head. "They weren't very cozy. On the tape, Ronnie told James his boss wouldn't like it if he didn't say Benny's house fire was homeowner negligence."

"His boss, eh? I'll see if we can identify Ronnie." He walked around the desk and took her by the arm, pointing her toward the door. "In the meantime, you need to go home and rest."

"Sure, Skip, as soon as I—"

"As soon as you nothing. Go home."

"I just need to—"

"You need to go home."

Between Detective Thompson and her boyfriend, she felt surrounded by obstinate men. "Fine, I'll go home. We on for dinner?"

"Yes."

"Good." She grabbed the doorknob. "I'm having a Grey Goose dirty martini tonight. On your tab."

CHAPTER 24

Back at home, Peri sat with her notes and a mug of coffee, and wondered where else she could go for information about this case. Somebody didn't want her to find out about the insurance policy. No doubt, the same somebody faked the investigator's report to make the policy unenforceable.

On the other side of the coin, someone else was feeding her information, first with the safety deposit box, then the envelope of clippings. She opened her notes and looked at what she'd written. Her scribbles took a moment to decipher, as they were made when she was completely sleep-deprived.

As was her habit, she opened her laptop and entered her notes into her computer, scanned the articles in, then backed up her files to her online account. Skip said she needed to rest, but she didn't see how that was going to happen if her mind was spinning at warp speed.

What she needed was answers. She got the clippings out again and studied them. Something Mrs. Murray said bounced back into her memory.

Babette Bennett Murray.

Peri looked at the photos with the magnifying glass. They were grainy and difficult to see any details, but there might be a similarity between Babette and Hester Bennett. *Perhaps Jason could work some photo magic on them to make them clearer,* she thought.

In the meantime, she had heard Mrs. Murray was receiving visitors today, to express their condolences. She should express hers.

Jumping up from the couch, Peri went into her bedroom and changed clothes. To be taken seriously, she needed to look serious, so she chose a black sheath dress and even wiggled into a pair of pantyhose. The June afternoon promised to be smothering, but she got out a pin-striped jacket, too, to present a polished look. There was something about Babette Bennett Murray that demanded upscale mourning.

After styling her blonde hair into a simple bun at the nape of her neck, Peri picked up her tote and headed out the door. She plugged the Murray home address into her phone's navigation tool, got into her car, and drove off.

Irvine, California, was a planned community, a city that carefully reserved spots for housing and spots for businesses and never allowed the two to mingle. The housing consisted of everything from apartments to million-dollar homes, yet their complete separation from mini-marts and strip malls did not prevent gang and criminal activities.

It looked nice on a map, though.

Peri worked her way down the interstate, getting off at Culver Drive and heading northeast toward a fashionable set of houses on a manmade lake. She pulled her car to the curb several driveways away from the Murray home, a gray two-story, over-landscaped with a maze of brick planters, and exploding with flora, from flowers to full-sized trees. A number of cars were parked up and down the street, even though there were signs everywhere indicating the homeowners association's disapproval.

She hoped the association could have a little compassion for the loss of one of their members. As she got out of her car, she smoothed her dress down and put on her jacket.

The front door was open, marked with a black wreath, a curious fixture from the past. Peri wandered into the house, glad she had dressed for the occasion. The foyer and adjoining rooms seemed to be stuffed with small groups of sophisticated people, drinking what appeared to be punch or coffee, all out of proper glass or china. No Styrofoam cups here.

On her way through the house, she tried to take in the furnishings as well as the faces, nodding in sympathy as she passed. A combination of smells hit her sensitive nose. There was something rich and beefy, wrapped around a sweet, cinnamon scent, with a hint of bacon from somewhere.

An older woman walked toward her, flawless and aristocratic in her years. Her skin, while showing its wrinkles, was moist. Her makeup was natural, and her silver hair was coiffed in waves that balanced her long face and accentuated her high cheekbones. She offered a manicured hand to Peri as she approached.

"Hello, I'm Carol Sykes Bennett, James's mother-in-law."

"Peri Minneopa." She took the woman's hand for a brief, gentle handshake. "I knew James a long time ago, and wanted to pay my respects."

Carol Bennett looked at Peri, her eyebrow raised. "Aren't you the woman who—"

"Yes." She cut her off before she had to formulate the rest of the sentence. "I was meeting with James when it happened. I'm still just in shock."

She hadn't planned on being recognized as the woman who woke up next to the dead guy. As far as she knew, that information hadn't been released. There was nothing to do now but take a breath and wait for the fallout.

The older woman linked her arm in Peri's, as if they were old friends. "Tell me, Dear, how did it happen? We are devastated. Answers of any kind would help us."

"I had stopped by to discuss my client's report with James." She stopped, wondering how much she should divulge. "I felt myself grow sleepy, and remember seeing his eyes close. Then I awoke, several hours later, to find…" She trailed off, unable to finish.

Mrs. Bennett patted Peri's hand. "It must have been awful. Whatever could have knocked you out?"

There was a digging tone in the woman's voice that made Peri suspicious. "I'm not sure. The police are testing everything they found in the office, though."

The woman nodded. "Let me take you back to my daughter. I'm certain she'll want to see you."

They walked through the formal dining room, which had been set up as a buffet. The food Peri had detected was artfully arranged on the table, along with the good china, silver, and linens. Drinks were on the credenza.

The house was decorated in neutral colors, understated and classic, with high-end furniture in soft mocha tones and sleek lines. As they passed by the credenza, Peri saw family photos on the wall.

One of them caught her eye. Two adults and two children, dressed in Sixties party attire, sat in classic photo studio pose. The man wore a dark suit, the woman a chiffon dress with a rolled v-neck. The children were in similar outfits and looked like miniature adults.

"What interesting pictures." She pointed. "I assume this is James's family?"

"No, that's my husband's side. That's my George, with his sister, Hester, and their parents, Leland and Norma." She prattled on a bit about their meeting in college, and Hester's marriage to George's best friend, Carl McHale, producing a son named Ronald.

Peri's ears perked up at the name. Perhaps this was the infamous Ronnie. She was shocked to hear he shared the same last name as the boy who died. Perhaps this woman liked to talk, and could be persuaded to tell more. "I love family stories. It sounds like you have a lot of good memories."

"Oh, yes, there was always something happening, although it wasn't always good." She motioned to a photo on the left. "That's my husband's family and my father-in-law's business partner and his family. Burton and Gretchen Smith, and their children Vincent, Burton Junior, and Emily."

Another frozen slice from the Sixties, the outdoor photo showed two men in gray suits, standing beside women in pencil-thin sheath dresses. She recognized Burton Smith at once. He looked only slightly happier in the picture than the last time she saw him. The children stood in front of them, dressed in their Sunday School finest. The lady identified as Gretchen Smith held young Emily in her arms.

Mrs. Bennett let her hand linger at the young girl's face. "Such a sweet girl, and such tragedy. I knew her, used to babysit her. She ran away from home when she was eighteen. Never heard from again."

Peri thought about her brother. "Wow, that must have been hard on the family."

"Yes, it was hard on everyone." Mrs. Bennett broke from her reverie, and smoothed her own slim, charcoal suit. "Now, let's find my daughter."

They followed a small stream of people into the kitchen, and found Babette sitting at the island. She was magnificent in mourning, her black dress as elegant as Hepburn in *Breakfast at Tiffany's*, her rich brown hair in a simple twist, her makeup subdued. She held a tissue, and Peri could see the redness in her eyes, even if she was otherwise perfect.

Several women were gathered around her, mouthing words of nurture and consolation, but she seemed to be only half-aware of what they were saying. Instead, she was scrubbing at a spot on the granite top of the island. Peri couldn't tell whether the spot was real or imagined.

"Mrs. Murray?" Peri extended her hand. "We met the other day. I'm—"

"Yes, I know who you are. You were in the room with James." She reached out, grabbing Peri's hand. Her fingers were strong, almost vise-like. "You poor thing, how are you?"

"I'm okay, but I'm so sorry. I came by to offer my condolences."

Babette nodded. "Can I offer you something?" She still held Peri's hand. "There's food in the dining room. I do apologize for the casual service. I believe people are helping themselves."

"No, thank you. I can't stay, I really just needed you to know how sorry I am about James, and to say I know the police will do their best to find out who did this. I've already told them that I'll help in any way I can."

"Of course, thank you. Are you sure I can't get you something? Coffee?" She gave an odd little smile. "Tea?"

Peri tugged on her hand a little, until the woman released it. "Thank you, no, I've got to be going. I'll see myself out. Again, I'm sorry for your loss."

She turned and retraced her steps toward the front door. As she neared the foyer, she saw James's secretary, Emma, enter the house. She was, as always, dressed in a sophisticated suit, and beautifully groomed. At the entrance, she paused and looked around.

Peri started toward her when she heard a crash to her left. She looked over to see a cup and saucer in pieces on the polished, parquet floor, and Mrs. Bennett standing over it, staring at Emma. Her mouth was slightly open, her face pale. Peri looked back at Emma, who casually glanced at the older woman, then continued toward Peri.

"Miss Minneopa, I didn't expect to see you here."

"Please, Emma, call me Peri. You seem to have given Mrs. Bennett a fright."

"Mrs. Bennett?" Emma gave another momentary look at the other woman. "Is that Mrs. Murray's mother?"

"Yes, haven't you met?"

"No. She's never visited the office." Peri thought she saw a sly smile on Emma's face, but she wasn't certain.

"By the way, did the police contact you?" Peri asked.

Emma nodded. "I gave them my statement this morning. They were asking me a lot of questions about that chamomile tea, I tell you. They showed me pictures of the office. What a mess. I never left that tray on the desk. It was in Mr. Murray's office when I left." She leaned in, a worried look on her face. "You don't think they think I did it, do you?"

"Emma, right now, we're all under the magnifying glass. Just be honest with them, no matter what."

Peri walked back to her car, thinking it would be a lot easier for the secretary to be upfront with the police. Emma hadn't broken into the office.

CHAPTER 25

"I wouldn't say she was frightened, exactly," Peri said, between bites of her pulled pork sliders. "But Mrs. Bennett was definitely startled to see Emma."

"Um-hm."

She looked up to see Skip watching the Angels game. They had stopped by Brian's, a local bar favored by the community for its barbecue as much as for its multitude of big screen televisions, all turned to the latest sporting events.

"So there was nothing else to do except borrow an ice pick and stab her in the eye." Peri watched her boyfriend as she said this.

"Right. Wait, what?"

"You're not listening to me."

"Because you're blathering."

"I'm not blathering." Peri took a sip of her amber ale. "I'm trying to talk through this case. For Pete's sake, I'm trying to piece all these things together and make it mean something."

"Tell you what, Doll, we just got the video footage the kid shot with his cell phone the night of the fire. Jason's pre-processing it, then we're going to sit down with Nick and study it. You're welcome to sit in and see if it leads you anywhere."

She sat up, smiling. "That would be great. When are you going to do it?"

"Probably not tomorrow, but maybe day after. I'll let you know."

"Oh, Skipper, if I wasn't just sticky with sauce, I'd hug you right now."

He smiled. "If we were home, I'd know how to fix that."

She laughed. "Should we take some of the sauce to go? In the meantime, I think I need to dig into the insurance company and all its players. Those clippings were about the men as well as the company. And I got the weirdest feeling a couple of times with Babette and her mom. The things they said…"

"I know this will fall on deaf ears, but be careful, Peri. Someone stabbed Murray and tried to stage it to look like you did it. You know what I think about people who've already killed once."

"They don't mind doing it again."

"Have you heard from Detective Thompson?"

"He said he'd let me know the tox results, but he wasn't as forthcoming with whether there was a report or not." She shook her head. "Seems like he still thinks I could have killed James. Damn police department protocol."

"Yeah, damn police protocol that keeps the court from throwing out evidence."

"Oh, speaking of evidence, I think maybe the 'Ronnie' on the audio file and in my photos may be Ronald McHale, grandson of one of the partners in the insurance company." She lifted her beer in salute and finished it. "And I'd like to know if he's related to the Yorba Linda McHales."

"We can look into it." Skip called over to the server for the check. "We may not be able to use the audio, but the photos are legal."

After paying for dinner, they walked to their cars.

"Your place or mine?" he asked.

"Let's go to yours for a change."

It was a five minute drive to his ranch-style home in a neighborhood across from Tri-City Park. Skip pulled into the garage, while Peri parked in the driveway, then they entered the house from the back door. He turned on the TV in the family room while she went to the kitchen.

"Want another beer?" she asked.

"Sure." He clicked through the channels until he found the news. "I'm out of Grey Goose. Sorry."

"Well, I can't afford it this month. I mean, Benny's paying me for working his case, but I'd be more comfortable if I had something else on the horizon."

He walked over and took his beer, wrapping his free arm around her waist. "You could always go back to cleaning houses."

"Ha ha, you wish." She leaned into him, her face turned toward his. "I like this job. I like sitting in a car with my camera in my lap, instead of kneeling over a stranger's toilet, scrubbing the inside."

"Please don't tell me you're getting hooked on the danger."

"Absolutely not." She reached up and kissed him. "Trust me, I like the easy cases."

He kissed her back, his lips tender. "I can be easy."

She laughed and put her beer down, then ran her hands across his back as she put her lips to his. They stood for a few moments like this, enjoying each other's caress, until Skip lifted her and walked to the bedroom. They found their way to the bed, making love until at last they were too finished and too tired to start up again.

"Oof," Peri exhaled.

"Am I too heavy?"

"No, it's just, I feel extra warm, like one of my hot flashes is around the corner."

Skip rose and pulled her up. "Let's wash up and get some sleep, then."

A quick shower later, they slipped back into bed. Peri rested her head on Skip's chest, listening to his heart as she fell asleep, thinking of family trees.

* * *

Investigating Bennett and Smith Insurance Company was not going to be just an easy day on the Internet. Peri knew her best bet for information would be from the newspaper that printed the articles she had received.

By nine a.m. she was in her car, heading south on Interstate 5 toward Santa Ana. Her destination was the Orange County Register, a few miles down the freeway, hidden off Grand Avenue. Twenty minutes later, she arrived at a pale brick building with a small door on the left corner.

The small door led to a large room, almost warehouse-like, with five-foot partial walls breaking up the space. A long front desk sat in front of the walls, with forms and information on one half, and a computer on the other. A receptionist sat at the computer. She was a dark-haired, dark-eyed young woman.

"Can I help you?" Her smile was warm, and her eyes sparkled.

"I'm looking for old news articles about certain events and people," Peri said.

"Oh, I am sorry. We don't allow the public access to our archives. But you could try one of our local libraries. They usually have our news articles on file."

"Thank you, I understand." She turned to leave, then stopped. "Can you tell me if a reporter named Sam Todd still works here?"

The girl opened a side drawer and ran her finger down a list of names. "No, I don't see that name on our directory."

A gruff male voice spoke from behind the half-wall. "Who's asking about Todd?"

Peri saw a gray-haired gentleman walk around to the desk, cleaning his glasses and putting them on before looking her up and down and extending his hand. "Bruce King."

"Peri Minneopa," she replied, and watched his eyes squint, just as everyone who heard her name for the first time. "Call me Peri. Do you know how I could get in touch with Sam Todd?"

"Why are you asking?" His face, set in a permanent state of frowning, did not reveal anything.

"I recently read some of his articles, from a few years ago, and I had some questions."

"Sam Todd died back in 1992."

"I'm so sorry." She was also disappointed, although she wouldn't tell Bruce.

"Car accident. Driven off the road by someone. Police thought it was a drunk driver."

"Do you think it was a drunk driver?" she asked.

"No, I don't, not that anyone would listen to me. Sam liked to chase provocative stories. I think he chased the wrong one." Bruce put his hand up in a stopping motion. "I've got the articles, let me show you."

He disappeared around the wall and returned some moments later with a folder. Inside there were at least ten articles about Todd's death. Peri didn't read them in depth, but caught headlines proclaiming everything from the initial assumption that he'd fallen asleep, to a rather screaming title accusing a local mob boss of assassinating him for digging too deeply into their finances.

"Sam was kind of a numbers guy. He could sniff out shady business dealings better than any IRS agent."

"And you think maybe it was this mob boss?"

Bruce took the folder back, and looked around briefly before answering. His voice softened to a near whisper. "Not really. I think it had more to do with the insurance company he was investigating. They stood to lose a chunk o' change if his snooping led to any formal allegations."

"Bennett and Smith?"

He nodded. "How did you know?"

Peri looked at him, wondering how much she should spill to a reporter. "Off the record?"

"I got no death wish."

"I'm a private investigator, working for a client whose home burned down. Bennett and Smith won't pay up. They say the damage was due to homeowner negligence."

"Let me guess," Bruce said. "Fire investigation report looks suspicious? Policy is for a much larger amount than the home could ever be worth?"

"Exactly."

"Wait here." He disappeared again for several minutes. When he reappeared, he was carrying a storage box, which he thrust into Peri's hands.

"These are Sam's notes. For awhile after he died, I thought I'd finish what he started. Then every time I opened the box, I'd see my wife and kids staring up at me." He shook his head, his frown deepening. "I'm no coward, but I had to take care of my family."

"I understand, Bruce. And I'll take good care of these."

"Just find the smoking gun. I'd like to think Sam's at peace, but I know he won't be until this is solved."

* * *

Peri drove home with more questions than answers. *Great,* she thought, *more papers to sift through, as if Benny's mess wasn't enough.* She checked her watch. Four-thirty. Traffic would be a choking beast on the freeway, so she stayed on Grand until it morphed into Glassell, then finally Kraemer Boulevard, heading north toward Placentia.

It was still a herky-jerky experience as the cars around her stopped at each red light, then rolled unsteadily forward as they were given the signal to go. Two hours earlier it would have taken her fifteen minutes to get home. At this time of day, she'd be lucky to get home within an hour. The afternoon sun bounced off the surrounding strip malls and mini-marts, sending its rays straight to her retinas, and the heat battled her car's air conditioning, burrowing into her skin.

She finally pulled into her driveway just after five o'clock with a raging headache and a strong wish her house had a swimming pool. As she removed her seatbelt, her phone rang.

"We on for dinner?" Skip's deep voice rumbled through her.

"Hey, Skipper, I just pulled into the drive." Peri walked around to the passenger side, and grabbed the box with one hand, holding on to her phone with the other, her tote swinging from her arm. "What's on the menu tonight?"

"I don't care. How's cheap Chinese sound?"

She set the box and her tote on the front steps and dug her house key out. "Works for me." As she pushed the key toward the lock, her front door gave inward.

"What the—"

"What the what?" Skip asked.

She heard a shuffle, thump, and crash inside and stepped back. "Are you doing anything right now?"

"Just finishing a report. Why?"

"Oh, it might be nice if you could swing by." More thumps from behind her front door made her step off the porch, into the lawn. "Someone broke into my house, and I think they're still here."

"Peri, get in your car now and drive away, down the street. I'm sending a squad car, and I'll be right there."

CHAPTER 26

Peri stood on the lawn for a few seconds, stunned, then grabbed her box of information and locked it in her car. What she needed now was a weapon.

Where did I put you, she thought, looking down the side of her house by the driveway. At last, she saw a garden spade leaning against the wall. She grabbed it and ran back to the front, just in time to see a large man running off with her tote and her laptop.

He may have been big, but she was a runner. It took her ten strides to catch up to him and tackle him from behind. The spade flew from her hand as they both hit the ground. He tried to scramble up, but her momentum carried her forward and she was able to push his shoulders down and dig her knee into the small of his back. He groaned.

"Give me my tote," she said as she reached around and grabbed a handful of pink snakeskin.

The man turned to wrench it from her and she saw his face for the first time.

"Ronnie? Ronnie McHale?"

He looked at her, his expression moving from anger to dullness, back to rage. She took his moment of confusion to pull hard on the tote and get it back from him. He began to squirm and buck his body, making it difficult for her to keep him on the ground. She leapt to her feet, and grabbed her only weapon, the spade.

"Stay right there," she said, shaking the spade at him.

"I don't think so." He backed away, looking around, then stared at her. "I should've taken you out, too." Turning, he ran toward Bradford Street.

Peri stopped for a moment, her breath knocked back by his words. She began to lope in his direction, wondering if she really wanted to catch him again. Did she really want to tackle a man who just said he should have killed her? Was this his admission that he had killed James? Her pace slowed, as a familiar gold Toyota truck flew past her on Bradford Street.

As she strolled back toward her home, she looked through her tote. Nothing seemed to be missing. A patrol car with flashing lights sped by, then stopped and backed up to her. It was Officer Chou.

"Miss Peri, Detective Carlton sent us right over. What happened?"

She gestured toward her house, still two driveways away. "I was going to get in my car, like Skip said, but this guy ran out of my house, so I chased him. He tried to steal my tote." The part about obeying Skip was mostly a lie, but she didn't think it would hurt.

"Is that all he tried to take?"

Peri looked around and spied something on the grass in front of her, the grass where they had fallen together. A black rectangle lay on the mashed greenery. She walked over and picked it up. "This. He wanted my laptop."

She opened the notes on her phone. "I have his license. His name is Ronnie, probably Ronald McHale, but I wouldn't swear to it. He just left the scene." She gave them the license information as a black SUV roared into her driveway and squealed to a halt.

Skip came running toward her. "You okay? What happened?"

She told him what she had explained to the officer. He did not look as convinced.

"Really? If you were going to drive away, why are you holding a garden tool?"

"Well, I was going to my car and then I saw him take my tote, so I just grabbed the first thing handy."

"If you were going to your car, why was your tote on the porch?"

"Well, I was going to—to—hell, Skip, why do you ask me this stuff? You know I try to make it sound like I wasn't doing anything dangerous."

He sighed. "This is why I wanted you to get away. That man could have hurt you."

"You're right. I do need a gun."

"That is not what I'm saying at all." He rubbed his scalp. "Peri, you do not need a gun. You need to stop chasing after dangerous people."

"He had my tote." She held her laptop out. "He also got this."

The clasp on the laptop gave out and the computer swung open, revealing a cracked screen.

"Aw, hell," she said. "You can dust it for prints, but I recognized the guy who took it. It was Ronnie. Before he ran off, he said he should've taken me out, too. I think he murdered James."

"Okay, just stay here while the officers check everything out." He walked toward her house, muttering. "Maybe I should just save the argument and handcuff you to the car."

"I heard that." She matched him, stride for stride. "You know, we've never played around with your handcuffs."

His sharp glance stopped her words, as well as her feet. She watched him walk up her porch and through the front door. Chasing a burglar was bad. Catching him was worse. Her body still shivered from the struggle, and she knew, in addition to aching tomorrow, she'd be lucky if this was Skip's last conversation on the subject.

While she waited, Peri took some pain relievers out of her bag and a bottle of water. *Might as well get started now.*

Several minutes later, she saw Officer Chou and his partner emerge and wave her over. "We didn't find anyone else inside, Miss Peri. Looks like the lock was picked, scratch marks around it. You can go on in, make a list of whatever they took." Chou looked at his watch. "We'll need a statement, but that can wait until tomorrow, if you want."

"Thanks, both of you. I appreciate your help."

She bounded up the two steps to her front door, then paused. *Someone had been in her house. What would it be like in there?* She opened the door, took a deep breath, and walked through.

It wasn't as bad as she thought. Nothing had been rearranged in the living room. She moved toward the kitchen, peering around the corner. Everything looked okay here, too. Stepping back, her next stop was the bedroom. It was also pristine, so she went to the office.

Skip was standing, looking at the mess. Her file cabinet was open, folders out, papers everywhere. All her cables from her laptop were draped across her desk. The mirrored closet door was open and her glass jar of pennies was broken and scattered across the floor. A lingering smell of body odor grabbed Peri's nose.

"At least his search was localized," he said.

"Some consolation." She opened both windows and turned on the ceiling fan. "Think I can hire someone to sterilize my place?"

He put his arms around her and hugged her. "Sorry, Doll. Want to stay at my place again?"

"No. Yes, but no. Could you stay here?"

He nodded. "I'll even help you clean this up."

Peri reached up and kissed him. "I'll buy dinner."

She went into the kitchen to grab a broom and fish two beers from the refrigerator while he picked up the glass pieces and coins. Once the glass was swept, they started picking up papers and putting them all in a single pile.

"He was looking for my notes about the insurance investigation."

"You don't know that, Peri."

She pulled a runaway folder from under the desk chair. "I've got a living room full of home theater equipment, all untouched. I have jewelry. Not a lot, but I don't hide any of it, and it's still here. It doesn't even look like he was in any other room. This is the room that got hit, the one with all the papers."

Rushing to the mirrored closet door, she pushed it aside and pulled out the bag from Benny's house.

"Thank God I hadn't filed these yet."

She put the bag on the antique chaise, then sat down on the floor and reached over to Skip's pile of papers and began to sort them according to case. He sat next to her with the folders. They worked as a team, with her handing him stacks so he could find the correct folder and add them. They were almost finished, when her head popped up and she slapped his arm with the back of her hand.

"And why take my laptop without any of the cables? He didn't want my information. He just didn't want me to have it."

"All right, I'll admit it's a good theory. But where's the evidence?"

She rocked back to rest on the wall. "I don't know. I just know I've been swimming upstream on this case ever since Benny hired me. First, his papers are stolen so he can't contact his insurance. Then the company denies he's a client. Then there's a fake insurance report—"

"Allegedly fake."

"James Murray told me so. I'll swear to that in court."

"You're not only a witness, you're a suspect."

Peri sank her head into her hands. "I know." She raised her head and stared at the window in front of her. "I still see it, still feel it, like it just happened. The drowsiness, the lack of control and fogged brain when I woke. And James, slumped forward." She wiped at the moistness under her eyes with a shaky hand.

Skip put his arm around her.

"And now this." She waved at the room. "And my brother, and poor Blanche dealing with Nick…"

He kissed her on the temple. "I know, it's a lot on your plate. We'll catch up to Ronnie and see what he can tell us. I suggested cheap Chinese for dinner earlier, but what if I treat you to something a little more special? Orea? Cheesecake Factory? Any place you like."

"I love you." She leaned into him. "Orea sounds good."

He reached down and kissed her, nibbling at her lower lip. "Maybe a brief interlude first?"

"Can we have our interlude after? Right now, I think I might weep for no reason." She brushed his cheek with her lips. "It makes interludes so messy."

"Anything for you."

CHAPTER 27

After a relaxing dinner and a romantic end to the evening, Peri lay in bed, squeezing her eyes shut in an attempt at sleep. She spent twenty minutes flopping about to find a more comfortable position, then surrendered to wakefulness and eased from bed, trying not to disturb Skip. She threw on a large t-shirt and wandered down the hall, pausing at the door to her office. Taking a breath, she walked in and switched on the light.

The clock display said two-fifteen. Peri looked at the piles of folders Skip had helped her organize. It was hard to know whether anything was taken from the files, but she suspected Ronnie was only looking for Benny's information. She looked at the grocery bag on the chaise.

After a quick trip to the freezer for a pint of vanilla toffee ice cream and a spoon, Peri dragged the bag to the floor, sat down, and began digging into the papers and the ice cream.

The statements from the bank were on top. She picked them up and read them, scraping bits of frozen dessert from the container and relishing the sweetness on her tongue.

A small pang of invasion guilt stung her. Finances seemed so intimate. Previously, she had only looked for proof the insurance was paid. Now she was studying the credits and debits.

"Whew," she whistled. "Where are you getting all this money, Ben?"

The account was flush with funds. She was surprised that his expenses were not as high as she had imagined. For all his love of things Dean Martin, Benny's spending was not rampant. Some of his debits were large, but he seemed to only make one major purchase every six months. Most of his money was spent on eating at the few restaurants he enjoyed, along with automatic withdrawals for basic necessities, like household utilities and car insurance.

His deposits were on a monthly basis and came from a trust. Peri found nothing suspicious about any of it, until she saw a line item from May of this year.

Deposit from Phillip J. Nickels, $600.

She sat back, munching on a chunk of toffee. The Nickels did take Benny to Ohio with them. It wouldn't be unusual, in the electronic age, for Phil to transfer money over to Benny to cover some cost associated with the trip.

Except that Benny didn't even know where his bank was, let alone his account number. How did Phil have the information?

"Didn't get enough baklava?" Skip leaned against the door.

Peri raised the ice cream container in salute. "Ben and Jerry make excellent partners at two o'clock in the morning."

He chuckled and sat down next to her. "Finding anything?"

"Just this." She showed him the bank statement. "I need to talk to Phil."

"Why not Benny?"

"He didn't even know where his bank account was until this week." She dug her spoon back into the ice cream and lifted it. "How would Phil know where to transfer money?"

Skip reached over and directed the spoon to his own mouth. "Mmm, toffee. Looks like you need to get some sleep so you can be clear-minded when you call Phil tomorrow."

"You're right." She put the lid back on the container and stood up. "If I can."

She felt his hand caress her leg, moving up the back of her thigh.

"Need help?" he asked.

She smiled. "Let me get this back in the freezer. Meet you under the covers in a minute."

After a round of languid, delicious lovemaking, Peri relaxed into sleep, her head on Skip's shoulder and limbs entwined in his. It was a sounder rest than she expected, and she woke at eight feeling refreshed.

A quick run and a shower completed her morning ritual, and she sat at the kitchen table and dialed Phil Nickels. Nancy answered and said that he was on the golf course.

Peri returned to the bedroom to get dressed. Skip was guiding his belt from loop to loop in a pair of navy slacks, his striped long-sleeved shirt attempting to escape its tucking. She held the back of his pants and smoothed the shirttail down.

He smiled. "See you tonight?"

"Of course." She walked to the closet. "Hopefully I'll have a breakthrough in the case to talk about."

She felt the slight sting of a hand slapping at her rump through her robe.

"My little bulldog," he said as he left the room.

After slipping into a pair of tan capris and a royal blue top, she applied a little makeup, brushed her hair, and grabbed her tote. Her to-do list included talking to Phil, dropping in on Detective Thompson to bug him about the case, and buying a new laptop. She glanced at her watch. It was already ten o'clock, so she needed to get moving.

Peri jumped in her car and drove five minutes to the Alta Vista Country Club. The jewel in Placentia's crown, Alta Vista was a private course surrounded by million dollar homes in the west end of the city. The clubhouse, built in a craftsman-style of stone and wood, tapered columns and gabled roofs, contained a bar, a restaurant, and a rather large banquet hall that could be closed into sections for smaller events.

Phil was still on the course when she arrived at the club, but the bar was open, so she went in for a cup of coffee. She recognized the bartender, Alvin, from her previous visits. An older man, with dark, time-etched skin and graying temples, he was a great guy for conversation.

"Miss Peri." He greeted her with a lingering two-handed shake, as if welcoming a long-lost sister. "It's been awhile."

"Hi, Alvin. Got any coffee back there?"

He handed her a full mug. "So what's on the agenda for today?"

"I just need to talk to one of the golfers. Kind of a personal involvement in a case I'm working."

"Anything I can help with?"

She smiled. "I don't think so, unless you know anything about the Bennett and Smith Insurance Company."

"Bennett and Smith?" He scowled. "Bunch o' damned crooks."

"You've dealt with them?"

The big man took a towel and wiped the counter. "Nearly cost me my house."

He said nothing for several moments, as if he couldn't bring himself to tell the tale. Peri waited, sipping her coffee.

"Had a house fire five years ago. Not a big fire, only in the kitchen. About ten thousand in damages. I been paying my insurance every year for thirty years. Suddenly, they accuse me of setting the fire, claim the appraisal is padded, question every nickel, dime. They gave me the run around for six months. What was I supposed to do? Without the repairs, we couldn't stay in the house. So I'm paying out money I don't have, maxing my credit cards to fix my kitchen, while I'm on the phone every day arguing with that sonofabitch Smith—"

"Burton Smith?"

"Yes'm. Ended up with subpar work done by the cheapest bidder, two months behind on the mortgage and three months on the credit card, and finally settled with the insurance for seven thousand, which was just barely enough to pull me out of the frying pan."

He sighed, as if exhausted with the memory. "Bad enough my wife was sick with cancer. She didn't have a lot of time, but I think the stress shortened what she had."

"I'm so sorry, Alvin." Peri felt herself bristling at the insurance company. "They're fighting with a client of mine at the moment."

"Well, you fight them back." Alvin pursed his lips, then pounded the towel on the bar. "You bring them down. They need to be accountable."

"I'm trying." Peri felt a hand on her shoulder and turned to see Phil Nickels.

"You wanted to talk to me?" He looked dapper in his navy shorts, yellow polo shirt, and Callaway ball cap.

"Coffee, sir?" Alvin offered. "Or iced tea?"

Peri motioned toward one of the dark wood tables and leather-trimmed chairs in the bar and they took their drinks and sat down.

"How can I help you?" Phil asked.

She took Benny's bank statement from her tote and showed it to him. "You can help me figure out how you could deposit money into Benny's bank account."

"Oh, that's just an electronic transfer. They're really easy." His face smiled, but his voice wavered.

"I know it's easy to transfer money, Phil. I also happen to know that before this week, Benny didn't even know where his bank was, let alone his account numbers. How did you know where to put the money?"

"Well, I—" Phil's eyes widened, along with his mouth, before settling on a mask of defensiveness. "There's certainly no law against it. I've never withdrawn any money from Benny's account, and I don't know that it's your business."

"It may not be, but the more I dig into Benny's case, the more questions I end up with. I'm just trying to understand things. I don't care that you have access to his account. It'd just be nice to know why, to have one answer to one question."

For several moments, silence rested between them. She watched his face. He seemed to be struggling with what to tell her, his eyes staring at her one minute, then looking at his hands the next. Whatever pros and cons he juggled, at last she saw him relax into his chair. He'd come to a decision.

"Rob—Benny's dad, Robert—and I were friends years ago. When Benny was young, about ten I think, Rob called me one Monday morning and asked me to meet him at the bank. It was an odd request, but I trusted him and showed up. He told me he had to leave town, for maybe a long time, and couldn't talk about why. It was awful. He looked like hell, and I thought he was going to start crying every time his mouth opened."

"What did he want?"

"He asked me to sign on to his bank account and make deposits for him as he directed. He'd send a check to me and I'd deposit it to the account. Later, he began transferring funds to my account electronically, and I'd transfer them to Benny."

"Where did these checks come from?"

"Columbus, Ohio. Oh, and I wasn't supposed to tell anyone I was doing this, especially Benny or his mom, Beth."

"Phil, I ran across a picture of Robert and Beth Needles with the owners of the Bennett and Smith Insurance Company. Would you know why they were all standing around with champagne glasses?"

"Rob was their accountant. Worked for them until he left."

"Did you ever speculate why he left so quickly?"

"I had my suspicions." Phil looked at the table, his hand rubbing his iced tea glass. "For a long time, Rob loved his job. Then suddenly, he started acting a little nervous. Then the articles started appearing in the newspaper, saying Bennett and Smith were shysters who took clients' money and denied all their claims. That's when Rob went from bad to worse."

He nodded. "I think it was a week or so after the first article, Rob called me. The next day, he was gone."

Peri sat back in her chair and rubbed her temple. "Are you still in contact with Benny's dad?"

He stared at her, quiet and unsmiling. "Yes and no," he said at last. "The funds still show up in my account, and I still transfer them to Benny. But he doesn't call or write to me. I can't tell you whether he's alive for certain."

"You know, there's an envelope in Benny's things, addressed to him from his father. It's marked *In the event of my death*. I can't get Benny to even talk about his dad. Is there any chance you could?"

"I doubt it." He shook his head. "I don't know exactly how Rob left it with his family, but he didn't tell me much and I thought we were good friends. Beth was devastated. Cried, lost weight, nearly had a nervous breakdown. Nancy spent some time with her, but I'm sure Benny watched his mom's pain. It affected him."

"I can imagine." She thought about it."It makes sense. Talking about his dad hurt his mom, so the pact was made not to talk about him. Ever."

"Wish I could help more. I just handle the finances."

She gazed at him, a theory hitting her in the head. "You do handle the finances, don't you? You would have access to Benny's safe deposit box."

His face reddened.

"You sent me his key, didn't you?"

"Not me." He held up his hands, palms out. "It was Nancy. I tried to stay out of the middle, but when you told us about your problem locating Benny's accounts, she couldn't let it go."

"Did you also send the newspaper clippings?"

"What newspaper clippings?" His face did not reveal anything but sincere confusion.

"Never mind." Peri decided he was not her personal Deep Throat. "Thank Nancy for me. And thank you. You've helped more than you know. I'm glad Benny has you looking out for him."

She stood and shook hands with him, then left him there, looking like she'd just forced him to dig up a body he'd rather forget. As she walked out of the bar, three men walked in. She heard one of them say, "there you are," and turned to see them all moving toward Phil's table.

Good, she thought. *He should be with friends.*

Getting back into her car, she considered her next move. She had planned to drive down to the Newport Beach police station to talk to Detective Thompson, but perhaps she could catch him with a phone call and do some more digging into the box of notes Sam Todd had left behind. A reporter's legacy might at least give her another perspective.

The detective answered after a couple of rings. "Thompson."

"Detective, this is Peri Minneopa. I was wondering if there was any information on my case."

"Peri, I'm just reading the tox results now. It looks like you and Murray were both given GHB, and judging from the amounts in his body and yours, at the same time."

"GHB?"

"One of the common date-rape drugs, although neither one of you were sexually assaulted. It typically leaves a person without any memory of events after it's been ingested, making it hard for a victim to remember even their attacker, much less what happened."

"I'm guessing it was in the tea, right?"

"Yes. It wasn't in the canister, only in the teapot and cups. I've got uniforms out, picking up the secretary. Hers were the only prints on the pot."

"Emma?" Peri thought about the idea. "I honestly don't know her that well, but I never got any indication from her that she might be capable of murder."

"In your statement, you also said Mrs. Murray and a man named Ronnie were in the foyer when you entered Murray's office, is that right?"

"Yes. Detective, I believe Ronnie's last name might be McHale and he broke into my house." She told him of the incident and what he was trying to steal, then remembered her first meeting with James' wife. "You know, Mrs. Murray was putting on driving gloves when I met her. And Emma told me Mrs. Murray sent her away from the teapot that evening."

"Thanks, good to know. I'll get with Detective Carlton and see if we have any information we can trade to catch Ronnie."

"Oh, Detective? Did you find a report on Benny Needles' house fire hidden away?" She crossed her fingers as she asked this.

There was no answer for a few seconds. "No."

She ended the call and sank back into the seat. Damn. Without the actual report, it was all just hearsay and conjecture, as Perry Mason would say. She started the car and drove off. As she pulled out of the country club onto Alta Vista Street, her phone rang. She tapped her Bluetooth and answered.

"Hey, Peri," Skip said. "We've got Nick down here at the station, to go over the recordings from that night. He's asking for you to sit in with us."

"Recordings?"

"Yeah, turns out Max took more videos than he posted online. Can you come?"

"Almost there."

She ended the call and turned onto All America Way, which ran behind the Placentia Police Department. The parking lot was almost full, but she found one open space in back of the library and took that. She was so interested in seeing the videos that she had to tell herself not to run to the building. Sam Todd's files would have to wait.

One of these days, she thought, *I'm going to get from Point A to Point B without taking a detour.*

CHAPTER 28

Peri went to Jason's lab, where she found Nick Debussy sitting in front of the computer monitor. Jason stood to his left, Skip to his right, and Craig Daniels was behind him. They were watching the grainy, low-lit, shaking pan of a room, accompanied by semi-intelligible voices.

She recognized the room as Benny's kitchen. There were several voices, laughing, on the recording.

Nick pointed to the screen. "I think this is when we started looking around the house."

"Dude," one of the boys was heard to say. "This place is messed up."

Nick identified the voice. "That's Max."

"Yeah, this is like watching *Hoarders*," another said.

"Dylan." Nick confirmed.

The camera swung down the hallway like a drunk on a turbulent plane. Even Peri had to step back to keep her equilibrium. Dim lighting made it difficult to see more than shapes as the living room came into view, but a few details could be seen.

"Wow, how does anybody live in this?" a familiar voice asked.

"That was me," Nick admitted.

A shadow stumbled down the hall.

"Alex, dude, where you going?" they heard Dylan ask.

The shadow waved as it disappeared. "Star-gazing."

"That was Alex." Nick's voice choked.

The camera continued to sweep through the room, Max laughing, and several voices talking over one another about going back to the kitchen, finding another room, and getting the hell out. The video ended.

Jason cued up the next scene. Close-ups of Nick and his friends, Max and Dylan, showed them taking swigs from a bottle, then making faces at the camera. They appeared to be in the kitchen.

"Alex," Max called out. "Dude, where are you?"

"Yeah, come in here and get your face time," Nick said.

The camera moved, unsteady, down the hall. As the living room was passed, a flash of light burst from the left side of the frame and there was a scream of surprise.

"Fire," Max squeaked at first, then yelled louder, "*Fire!*"

From this point, the video matched what was already seen on the Internet. Bodies moved about, voices yelling about fire, and calling for Alex. As the camera swung past the fire to the darkness, a voice said, "I'm out." It sounded different from the others, calmer.

"Can you go back to the first video?" Peri asked. "Go to where they step into the living room for the first time."

Jason recued the first video, and they all stared at the monitor.

"There." She pointed. "Stop it there."

The frame was of one of the walls in Benny's living room. A gold couch was in the corner, behind a decorative table, filled with VHS tapes. Next to the table was a stack of what looked like record albums.

"What do you see there?"

"Couch... table..." Skip named the various items. "What?"

"Where's your case file?"

Jason handed her a manila folder, which she dumped on the table, and sifted through the papers and photos. Finally, she found what she was looking for, and held up a photo of the same scene.

"Where's the can of turpentine?" She pointed to the burnt cans in the picture. "Where's the paint can? They were in all the after pictures, but where are they on this recording? For that matter, where's the frayed lamp cord that was supposed to have started the spark?"

Three men and a teen leaned forward, staring at the screen. One by one, they backed up, then turned to look at Peri. She looked at Nick.

"Someone else was in that house with you."

"The voice," he said. "The one I thought was Alex..."

"Was the arsonist, more than likely," Skip told him. "The arsonist who set that fire and killed your friend." He turned to Jason. "Get that frame isolated and printed. And can you coax any better resolution out of it? I don't want any doubts there are no cans or lamps along that wall before the fire."

Nick spoke up. "Could I just, just see the part where the voice says, 'I'm out'?"

Peri knelt down to him. "Why, Nick? To see if it really sounded like Alex?"

He nodded.

"Oh, honey. Why don't I get you home so you can talk to your folks? Recordings can sound distorted. If it sounds like Alex, it doesn't prove it was him. If it doesn't, it'll make you feel worse."

Nick stayed in his chair and looked at her, pleading. "Aunt Peri, I need to hear it."

She looked at Jason and shrugged, so he cued up the section of the video and pressed Play. They watched a flare and heard a roar, then the voices. Nick whispered names as each spoke. Max, Dylan, him. At the last voice, he cocked his head and frowned.

"Nope. It wasn't Alex at all."

"Actually," Peri said, "that sounds more like Ronnie."

She put the papers in order. Her photos of Babette and Ronnie were on top of the stack. Skip picked them up and studied the pictures.

"Peri," he said. "Can you take Nick home? Craig and I need to go find Ronnie McHale." He turned to Nick. "Did you ever hear of Alex talking about anyone in his family named Ronnie?"

Nick shook his head. "We don't really talk about family stuff."

Peri would have preferred to go with them to look for Ronnie, but she knew Nick needed all the support he could get. Plus, getting permission to tag along with the two detectives would have been an uphill fight. Not that she shrank away from these tugs-of-war, but she decided to choose her battles.

She patted Nick on the shoulder. "You ready to go?"

The boy rose, his shoulders sagging, and followed her out of the room. He was silent as they went to the car, then curled his tall frame into her little Honda. She got in and started the engine, wondering whether to engage him in conversation or let him alone. His sadness was understandable, but so was her excitement at having a lead to chase.

As they drove down Chapman Avenue to Orangethorpe, she fiddled with the radio and the air conditioner, glancing at Nick every once in awhile. He sat low in the seat, his knees pushed up against the dash. She could see him chewing on the side of his lip, and every so often, he scratched through his hair with his long fingers.

At last, she couldn't stand it. "Nick, I want to thank you for all your help. I don't know how we could have gotten this information without you. Frankly, I was beginning to think we'd never have the evidence to help Benny collect the insurance money. I'm just so sorry you lost a friend."

He said nothing for a long time. As they turned down his street, she heard him take a large breath.

"Aunt Peri," he began, and then sighed again. After some seconds, he spoke up. "Why did all this happen? We were just trying to find a place to party. Why did Alex have to die? I feel like I want to go to bed and never get up. I'm so sad and angry and messed up."

"It's hard to say, Nick. I don't know why someone set that fire. They had to know you were in the house." She shook her head as she pulled into the drive. "It was awful, what happened to Alex, but it wasn't your fault. You stayed for him. You thought he was out. You were his friend and that's what friends do."

She turned off the engine and faced him. "I know you're a good kid, honey. I've watched you grow up. You're honest, you're polite, you work hard, I couldn't be prouder to know you. I know you can move through these feelings and learn how to handle them without checking out."

He looked at her, his face a blueprint of frustration. "Aunt Peri, I don't want to mess up, but I don't know what I'm doing half the time. I hate being the good little boy but I don't like disappointing Mom and Dad. What the hell is wrong with me?" His eyes were shining with tears he refused to release.

"There's nothing wrong with you, except you're a teenager. We've all been teenagers, and had all the doubts and the anger and the desire to please our parents and flip them off at the same time. I didn't know your dad growing up, but I knew your mom, and trust me, she and I pulled our share of crap." She reached over and hugged him. "Trust us, Nick. Talk to us. If not your folks, you can talk to me, or a counselor, or even to Skip."

She patted his cheek. "Now, let's go see your mom."

Blanche was scrubbing the kitchen sink when they entered. Peri suddenly wanted to put the whole family in bubble wrap and keep them safe.

"Beebs, I brought you a present."

Nick walked over and draped his arms around his mom in a hug. She hugged him back, squeezing until he sputtered.

"Mom, I can't breathe."

"You're a brave kiddo," she told him. "I'm proud of you for stepping up."

"Can I go to my room now? I'm kinda tired."

Peri watched him turn and shuffle to the stairs, then returned to her friend.

"I may not survive the teenage years." Blanche sounded exhausted.

Peri put her arm around her shoulder. "Is it margarita time?"

"You get the tequila, I'll get the ice."

Ten minutes later, the two women sat on the patio with drinks and a bowl of chocolate-covered pretzels.

"Sorry," Blanche said as she sat the food on the table. "I'm out of chips."

"Are you kidding? Chocolate, salt, and crunch may be the perfect food. And God knows, we need some chocolate right about now."

They sat quietly, munching and sipping, before Peri spoke. "He did good today. You should be proud."

"Proud? Of what, the drinking, the drugs, or the breaking and entering?"

"Yes, he made a mistake." Blanche frowned at her, so she added, "Okay, several mistakes. I can probably talk Benny out of pressing charges for breaking and entering, so it will just depend on what the police want to do. But Nick was really helpful reviewing the tape and identifying where they were and what they were doing."

"I wish I understood his choices. What the hell gets into that boy?"

"He's a boy. Who knows?" Peri laughed. "I seem to recall a few of our antics. Why did I dye my hair purple? I still don't know. What were you thinking when you dismantled your mother's vacuum cleaner and hid one of the parts so you could claim it was broken?"

"I was thinking I didn't want to vacuum the house 'cause we had plans."

"Yeah, plans to meet some guys from the other high school and score some beer."

Blanche raised her palm toward her friend. "Okay, I get it."

"Ah, Beebs, I don't know how to raise a kid. You and Paul have done a great job. I only know how to be a teenager."

She heard the patio door whooshing and turned to see Nick walking out, cell phone in his hand. His face was almost yellow in its paleness, his eyes bloodshot.

"What is it?" Blanche asked.

He handed her the cell phone. There was a text from a blocked number.

ITS UR FAULT HES DEAD. SHUT UP OR MAYBE UR FRIENDS R UNLUCKY 2

CHAPTER 29

"Blocked, eh?" Peri studied the message. "What a coward." She took out her own cell phone and pressed a number.

"Who are you calling?" Nick looked stricken.

"Skip."

"No, Aunt Peri, no, didn't you read it? They'll hurt Max and Dylan."

Blanche stood and hugged her son. "We'd never let that happen."

"Absolutely not," Peri told him, then turned to her phone. "Skip, Nick just got a threatening text on his cell phone from a blocked number... no, it's a blocked number... can't you just... oh, okay." She paused and looked at Blanche. "Who's your carrier?"

"Verizon."

"Verizon," Peri repeated to her phone. "Okay, I'll tell them."

Two pairs of impatient eyes stared at her as she ended the call. "Skip is asking the Brea police if they could send a black-and-white to watch over the house. Nick, you are to stay here. If you can stand to hang out in the same room with your family, it would be better. In the meantime, Skip will need access to Nick's cell phone to see if they can unblock that number. Usually they'd get a warrant, but if the account holder would give permission—"

"Consider it granted," Blanche said, and pulled out her own phone to start the process.

Nick's phone, lying on the table, vibrated with an incoming text. He jumped away from it, so Peri picked it up and looked at the message.

"It's okay, Nick. Well, not okay, but it's from Max. Says he got the same message you just got." She put the phone back on the table. "I'm betting Dylan got the same message, or will soon. Someone is trying to guilt all of you into shutting up."

Turning to Blanche, she asked, "Was Alex's cell phone found with him?"

"I don't know, I'd have to check the inventory."

Nick shook his head. "Alex didn't have his phone that night. He forgot it on the charger in his room."

Peri phoned Skip again. "Skipper, Nick just got a text from Max. Someone sent him the same message. Did you process Alex's cell phone when you were at his house?"

"I don't remember. Let me check." She heard papers shuffling and Skip mumbling for a few seconds. "No record of a phone."

"Thanks." She turned to Blanche. "I gotta go check on something."

"Peri—" Blanche sounded motherly in her warning. "Where do you think you're going?"

"To the McHale's. I think the only way someone got your numbers is if they had Alex's phone. And I think that someone might be related to them."

Blanche pulled up her five-foot, two-inch frame to block her friend's path. "As I recall, Matt McHale ordered you off his property the last time you paid him a visit."

"Pfft, like I haven't heard that before."

"Peri, the man threatened to get his gun."

"Again, been there and done that." She reached down and hugged the petite brunette. "Beebs, I'll be careful. I'll be tactful and respectful and all those 'fuls'. Don't worry."

She hustled out the front door, grabbing her tote as she went, and got into her car. It roared to life under her heavy foot, as she pointed it toward Fairmont Street and the McHale residence. In less than five minutes, she was parked along their curb.

No one was tending the flowers this time, so she had to approach the door. Although she'd shown her best friend a brave face, her finger had a hard time pressing the doorbell. She needed information from the McHales, but if Matt was still mad at her, or worse, if they were the ones who sent the texts, it could all end badly.

After a deep inhale, Peri exhaled and pressed. She heard the low, perfect pitch of a high-end doorbell. A large shadow was soon visible, approaching from the right. Matt McHale opened the door, glaring at her.

"I know I am not your favorite person," she began. "But Alex's friends need your help."

The glare remained. "Why the hell should I help them? If it wasn't for them, Alex wouldn't have been in that shack—"

"Mr. McHale." She barked his name. "What Alex and those boys did wasn't right, but it was teenage impulse." She saw a muscle in his face relax, so she continued. "They had no expectation that a fire would break out. I've just seen evidence on a video that it was intentionally set."

McHale's face went from glowering to shock in a heartbeat. "Wh-what?"

"Can I come in?"

He swung the door wider and stepped aside. "Just keep your voice down. Christine and the girls are asleep."

Peri walked in and he closed the door. She followed him into the great room and sat on one of the couches, as he indicated. He took a seat across from her, his arms folded across his chest.

"Mr. McHale." She wasn't certain how to ask about Ronnie. "The fire investigator's report stating it was homeowner negligence was a fake. The investigator told me so, before he died. I think someone is working with the insurance company to keep from paying my client. After looking at the video, I'm also thinking, either someone set the fire to force a cancellation of my client's policy, or to somehow trap these boys."

She looked at the floor, thinking. If Ronnie set the fire, did he know Alex was going to be the *collateral*, as he called him on the tape? Was it possible that Matt ordered the fire? She decided to keep Ronnie's name out of it until she knew more. "Although why they would want these particular boys dead I don't know."

"Why are you telling me this?" McHale sounded guarded.

"Because your son's friends have been helping the police try to figure out what happened that night, and two of them have gotten threatening texts within the last half hour. I think the only way someone knew their cell phone numbers and their relationship with Alex, is if, one, they were there that night, and two, they have access to Alex's phone."

"I assume Alex's phone must still be in evidence with the police." His voice took on a hard edge. "You should be looking at the authorities."

"No. Nick said Alex forgot his phone that night. It should have been in his room, on his charger."

"Well, then those detectives took it—"

"No," she interrupted. "Sorry, but I called. They didn't take it into evidence."

He sat, silent, his face slackened. Suddenly he looked at her. "You can't think I did this, or, or my wife."

Peri stared back at him, her eyes narrowed. "No. You are suing my client, but I think that might be out of your pain, your desire to do something so Alex's death doesn't look so random and meaningless. I can't imagine you'd hamper an investigation into your son's death. Who else has been in your house lately?"

He shrugged. "Who hasn't? We've had a steady stream of people stopping by to pay their respects. We're planning Alex's memorial service and will have people back to the house after, so Christine's got all kinds of cleaners and caterers moving through here. Hell, even my cousin, Ronnie, stopped by. I hadn't seen him in probably five years."

237

"Ronnie McHale?" She took one of the pictures of him and Babette out of her tote. "Is this him?"

He looked at the photo. "Yes, that's Ronnie, with Babette. She's from the other side of the family."

"When was he here?"

"A couple of times, actually. He was here the day after we got the news, then right after you... stopped by." His face flushed.

Peri pursed her lips. "Could he have been in Alex's room?"

"It's possible. The neighbors were over and I don't know that I kept track of everyone's movements in our home. You think he took my son's phone? Why would he do that?"

"Well, maybe you should check Alex's room before we jump to any conclusions. According to Nick, Alex told him he'd left his phone on his charger."

McHale rose and went down the hall. While she waited, Peri stood, to stretch her legs. A heavy glass bowl on the table caught her attention. She picked up the business card in the bowl and read it.

Ronald McHale, Private Investigations.
Phone 714-555-2667

"Ronnie," she said. "What have you been digging into?"

McHale returned to the great room. "It's not there."

She held up the card. "Mr. McHale, have you benefitted from your cousin's services?"

He said nothing at first, although his face reddened. "I don't think that's any of your business."

"Maybe not. Or maybe I'm suspicious of a cousin you haven't seen in five years suddenly showing up to pay his respects. I'm guessing he offered his services to you. He might have even hinted he had knowledge of the situation."

A look of understanding washed across McHale's face. "He did. Told me about the negligence. Offered to get me information about the homeowner."

"Did he show you the actual fire investigator's report?"

"No, he just told me not to worry about it. Said one way or another, it was going to be negligence."

"Thank you so much for the information. And thank you for your honesty." She turned to leave.

"What's this all about with my cousin?" he asked.

"I can't tell you everything. I can say that Ronnie McHale has had his hands in my client's business the past few weeks, including the fire. Maybe he stole Alex's phone, I don't know. But you've given me enough information to try to locate him and find out."

"Are you thinking my cousin might have been involved in my son's death?"

She wanted to cry out, hell yes, but she didn't dare. "It doesn't matter what I'm thinking. Evidence is what matters."

McHale pounded the wall with his fist so hard, he left a dent. "That sonofa—"

Peri grabbed his arm and shook him. "No, no, we don't know anything." She had to shout to make him even look at her.

"You can't let yourself think that…" She trailed off. Even though she suspected it, she couldn't admit it to him, just in case he was that kind of man, the kind who'd seek his own justice.

Her voice softened. "I don't want you to do something you'd regret. Let the police do their job."

"Matt?"

She looked up to see Christine in the hallway.

"What's going on?" She was frailer than the last time Peri saw her. Bones. All bones, with the tightest layer of skin, as if she was disappearing in her grief.

Peri turned to McHale. "Take care of your wife. I'm going to the police. We'll figure this out."

She gave his arm a reassuring squeeze and went to the door. As she opened it to leave, she looked back. He had joined his wife in the hall, and was helping her toward the kitchen. Peri thought she heard him say something about fixing her scrambled eggs.

Perhaps he sees now what he needs to do.

She left the couple and jumped in her car. Skip and Craig were off to see Babette Murray. The Debussy family was supposedly safe for the night, under the watchful eye of the Brea PD. It seemed there was nothing to do except go home and sift through Sam Todd's big box of data.

CHAPTER 30

On her way home, Peri swung by the local Best Buy and picked up the new laptop she had ordered. Fortunately, her homeowner's insurance paid for the replacement.

Thank God I'm not with Bennett and Smith, she thought.

As she drove down her street, she saw her neighbor, Ozzie, playing in his front yard with a younger boy, possibly a brother. They were chasing each other around with plastic light sabers, screaming and laughing. For a brief moment, she pictured herself and Dev on a summer day, chasing each other with the hose. He hardly ever wanted to play, so she relished those memories.

She saw a woman sitting on the front steps, young and pretty, her black hair pulled back into a long braid. She guessed that was Ozzie's mother, Selina.

Peri pulled into her driveway, gathered her tote, and walked back to the Gomez house. The woman on the steps stood as she approached.

"Hi." Peri waved. "I'm your neighbor."

"I know already." Ozzie had stopped chasing his brother and stood with his light saber prepared for battle.

"Mrs. Gomez? I'm Peri. It's nice to meet you."

They both smiled and shook hands.

"Your son dropped an envelope at my house, and I have a question for him, if that's all right with you."

"Yes, of course." She looked at the smaller boy. "Michael, leave your brother alone. Come in and help me set the table."

Michael dropped his toy and whined. "Mom, it's Ozzie's turn."

"Come on, mijo." She opened the door. "Your brother can wash up tonight instead."

He lowered his head and shuffled toward the house, kicking up dirt as he went. Selina opened the door for him, then remained at the top of the steps. Peri assumed she wanted to supervise her visit with Ozzie, who walked to the porch and sat down.

"I'm trying to figure out who gave you this envelope." Peri pulled it out of her tote. "Do you remember what the lady looked like?"

Ozzie nodded. "Sure."

She pulled the picture of Babette out. The newspaper clippings fell as she did. "Was this her?"

"Maybe." He took the picture from her and held it. "It looks a little like her, but her hair was back." He handed the photo back and slicked his hair with his hands. "Like this."

"Like, in a ponytail?"

"Yes."

Peri picked up the clippings that had fallen, and Ozzie grabbed one. "I think she looked more like this."

It was the picture of the Bennetts, Smiths, and Needles, from their celebration. "Which woman?"

Ozzie pointed to Mrs. Smith. Peri looked at the photo. Gretchen, Mrs. Burton Smith, had been dead for quite a few years. Even if she was alive, she would have looked much older than this picture.

"Are you certain, Ozzie?"

"Yes."

This is why police are so suspicious of eyewitnesses, she thought. "Okay, well, just to make certain, close your eyes and think about the lady."

The boy did as he was told.

"Okay, now tell me what you see."

He wrinkled his nose. "She is in her car. It is red. Her hair is dark, maybe it is black. She is wearing sunglasses."

"Does she look older than your mom?"

"Yes."

"Does she look older than me?"

He opened his eyes and looked at Peri. "Maybe not. I think maybe you are the same age."

"Ozzie, is there anything else you remember about her?"

He rubbed his nose and looked down at his shoes. "She gave me ten dollars."

She smiled. "You deserved every bit of it."

Peri stood and held her hand out. Ozzie took it, smiling, and they shook.

"Ozzie you've been a great help to me. Thank you." She looked up at his mother and smiled, then walked back to her home, wondering what it meant. As sweet and honest as he was, Ozzie could not possibly have seen Gretchen Smith. Still, Peri had the same feeling about her, that she'd seen her somewhere before.

It had to have been Babette who gave her these clippings. She was Leland Bennett's granddaughter, so she'd have intimate knowledge of the family and access to these newspaper articles. It would certainly make more sense than Gretchen Smith's ghost.

As she entered her house, she threw her tote on the couch and made a beeline for the refrigerator, where she pulled a pint of ice cream from the freezer. Skip wasn't going to be around for dinner, so she was going to dine with Ben and Jerry. She dragged the box from the newspaper office into the living room, sat down on the couch, and looked down at the beige folders inside.

Maybe I need some fuel, she thought, and dug into the ice cream. For a few moments, she lost herself in bites of strawberry, graham crackers, and the undertones of cream cheese. Today had been exhausting, and it wasn't over.

At last sated, she pulled a folder out of the box and began. Sam Todd was an organized guy. The notes inside were from a specific couple who had lost their home due to Bennett and Smith. The second folder held notes from another family, and the third folder yet a third victim. Each set of notes detailed dates and times, and contained copies of statements and reports.

Everything looked like a grand jury should have been investigating, and yet no charges had ever been filed. Nothing on the notes indicated any legal profession's involvement.

The last folder had a bunch of miscellaneous scribbles and clippings. She leafed through them, not really knowing what she was looking for, apart from color commentary.

One clipping caught her attention. It was a small article talking about Emily Smith's disappearance. According to the story, the eighteen-year-old had left her house for work and was never seen again. Her parents were asking for the public's help. Emily's picture showed a pretty girl, with straight, dark hair, parted high on the left side, sparkling brown eyes, and a full smile. She held a bouquet of flowers in the photo, and looked like an angel.

Peri got out the picture of Gretchen Smith and compared the two. Emily was a younger version of her mom. She sat back and ate another spoonful of ice cream.

"Disappeared, just like Dev. Wonder where you are now."

Her phone rang so she picked it up. Skip.

"Hey Doll, no one was home at the Murray house, so we were on our way back to the station when we got the call. They found Ronnie."

"Great," Peri said. "Maybe he can give us some answers."

"No, at least not in the usual way. Ronnie's dead. Single-car accident on Ortega Highway."

"Just like that reporter," she said. "How coincidental."

"Good news is, they did verify his name was Ronald McHale."

"Son of Carl and Hester Bennett McHale," Peri told him. "Grandson of Leland Bennett of Bennett and Smith Insurance Company, and cousin of Matt McHale."

"Well, aren't you just a walking genealogy lesson."

"I like to stay informed. Do they have an approximate TOD?" She was hoping it was before she implicated Matt's cousin to him, not after.

"At least a day, from what I hear."

She sighed, thankful she hadn't sent Matt McHale off to commit a crime.

"What's the sigh about?" Skip didn't miss a thing.

Peri told him of her conversation with McHale.

"The good news is," she said, "McHale is probably not Ronnie's killer. The bad news is, Ronnie couldn't have been the one sending those texts."

"We're still working with the phone company to get that phone number." She heard him groan and pictured him scratching his head in exhaustion. "I'm at the scene here, on Ortega. I still have at least another hour. You okay alone tonight? I'm just about spent."

"You know I enjoy your company, but I can make it one night."

She hung up and went back to the files, putting everything into the box.

"Might as well open up the new computer." Peri took her new toy out of its packaging and turned it on. She was happy to see all her programs, including a good security system. All she needed to do was get on the Internet and download her data from her online storage.

In the middle of downloading files, she sat back and gasped. Then she picked up the phone.

CHAPTER 31

Skip stood at the side of California State Route 74, commonly known as Ortega Highway. Over a hundred miles of winding road, from San Juan Capistrano in the south of Orange County, up to Palm Desert in the easternmost part of Riverside County, two lanes carried travelers through forests, mountains, and desert.

Speed on the curves took enough lives by accident. One more single-car crash shouldn't matter. It only mattered this was a man police wanted to question, and he'd picked the worst time possible to drive his car off the edge and into a ravine.

"You Carlton?" A young, slender officer in an Orange County Sheriff Department uniform approached the detective. "I'm Deputy Kane. Captain's just finishing up with the coroner, then she'll be with you."

Skip had worked with Captain Tina Stark before. Most people mistook her laid-back personality to mean that she was casual about her job. She might be affable, but he knew from experience, working with her was an exercise in precision.

He wandered toward the coroner's van, noticing it was Frank Tsu, not Blanche, handling the body. *It was just as well,* he thought. *It might be a conflict of interest to work on the body of a man who possibly tried to kill your son.*

Captain Stark was standing next to the van, pen and pad in hand, talking to Tsu. An athletically built woman, she showed traits of her mixed ethnicity, with her freckled, fair skin and tight African American curls.

Skip hailed her as he approached. "Captain Stark."

"Carlton, it's good to see you." She pointed to the still figure, now in its zippered bag. "I heard you wanted a piece of this."

He smiled. "I'm happy to let you lead the way. Unfortunately, I wanted him while he was still breathing."

"Suspect?"

"A definite person of interest. He was at the scene of a murder in Newport, and according to my girlfriend, she caught him breaking into her home and trying to steal her laptop."

"Sorry about that." She nodded toward Tsu. "Hopefully we'll know more after the autopsy, but I have to say, it doesn't look normal. No wounds on the vic, but there's no skid marks on the road to indicate he was out of control. Tox screen may tell us if he'd been drinking or doped, but there's no smell of alcohol."

"Rumor is he's about one day dead."

Frank Tsu stopped writing and turned to the detective. "Less than a day. It's been warmer and more humid than normal the past week. Decay speeds up. Also, not as much bruising as this kind of crash should cause. Indicates he may have been dead when he hit the trees."

Skip took out his own notepad and checked what he'd scribbled earlier. It looked as if this still got Matt McHale off the hook for the murder, but Ronnie could have possibly sent the texts.

Stark interrupted his thoughts. "Of course, suicide's always a possibility."

"I didn't know him," Skip told her. "But I'm guessing he wasn't the kind of guy to lose sleep about anything."

"Captain?" Deputy Kane trotted over. "They just brought up the truck."

Skip looked over to see the gold Toyota, its front end mangled, being held by a large hook on the back of the local towing vehicle. There was a lot of damage, but it was hard to tell if the truck had been going fast when it popped the curb and went over the edge. Newer cars tended to buckle and dent more easily.

"We'll take it back for processing," Stark said.

"Ma'am, we've already found one interesting thing," the deputy told her. "The gear shift was set to neutral."

The captain looked at Skip. "Well, suicide is off the table."

Deputy Kane held out a bag. "We also found two cell phones."

"May I?" Skip held out a gloved hand.

He reached into the bag and took out the phones. One had *Ron's Phone* as its banner. The other did not have a banner, but in flipping through its contents, Skip found pictures of Alex and his friends. He put the phones back in their evidence bag.

"Well this answers one of my questions." He turned to Captain Stark. "Can I get a copy of the autopsy results, and the crash investigation?"

"You bet. Glad to have another pair of eyes."

Skip's cell phone rang, so he pulled it from his belt and answered it. It was Peri.

"We should check James Murray's internet storage." Her voice sounded high-pitched and loud, an indicator of her excitement level.

"What?"

"I was just transferring my backed-up files to my new laptop. I store everything on an internet cloud now. Maybe James did the same. Maybe the real fire investigation report is there."

"Possibly, but we'd need a warrant to get to them."

"So get a warrant."

"In pursuit of what case, Peri? Murray's death isn't in my jurisdiction. Neither is Ronnie's. I'm here as an observer. My only possible murder is Alex McHale and Murray's files have nothing to do with him."

"Well get one of those other agencies to get the warrant. This is important." Skip held the phone out to keep Peri's voice from piercing his eardrum. He looked over to see Captain Stark smiling.

"Peri, we can discuss this later, but right now I am not your personal police department. You want to see that account? Figure it out." He ended the call and saw the captain had stopped smiling and started laughing.

"Sounds like you're wading in some hot water," she said.

"Yeah, my girlfriend happens to be a P.I. working a case."

"One that involves Ronnie McHale?"

Skip shook his head. "I wish it didn't, but yes. And when that woman needs information, she's relentless."

"Oh, honey," Stark laughed. "What woman isn't?"

CHAPTER 32

Peri sat and looked at her phone, fuming. She needed access to James Murray's computer, which was probably in the property room of the Newport Beach Police Department. If not access to his computer, then access to his accounts. Without that report, she imagined Burton Smith would be willing to spend years in court, and perhaps as much in fees, to deny Benny his insurance settlement.

There was nothing to do but call Detective Thompson and appeal to him. It was already nine o'clock, but if she tried to wait until morning, there'd be no sleep for her tonight. She dug his card out of her tote and dialed.

After the third ring, she heard his voice. "Thompson."

"Detective, this is Peri. I know you aren't comfortable sharing any information about James Murray's death, but I've got an idea and I need help."

"Actually, Peri, we've already arrested someone in that case. Emma Malone."

"The secretary? No, that can't be right. What kind of motive would she have?"

He didn't answer at first, as if considering how much he should tell her. "According to Mrs. Murray, money had recently gone missing from the office. There were traces of GHB on the teapot and the cups, and only Emma's fingerprints on the pot."

Peri felt the heat in her gut rising up to her face. "Well, according to Emma, James never kept money in the office. That's why he never installed a security system. He said there was nothing valuable to steal. I saw Emma at the office the day after the murder. She didn't even know he was dead."

"What were you doing at the office?"

Now it was her turn to clam up. "My car," she said at last. "I had to come back and pick up my car."

She hoped he didn't notice her sigh of relief. "In addition, Detective, on the night of the murder, Mrs. Murray had gloves on when I met her. She could have drugged the tea and never left a print."

"Listen. Peri. I've been a detective for twenty years now. Usually the easiest answer is the correct one."

"And usually the spouse is the first suspect."

"Actually, you were the first suspect."

For a few moments, neither of them said anything. Finally, Peri spoke. "Is Emma in jail now?"

"No, she's been released on bond."

"I don't suppose you could give me her address."

"I don't suppose I could."

Her patience meter hit the red. "Ah, throw me a bone, here, Detective. I don't think she did it. What am I going to do, except go talk to her?"

"Ma'am, I think I'm done giving you anything. You have a good night." The line went dead.

Damn, she thought, *me and my short fuse.*

Turning to her laptop, she went on another people search. Emma Malone lived in Costa Mesa. There was no phone number listed, so Peri wrote down the address and wondered how early she could show up at Emma's door tomorrow morning.

It wasn't nearly time for bed. She turned on the TV and found a favorite movie, *Sabrina*. Audrey Hepburn was so elegant, even as the pigtailed youngster before she went off to Paris and got a makeover. Peri watched her triumphant return to the estate and envied her lean body and long limbs. She absentmindedly stroked her own neck, wishing it was as graceful as Ms. Hepburn's. Even William Holden didn't recognize her.

As she watched, she thought about Dev, and whether the letter had been delivered. If it was him, it would be just his style to not answer. Having Endeavor for a brother had always been frustrating. She missed him, but she couldn't miss a man she didn't know. It pissed her off, that he felt so little affection for her and their parents, but underneath the anger, she hurt.

If he was truly gone, she was the last of the Minneopas. Maybe she should have had children. She turned the TV off and walked to the bedroom, trying to imagine herself as a mother.

"Yeah, I don't think so," she said, turning out the light.

CHAPTER 33

At eight-thirty in the morning, Peri had been up for two hours, gone for a run, showered and was on the road to Costa Mesa. She made her way down the 55 freeway to Del Mar Avenue and a neighborhood of boxy, well-maintained homes. There were no fancy façades to any of them, no extra additions, and most of them were the same tan color. She wondered how you recognized your own house among all the lookalikes.

Emma's house had rose bushes lining the boundary of her front yard and gardenias under the window. Peri found an empty curb and parked. She got out of her car and walked to the front door, inhaling the gardenia fragrance as she went and hoping Emma was in the mood for company.

A minute passed after she rang the doorbell. She considered ringing it again, or knocking, when the door opened. Emma stood, dressed much more casually than Peri had seen her, in denim shorts and a University of Arizona Wildcats t-shirt. Her dark shoulder-length hair was down, parted high on the left side.

"Miss Minneopa." She looked surprised.

"Please call me Peri. Could I talk to you?"

Emma opened the door and allowed her to walk in. The small living room was sparsely decorated, with light walls and blond wood flooring, making the area seem larger. A small burgundy couch and matching chair were by the bay window, their clean lines keeping the room's large perspective. There was a vase of fresh roses on the table between them, and an oval, glass-topped coffee table in front. Emma gestured to the couch.

"Please sit down. Can I get you some coffee? I'm afraid I'm on my second pot of the day."

"I'd love some."

She disappeared into the kitchen and returned with two mugs. Handing one to Peri, she sat down in the chair next to her.

"For the record," Peri said. "I don't think you drugged me, and I don't think you killed James."

"Thank you. I wish you could convince the police of that."

"Well, maybe we can. I was hoping we could help each other. Before he died, James told me the fire investigation report that was sent to the police and insurance company was not the one he wrote. His real report would show my client wasn't negligent, but without it, there's no way the insurance company will pay for the damages."

"I had nothing to do with faking any reports—"

Peri held her hand out. "No, I didn't think you did. But maybe you could help me find the real one. And I could help prove you didn't slip us any drugs or kill James."

Emma looked at her and smiled. "Now how do you think you're going to do that?"

"It might not be as easy, but here's what I'm thinking." Peri took a deep breath. "Okay, follow me on this. Babette told the cops money was missing, but you told me James never kept money in the office. I can't think of a motive for you to want to do him any harm. I mean, you're out of a job now, for Pete's sake. A simple review of your finances should show you didn't profit, and a review of James's finances shouldn't show any loss."

"That's what I tried to tell that detective."

"Babette, however, is a Bennett, of Bennett and Smith Insurance. They're the insurance company that doesn't want to pay my client. Interestingly, they insured the house for many, many times its worth. Coincidentally, the house was destroyed by fire, and oddly enough, a fake report says it was the owner's fault and they don't have to pay. I think the Bennett family has more to lose from paying out any policy. And James Murray's real report, showing no negligence, would have jeopardized their bank accounts."

She watched Emma's face lighten. "That's a possibility."

"I think we need to find the real report, then investigate Babette's finances and show how much she would have suffered if Bennett and Smith had to pay out a million dollars."

"But what about my prints on the teapot?"

"Babette was wearing gloves when I met her that day, and you said she sent you to adjust the thermostat while the tea was brewing. She could have easily slipped drugs in the pot without leaving evidence. If we can get hold of her bank records, and her phone records, maybe we can find where she bought the GHB."

"The what?"

"According to Detective Thompson, that's what James and I were drugged with." Peri sat her mug on a tile coaster. "Do you know if James backed up his files?"

"Yes, I did it for him. He has an internet account."

Peri smiled. "I love you, Emma." She looked over at the secretary, who had reached behind the flower vase for a coaster. Peri gasped, then smiled even larger as she recognized the face smiling behind the roses. "Or should I call you Emily Smith?"

The smile faded from Emma's face. "How did you know?"

"I didn't. Seeing you with the roses jogged my memory. You look like the picture in the paper, the one of you holding the bouquet."

Emma sighed, and rose from her chair. "Want more coffee? I'm guessing you're going to want the whole story."

She shuffled to the kitchen and returned with freshened, full mugs, handing one to Peri before sitting down. The wine-red of the Wildcats logo on her shirt popped against the chair's fabric. Peri sipped her coffee, waiting for the tale to begin.

At last, Emma spoke.

"I hardly know how to tell it, I've never told anyone, but I'll try. My dad and I never got along. I was a rebellious child anyway, but it was the Sixties, so I was happy to be a hippie and a feminist and get his goat at every turn. The trouble began when I started my senior year of high school."

She stopped here, as if mulling the words over in her mind.

"I assumed I'd be going to college. My brothers went, and I thought Dad would be glad to get me out of the house. I did my research and felt UC Santa Cruz was right up my alley. I still remember the morning at breakfast when I told him that's where I wanted to apply. He said, 'I'm not sending you to college. It's a waste of money. You'll just get married and have kids.'" She paused, her face flushed. "It was always about the money with him. So I decided, if I was going to be mad, he was going to pay for it. I found the lowest, sleaziest guy on the high school campus, and got pregnant."

"Wow," Peri said. "That's a long way to go to piss off your pop."

"I was young and stupid, and didn't care about me as much as I cared about embarrassing him. He was livid, at first, then he calmed down and told me he understood and it would all be okay. I should have known better than to trust him.

"The next morning, he asked me to go to breakfast with him. We got in his car, but he didn't drive to any restaurant. He drove me to a back-alley doctor, who gave me an abortion." Emma's face was beet red now, and her hands shook as she stopped to drink.

"Did you try to escape?"

She shook her head. "I didn't know where we were going or what the place was, until I was in the room. I couldn't believe my dad was doing this. The nurse and the doctor grabbed me and I felt a pinch on my arm. When I woke up, I was back in my dad's car, going home. It was done."

"Emma, where was your mom?"

"Where she always was, at the bottom of her favorite martini." She scowled. "That's when I really got mad. It took me a week to think of how to retaliate. I decided to blackmail him. He loved his money so much, if I couldn't embarrass him, I'd make him pay for what he'd done to me. I typed up a blackmail letter, one with enough details to prove I knew what happened. I pretended to be the guy who got me pregnant—I never told anyone who it was, anyway. I asked for a small sum of money at first."

"At first?"

"I guess I was afraid of him calling my bluff, so I didn't ask for a lot. Like, five hundred dollars. But he paid it. So the next month, I asked for a thousand. Again, he paid it. The last payoff was twenty thousand dollars."

"What happened with the last payoff?" Peri had taken her notebook out and was writing as fast as Emma talked.

"I couldn't live in his house anymore. The money did nothing to make me like him. As a matter of fact, I hated him even more. I decided on one last, big score, after which I'd leave town, change my name, and start a new life. It was August. It would have been my baby's due date. He usually left the money in a box somewhere. Every month was a different location.

"This time, he asked for a meet. Said he wasn't going to leave that much cash lying around by a dumpster. I agreed." She shook her head. "Why, I don't know, but I agreed. The plan was, we'd meet at the nursery out on Lambert Street and Valencia. He'd leave the briefcase by a specific tree, then get back in his car. I still didn't trust him, so I asked a girl I met at the mall to help me. She wore a hooded jacket to hide her face. I promised her a thousand dollars."

Peri saw Emma's eyes become glossy with tears. "I'm guessing it didn't go as planned."

"We rode our bikes to the nursery. She parked hers by the tree where he was supposed to leave the money. I hid, with my bike, back further in the nursery, then watched my dad's car pull up. It was around one in the morning. I saw him get out of the car, put the briefcase down, and return. The girl came from behind the tree and reached down to pick it up... I can still see it. He drove his car forward and hit her. Knocked her off her feet. Then he backed up.

"Peri, I watched my own father walk to the trunk of his car and come back with a tire iron. He beat that girl. He never pulled back the hood, never hesitated, just beat her to... to... I never knew before what he was capable of." She was crying now, so Peri reached into her tote and handed her a tissue.

"When he hit her with the car, the briefcase got smashed by the tire. It split open and the money kind of spit out of it. I was close enough to grab a lot of it without being seen. My dad didn't even try to find the money. He took the briefcase, got in his car and drove off.

"When I was sure he was gone, I picked up the rest of the money, and went home. The next morning, I got dressed and acted like I was going to work. Thank God my father didn't come down to breakfast. I walked to the bus station, bought a ticket, and started a new life in Arizona."

Peri finished writing and looked up. "What brought you back to the family?"

"Although I changed my name, I still felt really close to my younger brother, Bud—Burton Junior—so I kept in touch with him. I never told him why I did what I did, but he never questioned me and never told anyone, not even Vincent. When Bud first graduated from college, he did a summer internship for Dad. He found some really shady things going on at the company, things he'd write to me about. They were charging lots of money for policies that never paid out. I mean, *never* paid out.

"It nearly killed me when Mom died and I couldn't go to the funeral. Then Bud died last year. Dad was still alive, still stealing clients' money and jerking people around, and it just wasn't fair. I decided to come back and see if there was some way to set things right. Your client's fire gave me that chance."

Peri put her notebook down. "Okay, here's what I think we need to do, to start. Can you find that report on James's internet backup?"

"If it's there, I can find it."

"We take that report, my newspaper clippings, and your story to Detective Thompson. Do you have any proof that you used to be Emily Smith?"

She got up and left the living room, returning with a folder, which she handed to Peri. "My birth certificate and my application for a name change in Arizona."

"You did this all very legally, Emma. It should have been easy to find you."

Emma smiled. "It should have. According to Bud, my mother was distraught and called the police within a day of my disappearance. When they showed up, my dad took them aside and told them I was a runaway, troubled, that I'd gone off before and always came home when I ran out of money."

"So they filed a report and put it away."

Nodding, her eyes widened. "Bud told me something else, earlier that morning, Dad was at the breakfast table with the newspaper. He suddenly turned pale and grabbed at his chest, then got up and left. Bud looked at the paper and saw an article about an unidentified girl's body found at the nursery."

"Did Bud know what you saw?" Peri asked.

"No, I didn't want to burden him."

Peri stood up. "Let's go talk to Detective Thompson."

"Should I look for that report on Mr. Murray's account first?"

She thought about this. "No. We don't want the police to think you downloaded and doctored it. You can give them the information about how to access the account, and they can look into it."

"But what if it's not there? Or what if the report doesn't say what you hope it will?"

"Emma, that's the chance we've got to take."

CHAPTER 34

Detective Thompson was a quiet man. Peri presented her information, piece by piece, from the internet video, to the mysterious packages she received, to the pictures of Babette Murray and Ronnie McHale she snapped the night they broke into Murray's office. She paced as she spoke, dragging out papers for him to examine. The large, bald detective sat with no expression on his face.

At one point, Peri wondered if he was listening, but he said, "You know, technically, Mrs. Murray didn't break into her husband's office. She had a key."

"Does a key trump the police tape?"

His mustache flickered in the hint of a smile. "Does police tape trump picking a lock?"

Peri sat down and crossed her arms. "Well played, Detective. The thing is, I don't think Emma drugged us. I don't think she's got motive to kill James." She nodded toward Emma, who was sitting in the hallway, waiting outside the detective's closed door. "She had motive to keep him alive, trying to make certain his report brought Bennett and Smith to its knees."

Peri watched Thompson look out the window at the secretary, who was pressing her fingers into each other as if to release her tension.

"The other theory is, Murray's report wasn't going to make the insurance company pay and she killed him to replace the report with one that would."

"And that's why we didn't try to look up the missing report in his online account," Peri said. "I figured Emma could give your CSI guys the access and they could do their cyber-magic on it and figure out it's the real deal."

"What makes you think we'll find the report? Or that we're even interested in following this lead?"

Peri stood in front of the desk, her palms pushed toward him. "First of all, I don't know if you'll find the report. I don't know what you'll find. For all I know, there's nothing in that account. But James told me he didn't write the report that was sent to the police department. I have an audio file, yes, retrieved in an unorthodox manner, but it still shows a guy named Ronnie was threatening James to write it up as negligence, and James was unwilling.

"And of course you're not interested in this lead. You have a suspect." She pointed to Emma. "She is a viable one, even if she's the wrong one. You've done the work, probably handed it off to the D.A. by now and you want to move on to the next case. I totally get it."

Sitting again, she rubbed her forehead. "You're overworked, understaffed, overwhelmed, and happy to get one case solved because there are more out there. I know this. I also know I'm not one of your citizens, just a random victim of a crime here."

The detective got up and moved around the desk. "Look, Peri, the Newport Beach police take you seriously as a victim. We want to catch the guilty party and give you closure. But this—" He picked up her papers. "Even if I didn't believe the easiest answer is usually the correct one, I just don't have the resources to check it all out. Do you know how long this would take? We've already spent a lot of time processing the original scene of the crime."

"I know." She gathered her evidence and put it back in her tote. "Thank you for listening, Detective."

Peri looked over at Emma, who stood. The detective escorted them back to the reception area.

"Good luck," he said.

The two women walked back to Peri's car. "Good luck, my ass," she told Emma. "Luck is for people who don't know how to work it."

They got in and prepared to drive away, buckling seatbelts and turning on air conditioning.

"I guess I better talk to my attorney," Emma said. "Would it be okay if she contacted you?"

Peri didn't answer at first, thinking about her options. "What? Oh, sure, I'll talk to the attorney. Have you got time for a trip to Placentia?"

"Sure. Why are we going there?"

"To get the Placentia police involved." She put the car into gear and drove onto Jamboree Road, past the luxurious lawns and Back Bay, toward the freeway.

"How can they be involved? Mr. Murray was killed in Newport."

"Oh, they won't investigate his murder. But maybe we could convince them to look into the insurance fraud and arson. That's definitely in their jurisdiction."

* * *

Skip seemed a little more receptive to Peri's theory, at least in his body language. She watched him nod and lean forward as she dragged out the pieces of evidence and repeated her theory to him. This time, she included Emma in the presentation, having her tell her story of blackmail and murder.

"Detective Thompson doesn't really want to hear it," Peri told him. "He's got his murderer in Newport Beach. But you've got insurance fraud and arson here in P-Town."

Skip looked down at papers on his desk, then at Emma. "Just out of curiosity, where were you yesterday, between six a.m. and noon?"

"I was a guest of the Newport Beach Police Department, Sir."

He stared back at the papers, shuffling through a few pages. "Miss Malone, is it? Would you excuse us for a moment?" He motioned for Peri to follow him out of the office. She obeyed, and he closed the door.

"You know how I like to play devil's advocate to your ideas, Doll." He held up the folder. "But I have the autopsy report from Ron McHale here. Before he took Mr. Toad's wild ride, someone suffocated him. And guess what they found in his system?"

"GHB."

He nodded. "Our number-one suspect in the insurance fraud is drugged with the same stuff Emma here supposedly fed you before she stabbed her boss."

"Except that she was in jail at the time."

"I suppose she could have spiked something he didn't eat or drink right away—"

Peri interrupted. "But if someone was trying to kill him, they'd want to know when he was drugged so they could suffocate him and stage his little accident."

"She could be working with someone."

"I suppose." Peri looked in the office window at the slender brunette, dressed elegantly in white slacks and a burgundy striped top. "But her story is a woman who ran away and spent her entire life basically alone. No family, no husband, no kids, at least none that she's talked about. That doesn't strike me as the person who'd work with anyone."

"Her brother."

"Who is dead."

"Then her other brother."

"She's not talking about Vincent." She watched Skip's expression. "Look, as far as I can tell, she has no motive to kill Murray, or to help defraud Benny. She's more likely to want Ron dead, but she was in jail at the time."

"Okay." Skip sighed as he said it. "We can at least look for that report. I'll get Jason."

As Emma met with Jason, to give him access to James Murray's backup account, Peri sat in Skip's office, reading various notes on his desk, her foot tapping a beat on the leg of her chair.

"Would you just cool it?" Skip sounded annoyed.

She looked up to find him staring at her. "What?"

He waved his hand. "The foot-rapping, nervous-snooping thing you have going here. They'll be finished when they're finished."

"I need them to find that report. I know it's there. James was a lot of things, but liar wasn't one of them. I figure I take it back to Smith and…" She stopped talking and thought.

"Yeah, and then what? He finds another reason to stall, or dribble the least amount of payout possible, like you told me he did with Alvin. Benny may have to take him to court."

She sat back and relaxed. "You're right. I need that report, but it's not a magic bullet."

A jaunty tune cackled from her tote, so she retrieved her phone and answered.

"Miss Peri, I got news." Benny's voice sounded bright.

She waited for him to tell her, but there was silence until she prodded. "What is it, Ben?"

"Mr. Campbell called. My attorney."

Yes, I know who he is, she wanted to yell, but didn't.

"He said that family called. The McHales. The awful people who were suing me. Well, I guess really they didn't call Mr. Campbell. Their attorney called him. But it's the same thing—"

"What did they want?"

"Oh, yeah," he said, as if he forgot why he was calling. "They're not suing me anymore. Isn't that great?"

"That is good news."

"We should go out and celebrate. Can we go back to Amelia's tonight?"

She was a little surprised by Benny's request. He was not a man who thought in terms of 'we'. "I'd love to, but I'm kind of busy at the police station, trying to find evidence to make the insurance company give you your money. We might have to postpone—"

"Oh, do that instead," he told her. "I need my money."

The call ended. Peri delivered the news to Skip.

"Well, I guess I made a dent in the McHale family. If Matt's cousin set the fire that killed their son, they've got a whole new target to pursue. Of course, I don't know if they know Ronnie's dead yet."

A sharp rap was heard on the door before it swung open and Craig Daniels entered. He smiled at Peri.

"Hey there, haven't you gotten tired of this guy yet?"

"If I do, I'll let you know." She threw the empty flirt at him, knowing he was an eternal skirt chaser.

"Chief would like to see you," he told Skip. "We're having a conference call with the OC sheriff's office to talk about the Ron McHale case."

Skip nodded and picked up the pictures of Ron with Babette Murray. "I think we should bring the Newport police in on this. Even if they think their case is closed, it would be a favor to let them know what our dead guy was doing in their jurisdiction."

Peri smiled. "Absolutely. I'll just wait here for Emma."

The two men left her alone, so she gathered her notes and evidence from Skip's desk and put them back in the envelope. She opened her tote and saw another envelope, the one from Benny's house, with his family pictures and his dad's letter. Her gut told her the letter was important, but her moral compass told her that only Benny could open it. She had been hoping to talk him into reading it, so she carried it with her, waiting for her opportunity.

Taking it out, she read the instructions again. *In the event of my death.* She had no clue. Benny wouldn't talk about him. Phil Nickels didn't know, and didn't know how to find out.

Just like Schrodinger's cat, Benny's dad was dead and alive.

She could do some more investigating and find him. Or she could shut off that little voice telling her it would be wrong to snoop in someone else's correspondence. It could be a letter of regret and explanation, a plea for forgiveness, something completely intimate. She shouldn't read it.

Unless reading it would ultimately help Benny. He had been hurt by his dad's absence. Now he seemed angry, but at the bottom of that anger was his original pain and confusion. It might do him good to hear that his dad regretted leaving. If his dad had no regrets, well, that was something she could spin, too, if it made Benny feel better about his family.

Armed with an excuse and a way to justify it to her soul, Peri took Skip's letter opener and slid it under the flap. The glue was old and had decayed, making the envelope open with ease. She slipped out a fat letter, several pages, and slowly opened it, taking deep breaths as if she were breaking into a locked room.

Robert Needles's handwriting was neat, on lined paper. A blue pen had been used, and there were no smudges or crossed-out words. Peri imagined Mr. Needles writing it all out in pencil, then carefully transferring it to its final version. In his own way, Benny had picked up a certain amount of meticulousness from his father.

As she suspected, the first part of the letter was an acknowledgment of the pain he caused and a plea for forgiveness. He assured his son of his love and how much it hurt to leave him and his mother. But, as always, there was a good reason.

This is what Peri wanted to know. As she read, her eyes widened and her mind reeled like a thousand cogs, moving all the pieces into a final picture. By the end, she sat back, her hand over her mouth, astonished. She'd had the answer in her possession all the time.

The office door opened and Jason walked in, with Emma. He held a folder out to Peri.

"We found the real report," he told her. "It definitely rules out homeowner negligence."

She held up the letter. "And I found the biggest piece of the puzzle."

CHAPTER 35

Dear Benny,

First of all, I want you to know I've loved you since before I held you in my arms, and I will love you always. Your mom and I didn't think we were going to be able to have children, so when you came along, it felt like a miracle. I know a lot of people think you are a quirky boy, but I love your special ways of doing things. I love that you wash your hands ten times before dinner, and you eat each food separately and turn your plate clockwise. I love that your prayers at night include anyone you've seen during the day, even if you didn't know them.

All I wanted was to have a quiet life with you and your mom. We didn't need to be rich, just comfortable. I'm an accountant, so I thought that would be easy to do. I got a job at an insurance company, Bennett and Smith. We had a nice house in a good neighborhood with good schools and a church close to us. It was all good.

And then it all went wrong. Mr. Smith needed to pull a little money out of the company fund. I guess it was his company, he had a right to the money, except he didn't want Mr. Bennett to know about it. He said he could put the money back at the end of the month. I just had to cover the missing funds in the books until then. He promised, plus, he was my boss. What was I supposed to do?

One month turned into three and he kept borrowing more from the company, so I was hiding bigger and bigger debts. I was losing sleep from the dishonesty. One morning I went to work and Mr. Smith met me at my office. He had told Mr. Bennett about the "loan" and it was all okay. As a matter of fact, Mr. Bennett expected the same treatment.

Suddenly, I went from being a nice, honest company accountant, to a sleazy bookkeeper who kept two ledgers. I was getting well paid, but I felt like I'd lost everything. I couldn't even look your mom or you in the eye. I wasn't the kind of dad you could look up to.

After a year, I was contacted by a reporter, Sam Todd. He was collecting evidence that the company was weaseling out of paying policies. He had stories from people who had legitimate complaints. Even though I wasn't part of those decisions, I felt guilty, and I knew if the reporter continued to dig, my crimes would be discovered.

I called a meeting with Mr. Bennett and Mr. Smith. I explained to them I couldn't do this anymore. I would never tell anyone what was going on at the company. Not only was I loyal, but I was in as much trouble as they were. But they needed to find a new accountant.

They were actually pretty nice about it. All I had to do was buy one of their outrageously priced, completely uncollectable insurance policies. It was steep, but I could do it. Oh, and one more thing: I had to leave town, without you and your mom. Mr. Bennett seemed okay if I stayed, but Mr. Smith sounded like he didn't trust me not to spread the word around town about their bogus policies and questionable accounting practices. If I left with my family, I would feel safe to talk. If I left you both behind, I couldn't guarantee your safety unless I kept my mouth shut.

It was their insurance policy against me. Oh, Benny I love you so much, and your mom. If anything happened to you, I couldn't live with it, especially since I got us into this mess.

I took the deal. I'm living under an assumed name in a little town in Ohio. I got a job in a bank, and I'm putting everything I can in an account that a friend of mine has access to. He'll funnel it into your account, so you won't run out of money. I'd like to know how you're doing, get updates or maybe pictures, but I don't dare.

I love you, Benny. I wish I was there.

Your dad, Robert Needles

Emma sat, nodding, her manicured hands rubbing together, as she listened to Peri read the letter aloud.

"It makes more sense now," she said. "Where Dad was getting the money."

Peri rose, picking up Murray's last report, along with the letter. "We need to let the police in on all this. Then I'm going to visit your dad. Care to join me, or should I take you home first?"

274

Emma looked at her, arms crossed. "I think I'm in enough hot water, and I don't care if I ever see that man again. You can take me home."

"Oh, all right. Wait here. I'll be back." She dashed out the door, down the hall to the chief's office.

The door was still closed, but she could see Skip, Craig, and Chief Fletcher sitting around the phone. She wondered if knocking would disturb them more than walking in unannounced. She decided they would be disturbed no matter what, so she pulled the door open.

The three men turned to look at her as she heard a female voice on the telephone talk about pulling LUDS for Ron McHale.

"So far, most of his calls are going to either a Burton Smith or a Babette Murray," the voice said.

Peri couldn't contain herself. "I bet he was working for Smith."

The female stopped talking.

"Captain Stark, Peri Minneopa just entered," Chief Fletcher said, narrowing his eyes at Peri. "She's a private investigator."

"I'm sorry to burst in, but I just found a piece of information I think is important to Ron McHale's murder." She wasn't really sorry to burst in, but she was a little sorry to be so annoying to Skip's boss.

"Jason found the real fire investigation report written by James Murray. The one that was sent to the police and fire departments was a fake. I'm betting Ron McHale wrote it. I have an audiotape of Murray talking to someone he identified as Ronnie, and Ronnie is trying to force him to say the Needles fire was homeowner negligence. This report shows otherwise."

She gave the papers to the chief, who glanced through them.

"The top sheet shows the date it was last accessed," he said, and showed it to Skip.

Skip read it. "The day before James Murray was murdered."

Peri continued. "I also spoke with Ron's cousin, Matt McHale, who said Ron told him the report would call it negligence."

"So you're saying Ron was involved in insurance fraud," Captain Stark said.

"It would make sense," Skip told her. "His primary phone calls are to the owner of the insurance company, as well as to the granddaughter of the late partner. He is at the scene of a fire, telling the fire investigator how to rule on the cause, and he's giving information to the parents of the boy who died in the fire."

"I also found this," Peri laid the letter on the desk. "It's a letter from Robert Needles to his son, Benny, describing how he was forced to keep two sets of books at the insurance company when he was their accountant. I think Ron was working for Bennett and Smith to keep them from paying out any claims so they could continue to rob from their customers. I assume the Placentia Police Department wants to investigate."

She thought the three men couldn't have looked more surprised if a panda had walked into the room. Skip took the letter and skimmed through it, then handed it to Chief Fletcher.

"Think we can get a warrant?"

"Go make the call." The chief turned back to the phone conversation. "Captain, we may be looking at murder having to do with insurance fraud. I think one of our departments needs to talk to Burton Smith and Babette Murray. How would you like to divvy up the work?"

"Why don't we take the grieving widow and let you have the insurance agent? Then we'll get together and compare notes."

"Sounds good." He ended the call and turned to Craig Daniels. "Get the warrant and I'll send a team over to Smith's office. See if they can find those books. And bring in Smith for questioning."

Peri reached over to take the letter from him, but his fingers didn't give. "By the way, where did you get this?"

"It's Benny's, Chief. Here's the envelope." She handed it to him.

"Did Benny open it?"

"No. I did."

He glared at her. "With his permission?"

"No, Chief. Benny won't talk about his dad, won't give me permission to investigate his dad, nothing. I knew his dad worked for the insurance company. I knew, from interviewing Phil Nickels, that he left town quickly, under duress. I'm not proud of opening that letter, but I was desperate for information."

She heard the sigh of disappointment from him. It wasn't the first time she'd heard it from someone.

"Peri—" He sounded frustrated.

She had heard that voice before, too. "You have to admit, I hit the jackpot."

"We'll talk about it later." He pulled the letter and envelope away from her. "Right now, this is evidence."

"I know it's evidence, Chief, but could I hold onto it a little while? I've got to tell Benny what I've done. I think, if I don't have it in my hands when I confess..." She shrugged.

He looked at the letter, then held it out to her. "Make a copy of it, just in case. Then do what you have to with Benny."

"Sure." She put her hand on the doorknob, then turned. "Chief, I was thinking. If you called Detective Thompson at the Newport Beach PD and told him what we've found, perhaps he would listen to you and look at someone else as a murder suspect."

"Why do we care about a murder in another jurisdiction?"

"Because I was there." Peri nearly shouted. "I was in the room with James and I fell asleep and I woke up with him dead and I keep seeing little pieces of the night and having sensations, but I can't remember it. Thompson wants to blame Emma because she was the last one to handle the tea, but it doesn't make sense and they won't consider any other theories and I just don't think Emma did it and I want to know who did."

He walked forward and reached toward her arm, grabbing her hand instead. "I'm sorry you went through—"

"A man's hand." She looked down, a flash of memory streaking through her. "There was a large hand around mine, pressing it onto something cool." She closed her eyes, flexing her hand. "Cool and round."

Chief Fletcher motioned for her to sit down. "Let me call Thompson right now." He moved to his desk and flipped through a directory.

As they listened to the ring, he looked at her and put his finger to his lips. Detective Thompson answered. The chief introduced himself and explained the case they were working on.

"Detective, I don't know what kind of evidence you have on Emma Malone, but we're looking at Ron McHale's last days and we're pretty interested in what he was doing at James Murray's office, not to mention his many calls to Murray's wife. Perhaps we could get a look at what you processed at that scene?"

"Sure, we're happy to help. What we have on Emma Malone is that we found GHB residue in the cups and the teapot, and her fingerprints on both."

"Were they on the murder weapon?"

"No, the only prints we found there were Peri Minn—Minnie—"

"Minneopa?"

"Yes."

Peri nearly gasped, but stifled the sound.

"And you didn't consider her a suspect?" Chief Fletcher shot her a warning look as he asked this.

"Not for long. She was definitely drugged at the same time, and her prints weren't consistent with someone who had held the letter opener to stab the victim. We also found a few drops of blood that didn't match the victim's, on the letter opener and under Peri's fingernails."

"Did you find a match?"

"The lab results should be back today. We believe it will match our suspect."

Peri tapped the chief's hand and mouthed *Ron* at him. He narrowed his eyes, so she grabbed a pencil and wrote, *Ron. Test.*

"Detective, if it doesn't come back as Emma's it might be a good idea to test against Ron McHale's. He seemed to be into some bad business."

There was silence for a moment. "That may be a good idea, Chief Fletcher. I just got the report. The blood isn't Malone's."

"We've got the report on McHale's blood and tox results. I can fax it over to you." He took down the fax number and ended the call before turning to Peri.

"You can take Emma home now. I know I'm not your boss, but, I'd really like it if she didn't know about those lab results yet."

"Don't worry, Chief. I can keep a secret."

CHAPTER 36

Peri drove back to Emma's Costa Mesa home. Her passenger looked out the window, her face without expression.

"I suppose it was hard to leave," Peri said.

Emma nodded. "My dad was mean. Cruel, in fact, especially when he was defied. My mom was too busy self-medicating to help any of us. Still, there was a feeling of family I missed. I wanted what I never had with them, and in some sense, wanted to return to try to find it."

"I'm frankly surprised you and your brother were able to remain in contact without your parents' knowledge."

"I know. Mom might not have noticed, but Dad was nosy and manipulative. It would be like him to buddy up to his sons and then use what they told him against them."

"Did you ever get to see Bud face to face? Or was it just through the post office?"

"Oh yes." Emma ran her nails through her hair. "The first time, he had to jump through a hundred hoops to make certain Dad didn't know where he went. Contrived a visit to ASU to see a high school friend and had to actually pay the so-called friend to uphold the illusion."

She chuckled. "After he got away with it once, Bud came to visit all the time."

"Why not Vincent?"

"He was so much older. By the time I wanted a brother to bond with, Vince was in college. Bud was there for me."

"What did you end up doing in Arizona?"

"I got my bachelor's, then my master's at ASU, and worked as a counselor for at-risk children."

"No children of your own?"

"No. I've had a difficult time with relationships. Trust issues."

"I understand." Peri thought about her own family and wondered if her letter had reached its destination. *Devlin Young of Las Vegas, were you really Endeavor Minneopa?* "I'm sorry about your brother."

"Cancer," Emma said. "He tried to keep it from me, but I knew when he came to visit me last year. So thin, and the way Steven, his partner, hovered around him." She sighed. "The hardest part was trying to play along with him and act like he was fine. Steven said he wanted it that way."

"I guess he wanted to live on his terms."

"And die." She turned to look out the passenger window again. Peri thought she saw her hand flutter up to her face, perhaps to wipe away a tear.

They pulled into the driveway and Emma opened the car door. "Thank you, Peri. I hope your client gets his money. I hope there's enough money for all those insurance clients to get what they deserve."

Peri watched her unlock the front door and enter her house, then backed out and retraced her route to the 55 freeway, toward Placentia. She felt heavy, as if the earlier excitement of finding the documents had worn her out. The clock on her dash read three-thirty, which was a shame. If it were earlier, she would have gone home for a nap.

Skip was still at work, she imagined. Perhaps he had Burton Smith at the station. She wondered whether Smith was confessing or spinning tales. Might as well drive through the parking lot and see if Skip's there, she reasoned. I have a right to know what Smith plans to do about Benny's insurance.

Crossing her fingers, Peri drove toward Chapman and Kraemer.

She pulled into the parking lot and rolled up one aisle and down the next. Skip's SUV was against the wall, in one of the reserved spots. She found an empty space further away, across from the library and parked her car.

Once inside the building, she went on a hunt to find Skip. Her first stop was his office. It was empty, but she saw her favorite CSU, Jason, hustling down the hall.

He slowed when he saw her and smiled. "They're in Interrogation. I was told you could come in if you stood in the back quietly. The word they told me to emphasize is 'quietly'."

"Does 'they' refer to Skip or Chief Fletcher?"

"Skip said it. But the chief was nodding."

He was on the move again, walking toward the interrogation room. Peri joined him.

"I'll be as silent as Theda Bara," she told him.

"Who?"

"A silent movie star."

"Oh, yeah. I always wanted to know, when you went to movies in the old days, was the theater just quiet? Or did they have someone playing music, or reading the lines or something?"

She looked at him, scowling. "I'm older, Jason. Not antique."

"Sorry," he whispered as he opened the observation room door and invited her to walk ahead of him.

Chief Fletcher was alone in the room. He nodded at Peri and Jason as they entered. Jason handed him several papers and leaned in to murmur something. She wanted to lean in, also, to hear what he was saying, but stopped herself. Instead, she watched their body language. Jason appeared to be excited about his results. The chief looked somber, raising his eyebrows slightly as he read. Then he looked at the CSU officer and gave a quick nod, sending Jason out of the room.

Throughout their exchange, questions and answers had been stuttering in the background, coming from the next room, where Skip and his partner, Craig, sat around a table, with Burton Smith between them. A middle-aged man in a dark gray suit sat to Smith's right. Peri guessed this might be his attorney.

Craig sounded as if he was trying the Reasonable Cop approach. "Mr. Smith, we're just trying to understand why Ron McHale's phone records show at least one call a day to your office, and several calls every day within the last two weeks."

Smith and the suited man exchanged glances. The suited man nodded.

"How should I know? People call the office all the time. I don't always answer." Smith was not making this easy.

"Well, someone answered his calls. They typically last between five and ten minutes."

"I'm going to ask again," Skip said. "What was your relationship with Ron McHale?"

"And I'm saying it's none of your business. It was nothing. He was related to my former partner. That's all."

"This has been asked and answered, detectives," said the attorney. "Move on."

Peri saw their door open and Jason enter. He handed the papers to Skip and pointed to something on a couple of sheets. Skip nodded at him, and turned to Smith, placing one of the papers in front of him and his attorney.

"Even if I believed you, I don't believe in coincidences. In addition to your phone calls, would you like to explain how every other Thursday you withdrew twelve hundred dollars from your account, and every other Friday, McHale deposited the same amount into his bank?"

Smith said nothing, but Peri watched his face turn red and his jaw tighten.

"And it would seem you have a long relationship with your partner's family." Skip laid another paper on the table. "Ron's dad, your late partner's son-in-law, used to be on your payroll."

"So what?" Smith frowned.

"So nothing, I guess," Craig told him. "Except that we also have a receipt from Ronnie's truck for one can of turpentine and one can of paint, purchased the day of the fire."

Skip stood and began touching each finger, speaking with each count. "So we have a receipt for turpentine and paint in Ronnie's car, a tape of Ronnie threatening James Murray, and a correlation between his income and your debt. We also have a fire at a house you insured, and a policy that could be voided if the homeowner was negligent."

Peri gasped. "I thought you couldn't use my tape. Illegally obtained, blah-blah-blah."

"We can use it now." Chief Fletcher's voice was even, emotionless. "If we need it later, we'll let the court decide if it's admissible."

Craig picked up the papers and looked at Smith's attorney. "I think the D.A. can tell a jury quite the story, don't you?"

"Are you going to charge my client or not?" Smith's attorney said at last.

Craig looked at Skip. "What do you think? Should we charge him?"

"Maybe we should."

Smith sat back and smiled. "Good luck proving anything more than coincidence."

"Oh, I forgot one little thing," Skip told him. "We also have a letter from your former accountant. He was kind enough to tell us about the two sets of books you keep. You know, you really should've hidden the second set better. Our CSU found it within thirty minutes."

Smith's face was purpled in rage. "You had no right—"

Craig pounded his hand on the table, as his voice rang out to match Smith's. "We had a warrant."

Peri was enthralled by the progression of tense bodies and flushed faces, to a kind of physical alertness, as if ready to either relax or explode. Finally, she heard Skip's voice, melodic, calm, soothing.

"You're not a young man, Burton. You're not in a position to fight this in the courts for years with little chance of prevailing. As soon as your other clients hear about what you tried with the Needles fire, they'll be finding an attorney who specializes in class action suits. If you're lucky, you'll find a way to spend your last dollar on your last day. I'm guessing, what with legal fees, you'll be in the red, and possibly in the street, if you're not in jail."

Peri saw Smith's bushy eyebrows scrunching low over his bent nose. His shoulders dropped a little.

"Not a young man? You have no idea." His attorney leaned over to him, but Smith pushed him back. "Robert Needles. He was a good accountant, but weak. Couldn't handle it when that reporter started snooping around."

"Mr. Smith," the attorney said. "I really need to remind you—"

"Shut up." Smith turned to Skip and Craig. "It doesn't matter. I'm dying. Lymphoma, diagnosed too late to do anything except say my prayers. It's okay, no one will miss me. I do have one son who's still alive, but he hasn't talked to me in twenty years. Detectives, I've spent my entire life being a sonuvabitch. Don't think I'll be able to turn that around in the few months I've got left, but I thought, for Vincent, I should clean up my own mess.

"I decided to close shop. Not just close it. Delete it. Remove it from the face of the earth. First, I cancelled all my clients' policies and referred them to other agencies." He chuckled. "Bet they're all shocked to find out how much I was gouging them. The plan was to shred all the papers, wipe Bennett & Smith off the map, and write one last, big check to Vincent.

"But what to do about Robert Needles? I couldn't cancel his policy. It would remove his reason to stay silent about me. Oh, I don't care about myself, I'll be gone. But Vincent... I didn't want him to live with what I did."

He stopped and pulled out a white handkerchief, then blew his nose on it before stuffing it back in his pocket. "I know what I am. I'm a grifter, a con man, and even worse. I decided to burn the Needles house. It would look like negligence, I could deny the claim, cancel the policy and be done with the family."

"Wouldn't that void your agreement with Robert Needles?" Craig asked.

"Yeah, well, I was betting that the method of policy cancellation would frighten him too much to say anything."

"It probably would have worked if those boys hadn't broken in," Skip said.

"Damn that Ronnie," Smith said. "We had the Needles' son's schedule. He knew those boys were in the house. He could have waited one more day."

Skip looked up from his notes. "And James Murray?"

"All I told Ronnie was to make sure the report said negligence. I never said to kill anyone. Babette called me the next day, crazy angry."

"Did you kill Ronnie?" Skip asked.

"Ronnie's dead? No, no, I didn't do that. How'd it happen?"

Skip was silent, so Craig said, "Car crash on Ortega."

"Fitting." Smith chuckled again. "That's how his old man took out that reporter."

Both detectives looked at the old man, who shrugged and said, "I told you I was a sonuvabitch." He blew his nose again, then added, "Robert was weak, but he was honest. Tell his son I'll pay him his million. Maybe I'll get a little karma."

Peri watched Skip push himself from the table. His mouth twitched downward, exactly once. She could tell he was thinking about everything Smith had just said. Craig also stood up, and the two detectives escorted Smith and the lawyer from the room.

"Well, Benny will be glad to know he'll get his money," she said. "I just hope someone can guide him through rebuilding his house before he starts to re-stock it with Dino."

The chief walked toward the door, so Peri joined him. As he opened it, his cell phone rang. He stepped aside and allowed her to exit, just in time for her to meet Burton Smith in the hall. Smith's eyes brightened with recognition.

"You." He spat the word. "Did you do all this?"

"Absolutely not," Peri told him. "The PPD did all this. I just tattled."

"Be careful with him, Peri," a voice said from down the hallway. "He's capable of some pretty awful things."

Everyone turned to see Emma Malone, aka Emily Smith, walking toward them.

"Emma," Peri said. "I left you at home."

"I know, but I decided I wanted that family reunion after all."

Burton Smith staggered back. "Emily—"

"Hi, Dad." Her voice was mocking. "I guess after you've murdered someone, lying and stealing and being a general dirtbag comes pretty easy."

"Murder?" Chief Fletcher asked.

"I never laid a hand on Murray," Smith said. "Or Ronnie."

"Not them," she told the chief, then turned to her father. "I'm talking about a young girl murdered thirty years ago in Brea. I was there that night, Dad. I watched from behind the trees while you beat that girl to death." Emma was shaking, fighting tears. "You didn't even blink. You just got back into your car and drove off."

Smith stared at his daughter, his hand clawing toward his heart.

"Did you think you'd killed me? Were you happy to get rid of me?" She lunged at him, both hands beating at the air.

Skip stepped in and caught her, pulling her away and calling for help. He blocked her while his partner maneuvered her father and his attorney toward the booking area. Officer Chou appeared from around the corner to be an escort with Craig while Skip calmed Emma.

"Miss Malone, we'll be turning this over to the Brea police," Chief Fletcher told her. "We'll expect your cooperation."

"Don't worry, sir. I think I've been waiting for this day."

The chief turned to Skip. "I just got off the phone with Detective Thompson. The unknown blood on the letter opener matched Ron McHale. They're reviewing the rest of the evidence, and Babette Murray is in their office now, being interviewed."

"Is she saying anything interesting?" Peri asked.

"Not so far. Thompson doesn't think they'll get much out of her. She's ice-cold, gives as little information as possible, sticks with her story. They're working on a warrant."

Peri looked up at Skip. "Did you find GHB in Smith's office?"

He shook his head. "We're getting a warrant to check his house."

"Well somebody's got to have remnants of it, somewhere." She frowned. "Who's checking Ron's home?"

"That would be the OC sheriff," Chief Fletcher said. "They'll call if they find anything. In the meantime, it sounds like Newport will be dropping the charges on Emma Malone."

"Thank you," Emma said, then turned and hugged Peri. "And thank you for not giving up."

"So Benny will have his money," Peri said. "It looks like either Babette or Ron McHale drugged me and James, then Ron stabbed James. Burton Smith hired him to do it. But who killed Ron?"

"We don't need to know right now." Skip put his arm around her shoulder and began to steer her toward his office, away from the chief. "Newport and Placentia will work together on finding out if Smith had anything to do with ordering Murray's death. The OC sheriff's office will do the investigation on Ron McHale, and they'll keep us in the loop. I'm pretty sure this is where your involvement ends."

"But the loose ends, Skipper. All the loose ends."

"Will be tied up by someone else." They stopped by his office door. "How about dinner tonight? We'll celebrate, wherever you want."

"El Farolito? I'm starving for fajitas and a margarita." Peri turned to Emma. "Would you like to join us for a little fiesta?"

Emma smiled and shook her head. "Thanks, but I think I'd like to go home now. It's been a little stressful." With one more hug for Peri and Skip, she walked out of the station.

"Call Blanche and see if they can join us," Skip said.

"I'll meet you there at seven." She gave him a quick peck on his cheek, then moved toward the exit. Halfway to the door, she stopped and turned back. "Benny. Is it okay if I invite him? He probably won't come, since it's not Italian, but he should be included in the party."

Skip smiled and shook his head. "Okay with me, Doll, but you're responsible for helping him navigate the menu."

"I just need to keep the staff from killing him." She continued on her way out, to the parking lot and her car. There was just enough time for a quick shower and a few phone calls before dinner. If she was lucky, she could sneak in a catnap, too.

CHAPTER 37

The sudden blast of a song jolted Peri from sleep. She leaped from the couch, picked up her cell phone and looked at the ID before answering.

"Hi, Benny."

"Miss Peri I forgot to ask you what I'm supposed to wear tonight."

"Tonight?" She looked at the clock. It was after six. "Crap, I fell asleep. Just casual wear, Ben. I may be running a little late, but I'll be there."

After a quick debate about business casual versus golf casual, she managed to extricate her ear from Benny's questions and end the call. On her way to the bathroom, she grabbed a towel and a change of clothes, and raced through the process of making herself presentable, cursing all the way.

"Damn. It. I just sat down for a minute. I shouldn't have been that tired. Crap. I'm going to be late. I hate this top, but I don't have time to change." She smoothed the white v-neck blouse over her tan slacks and slipped on a pair of shiny gold flats. Checking the time on her cell phone, she cursed again and rushed toward the door.

El Farolito, at the edge of Placita Santa Fe, was an establishment of the local community, still run by the original family. Along with several other family-owned Mexican restaurants, they competed for the hearts and appetites of local customers.

Peri drove down Bradford Street. At Chapman Avenue, she saw young people wandering around the doors of the corner church, a tall white stucco building that reminded her of a mission. A banner in front announced their Friday night youth meeting.

Friday night, she thought. *I'll never find parking in the Placita.*

A quick lane change let her turn left at the light and head down Chapman. She slipped around the corner to Kraemer, then Crowther Avenue. Across from the complex where the Bennett and Smith Insurance Company was hidden, there was a parking lot. Most people didn't use it, because it meant walking over the bridge that crossed the railroad tracks, and that meant either climbing stairs or waiting for an elevator.

Plenty of empty spaces awaited, so she slid into the closest one and hurried up the flight of stairs. The bridge itself was enclosed by iron bars and mesh, making it impossible to fall onto the tracks, and a little difficult to see through. A few people paused to look down, however. At both edges, there was a small open area, with just an iron railing, that reached around the elevator platforms to the stairwells.

She thought about how interesting it would be to watch a train pass by underneath, but hurried on.

Exiting the stairwell, Peri rushed toward the white building, still gleaming in the disappearing sun, the neon light of the *El Farolito* sign still unlit. She pulled open the large wooden door and entered.

The smells of traditional Mexican foods wrapped themselves around her sinuses, and even into the pores of her skin. Chiles of all varieties, warm corn smells from the tortillas and tamales, tomatoes, spices unknown to her by name but familiar by taste, reminded her that she hadn't eaten since the morning.

Frantic hands waving about caught her attention. She saw Blanche smiling and walked to the table, nodding at the hostess and pointing toward her friends. Blanche rose to hug her. They squeezed each other like they had been apart for years.

"I love impromptu parties," Peri said.

"I'm just glad we could all get the night off." Blanche's raspy voice sounded carefree.

Peri gave Blanche's husband, Paul, a quick kiss on the cheek, then moved to Skip for a more familiar embrace.

"Hi, Benny." She patted his shoulder as she sat down next to him at the round table.

He shoved a menu at her face. "Miss Peri, what should I order here?"

"Well, I'm starting with a margarita." She said this to the server who had just walked over, then turned to Benny to look over the selections.

After a multitude of questions and a little grousing about the lack of pasta or marinara sauce, she convinced him to try the chicken enchiladas. Orders placed, Peri leaned forward and reached for a crispy tortilla chip to load with salsa.

"So, how's every little thing?" she asked.

"The little things are fine," Paul said.

"The big things aren't doing so bad, either," Blanche added.

"I got the weekend off," Skip told her. "Want to go do something?"

A tall, familiar figure interrupted them. Nick Debussy approached the table as if it might leap up and smack him. Blanche and Paul rose and led him around to Benny.

"This may not exactly be the place," Paul said. "But we knew you'd be here." He stepped back, his hand on Nick's shoulder.

Peri couldn't tell whether he stepped or was pushed, but Nick moved forward. "Mr. Needles, I'm Nick Debussy. I'm one of the guys who broke into your house the night it burned."

Benny's face passed from happy to sad to angry with glacial slowness. "You were in my house. You had no right to be in my house."

Nick looked frightened, but continued. "I know, Mr. Needles. I wanted to tell you how sorry I am. I'm not just sorry your house burned, and I'm not just sorry because I got caught. I'm sorry because I knew it was wrong when we did it and I did it anyway. I went along with my friends. I didn't think for myself. I'm sorry, Mr. Needles. I'm very sorry."

Peri laid her hand on Benny's shoulder. "Ben, he did help the police find the man who set the fire."

"My house burned. My things, my Dean Martin things, burned." His face was red, his jaw stiff. He looked at Nick, who lowered his gaze. "You helped find the man who did it?"

Nick nodded, and Peri saw Benny's face relax.

"Okay." His left hand slipped into his pocket.

Peri knew he was rubbing his ashtray. "I know it upset you to have them in your house, but since Nick was so helpful, maybe you don't have to press charges against him for breaking in. After all, if the boys hadn't been there recording it, we wouldn't have known who set the fire."

Benny's head jerked up as he looked at Peri, then Nick, then Peri again. "Charges? Why would I press charges? I don't like the police station."

Now Nick relaxed. "Thank you, Mr. Needles. I mean, I did something wrong and I totally accept the consequences. I wasn't here to ask you not to have me arrested. I was just here to apologize."

Benny nodded.

"Did you want to join us for dinner, Nick?" Peri asked. "We can get another chair."

"No, Aunt Peri, I have stuff to do." He exchanged looks with Paul. "But thank you." He mumbled good-byes to everyone and waved on his way out the door.

Blanche smiled and nodded toward her son. "Paul's having him do a little Debussy Community Service—cleaning out the garage."

"He's a good kid," Skip told her. "He'll work it all out."

She shrugged. "At this point, there's not much we can do to reset his course."

"Kids," Paul added. "Seems like you can steer them as much as you want, they're still going to be who they are."

Peri nodded, thinking of her brother. She'd always just accepted Dev for being who he was, but tonight she wished she had tried harder to maintain contact, even if she was the only one doing the work. Suddenly, she stood up.

"Excuse me, I'll be right back," she told her friends, and turned to catch up with Nick. "I've got an idea for a way you can show Benny how sorry you are."

She and the teenager discussed her plan, Nick nodding and smiling. He left the restaurant, hurrying as if on a mission, and she returned to the table.

"I had an idea for another little community service project. Your son liked it."

Dinner arrived and the conversation idled while everyone ate. Peri watched Benny pick around the edges of the cheese, open the tortilla to see the chicken inside, and sniff every forkful before putting it in his mouth. After three or four bites, he turned to her.

"It's not Italian, but it's pretty good."

"I can't believe you've never eaten Mexican food," Blanche said. "This is southern California, for Pete's sake."

Benny looked at her, his jaw slackened and eyebrows creased together. "My mom cooked Italian. I like Italian." He resumed eating.

She changed the subject. "Well, you must be happy about the insurance payment, and Alex's parents, dropping their lawsuit."

He nodded.

"I still wish we knew who killed Ron McHale," Peri said. "Skip have you—"

He stopped her. "No. It's not in my jurisdiction. I'm just waiting for the OC sheriff's report. Unless they ask for my involvement, I'm not on the case."

"You're no fun."

"I might be," Blanche said. "I can tell you what the autopsy showed."

"I thought you weren't working that case," Skip said.

"I'm not, but Frank asked me to look over his notes. He's such a thorough examiner, he wanted to make certain, even though the tox screen came back positive for a large enough quantity of GHB to be lethal, the other signs pointed to strangulation."

Peri leapt at this information. "Other signs?"

"Petechiae under the eyelids isn't conclusive, but by the time he got back to the morgue there were definite bruises about the neck."

Now Skip was interested. "What kinds of bruising?"

"No fingerprints, if that's what you're hoping. General bruises from an unknown source. If I had to guess—" Blanche paused and stared at Skip, pointing. "And I'm not given to guessing, I might say a soft object, like a scarf or towel or necktie. Nothing abrasive, like a rope."

"Are you guys always this gross at the dinner table?" Benny asked.

"You get used to it," Paul told him.

"Sorry," Peri said. "So, what do you think the Angels' chances are for a championship this year?"

Pointing the conversation to anything but murder was difficult, but they managed it until the bill came for them to argue over. Peri laughed, watching Benny sit quietly and let everyone else do the heavy lifting. Money and plastic exchanged, the five friends exited the restaurant and said their goodbyes on the sidewalk, next to the long line of people waiting for a table.

Benny waved and walked south toward Santa Fe Avenue, and the railroad tracks. Paul and Blanche moved in the opposite direction, having found a space in the restaurant's parking lot.

"Your place or mine?" Skip asked Peri.

"Yours. I'm out of beer. Which way did you park?"

He pointed across the street, to the El Farolito overflow lot.

"I'm across the tracks." She reached up and kissed him. "See you in a few."

Night had descended, but the neighborhood was well-lit, with neon signs from restaurants, colorful lanterns for patio dining, and plenty of streetlights to chase away the shadows. In normal southern California fashion, the day's heat had been banished with the sunlight, and the air was now at least twenty degrees cooler.

Peri hurried toward the tracks, impatient to get to her car and meet Skip. It had been a great day, and she wasn't done celebrating. For all of the people still out at the restaurant, the parking lot was quiet and the bridge was unoccupied.

She hopped up the two flights of steps to the bridge that spanned the tracks. The stairs wound left, then right, around the elevator, and to the bridge. She rushed around the corner, glancing at the time on her cell phone.

"Excuse me," said a woman's voice.

Peri turned left toward the speaker and felt something large and flat slam into the side of her face. She saw darkness, punctuated by starbursts of light, as she spun. A smaller body pressed into her back and something soft slipped around her throat, tightening. She couldn't breathe.

It was like being murdered with a fluffy mitten.

CHAPTER 38

Her attacker was pulling her backward, trying to tighten the noose, while Peri struggled to get her hands underneath and pull free. Her fingers pushed their way through what felt like a silk scarf. A rational corner of her brain was telling her she didn't have long to do this, as her windpipe was starving for air.

A sharp pain to the back of her right knee brought her forward and to the floor. She guessed her attacker was trying to get the scarf tighter on her carotid, where unconsciousness would be faster, with death on its heels. She worked harder to get her hands around the scarf and lift the pressure. Her heart was pounding faster, while her head grew lighter, and her limbs felt leaden.

With an enormous push, she flung herself backward. The back of her head made contact with something hard and she fell on top of a twisting, clamoring body. She rolled over and jumped to her feet, whipping around to see who was trying to kill her.

"Babette." Her voice could barely chirp out the name. The faint scent of perfume flitted around them, and Peri remembered the lady in the stairwell earlier. "What the hell?"

Murray's widow had scrambled up, dropping the scarf and letting it blow across the platform, where it caught in the wrought-iron railing. It waved there, red silk with gold chain designs, instantly recognizable as Hermès.

Peri looked at Babette, who watched the scarf flying, before glancing down at the drops of blood on her silk blouse. She wiped her hand across her face, then stared at the crimson coming from her nose. Peri stood, wondering what was going to happen next. She didn't have to wait long.

Babette ran at her, hands pushing from sinewy arms, her face contorted with rage. She caught Peri in the shoulders, sending her back toward the rail. Peri's hips made contact with the metal before she stopped the momentum and put her hands out to push back. She opened her mouth to reason with the woman, then realized she would not have time. Babette was attacking again.

The brunette shoved into Peri as Peri shoved back at her. They stood this way for a few moments, Peri's back half against the railing and half against the stucco-wrapped column that supported the platform. To her right was the entrance to the bridge. Below was the fence with spiked bars to discourage people from trying to walk on the tracks.

She pushed harder against Babette. At some point, she thought about screaming to attract someone's attention, but she found she was too busy trying to get this woman off her. Suddenly, Babette pulled away from her. Peri pushed back against the stucco column, sweaty and panting.

"Babette, I don't understand." Her voice was still a strain to produce. "I know you didn't kill James, but did you kill Ronnie?"

Babette didn't respond. Instead she reached down for her leather clutch. Peri believed that must have been what hit her in the face. Babette opened it and withdrew a knife.

"I didn't want to use this." She looked down at her outfit. "You just can't get the blood out of silk."

Peri stood to attention and backed toward the rail again. "Are you insane?"

She saw the murderous look in Babette's eyes, so she put her left hand out. "No, wait, that's not what I meant."

To say out loud.

"No. One. Hurts. My. Family." Her voice was even, her words enunciated, as she swung the knife. A whooshing slash nicked Peri's palm before she could withdraw. "See? So messy."

Peri looked to her right, thinking she could make a running escape over the bridge, but her attacker swept in to cut off that route. There seemed to be only one exit left—over the railing. She had mere seconds to consider her chances. If she hit the fence, she'd be impaled. If she didn't, it was about a twenty-foot fall. Broken bones, paralysis, or death, awaited, depending on how she landed.

None of those options were attractive; nevertheless, she stepped over the railing, onto the tiny hangover ledge. Babette smiled and rushed toward her, so she scooted to her right, toward the bridge. Her ballet flats slipped on the surface, causing her to swing from her hands, which were still gripping the railing. The metal felt cold and hard, and the cut on her palm stung. Her heart took a permanent seat in her throat, where it beat like a Keith Moon drum solo.

Knowing Babette would not stop until she was lying in a heap on the sidewalk, Peri flailed onward to the right, her hands grappling along the railing as she kicked her shoes off and climbed up with her bare feet.

At last, she had reached the bridge, encased in strong mesh, and held in place by horizontal and diagonal beams that formed backward N's. The ledge was much narrower here, causing Peri to grip with her toes and flatten herself against the mesh, hanging onto a beam, her fingertips digging for every spare crevasse between the beam and the mesh.

Every surface was hard and gritty with dirt. Her toes had gotten scratched from scrambling up the stucco wall and now the ledge bit at each scrape. The cut on her hand screamed at her, blood running down her arm.

She reasoned Babette would not be able to stab her through the mesh, and certainly someone would see her hanging outside the bridge. Looking back at the parking lot, she tried to find someone, to get their attention. The only people she could see had gotten out of their cars and were walking up Bradford Street, their backs to her. She tried to call out to them, but her throat wouldn't produce any sound.

Where are those Friday night southern California crowds when I need them?

Peri shifted across, far enough to stay out of the crazy woman's reach, planning to hang there until the cavalry arrived. She hoped they brought the dog with the keg around its neck.

Babette stared at her from the platform. Suddenly she threw down the knife, and removed her shoes.

Holy crap, she's coming after me. Peri moved her feet in slow, toe-gripping steps, across the ledge. Once her legs were sufficiently close to the next iron support, she slid over and grabbed the iron in her hands.

Babette crawled over the railing, testing the ledge, then calmly grabbed the first bridge support and stepped toward Peri. She also crawled across, laying her arms out to the support beam first, then following with her feet.

The two women followed this dance above the tracks, flattened to the bridge's mesh, creeping to the right with one half of their bodies, then reaching to clutch with the other. Peri's body ached, her toes were on fire, and her fingers cramped down to her elbows, but her fear drove her forward. At the halfway point, she tried to scream again, to get someone's attention. A thin wail came out, mostly swallowed by a distant rumbling.

If there were people below, she could not see them. She didn't dare look at anything except the woman chasing her. Babette was only two bars away, laboring to catch up.

Peri felt her body shifting downward. This meant they were getting closer to the other side, where she could climb over the rail, run down the stairs, and get away from this nightmare. She worked toward the rail as fast as her fear would allow. She had to reach it before Babette caught up with her.

Babette seemed to be leaving the world of caution in her attempt to get closer. She threw her upper body from bar to bar, pulling her feet along. A couple of times, Peri saw her feet miss, dangle, and scramble back to the ledge. As much as she didn't want Babette to catch her, it frightened her to see the woman nearly fall.

There was now only one bar between them. Peri could see Babette's jewel-green eyes staring at her, lit from the streetlamp to their right.

"Oh my god, you're filthy," Babette said, and pulled her body back to look at her own, grime-covered clothes. "I'll never get this out. You are such a nosy bitch."

The last sentence was harder to hear, due to the rumbling sound, which was now closer, and became obvious to Peri.

A train was on the way.

She had thought about being on the bridge when one went past. Perhaps she should have been more specific about being inside the screen. She grabbed the bar and squished her body tightly to the mesh, yelling at Babette to hold on.

If Babette heard her, it was too late. A freight train came roaring up the tracks. From the squeal of its brakes, Peri knew someone on board had seen her and Babette, but an engine pulling even a few cars was not going to stop instantly. The vibration shook the two women like rag dolls.

Babette fell first, onto one of the rushing freight cars. Peri closed her eyes, but not before seeing the woman's body bounce from the car and slip between the links onto the tracks. She clung to the iron, her hands burning, but the train was stronger and jostled her loose. As she reached out, trying to grab something, she heard a cry. She assumed it was her own.

Someone gripped her wrist. She looked up to see Benny, leaning over the rail, holding her with both hands, his face crimson.

"Miss Peri, you gotta help."

She swung her legs toward the bar and was able to grasp it with her other hand. He continued to pull her as she labored to get a foothold and boost her body to safety. The rattle of the train did not help their efforts.

Just as her legs found the strength to lift her upward, she saw something fall past her. She climbed to the platform and lay on the cold floor. Benny stood over her.

"Miss Peri, what were you doing? You're kind of a mess."

Peri laughed and cried at the same time. "Yes I am. And I'm thankful. I'm so thankful to you, Ben. I don't know what to say, except thank you." She pushed herself up, scooting her back against one of the columns. "I could just hug you."

"No you can't. You're too dirty."

She laughed again, then looked at the railing. "Was that your ashtray that fell? Oh, Benny."

"It's just a thing. It's not a life, like you."

"Wait—what? Who are you and what did you do with Benny?"

He looked insulted. "I love my things, but I know people are more important. Mom taught me that."

"Well, thank you. And when I get cleaned up, you're definitely getting a hug." She tried to stand, then sat back down, her body still shaking. "I suppose I'm too dirty to ride in the Caddy."

His expression said it all.

"Maybe you could go find my cell phone? I think I dropped it on the other side of the bridge. I need to call Skip."

Looking down, she saw the train had stopped and there were several men walking toward what was left of Babette Bennett Murray. One man began retching, so she yelled down, "Don't throw up on any evidence."

A stout man in gray workman's slacks, a plaid shirt, and a Yankees ball cap looked up at her. "What the hell happened here?"

"Long story," she told him. "I'd rather tell it once, when the police arrive."

Leaning back against the rough stucco again, she waited for her hero to bring her cell phone, tears running down her face.

CHAPTER 39

Peri was relaxing on the paramedic's gurney when Skip finally came to see her. He leaned forward and kissed her.

"This was really not the way I wanted to celebrate the end of a case," she told him.

"Me neither, Doll."

"The good news is, at least I didn't get shot, or a concussion."

"Yeah, you can't really afford too many more of those." He frowned, in a way she recognized.

"We're not having the conversation again, are we? About my line of work?"

He didn't answer right away. "No. I give up, for now."

"The paramedic says I don't even have to go to the hospital."

A young Hispanic man in a uniform walked from the front of the truck. "I did say she should check in with her doctor, though. Most of your injuries are minor, but I would like someone to keep an eye on that bruised trachea. Also, if you experience any nausea, headaches, disorientation—"

"I know, keep a lookout for any aftereffects of being strangled."

"Jason's processing the scene right now. I've let Captain Stark know to get a warrant for Babette's house and search her scarves for any trace of Ron McHale, as well as GHB. Did she say anything to you?"

"No confession, if that's what you're hoping for. It was all about getting rid of me. Oh, and she hated getting messy." Peri looked down at herself. Her clothes were completely blackened by her journey across the bridge, and crusts of blood had dried along her left side. "This outfit is going in the trash. If I could throw my skin in the trash, that'd go, too."

Benny walked to the gurney, holding Peri's pink snakeskin tote in one hand. "Jason told me to give you this."

Peri reached out to take it, but he didn't give it to her. Instead, he held up papers in his other hand. She recognized them, Benny's dad's letter.

"You had no right."

Skip mumbled something about checking in with the train's engineers, and left them alone.

"I know I had no right. I felt badly about opening it."

"I trusted you."

"I know. I didn't want to open it. I needed information. Forgive me, please, Benny. Your father's letter helped crack your case."

"It did?"

"He helped you get your money from the insurance agency. Didn't you read it?"

Benny shook his head. "It says to open when he's dead."

Peri smiled, understanding at last. "If you don't open it, he's not dead, is he?"

He shook his head again.

"Well, someone's been keeping money in your account all this time. I opened the letter, but not in the event of his death. It was more, in the event of an emergency."

Skip interrupted them. "Hey, Benny, the crew found something." He held out a clear, heavy object.

"My ashtray." Benny turned it over, rubbing off the dirt and examining it. "There's a new crack in the corner, but it's still good. It's still my ashtray."

He smiled, the tiniest grin, and returned the talisman to his pocket.

A familiar CSU officer loped up, a pair of slippers in his hands. "Hey, Peri, found these. Thought you might want to wear them home."

"Thanks, Jason. I think I've had enough barefootin' tonight." She turned to Skip. "How much longer until I can get a shower?"

"Let me check out with Daniels and I'll take you home. And no, you can't drive yourself. I'll get one of the other officers to drop your car at my place."

"Did I even try to argue?" She smiled. "Okay, don't answer that."

* * *

After a lengthy shower, a handful of pain relievers, and a good night's sleep, Peri awoke to a quiet day at Skip's house. She helped herself to the pot of coffee he had brewed when he went to work, and prepared some scrambled eggs.

The newspaper had been left for her perusal, although the sports section was MIA. She had finished skimming the latest book review, trying to find out whether the writer actually liked the book or not, when her cell phone played a perky tune.

"Aunt Peri, it's Nick. I got what you asked for. It's all done."

"Wow, that was fast. I'll pick you up and we'll go over to Benny's. I think you should be the one to give it to him."

"But you paid for most of it."

"Not all of it. And you're going to work off the rest of it, doing some chores for me, right?"

"Right."

Peri dressed quickly in shorts and a t-shirt, then pulled her hair in a pony tail and stuck her favorite Angels ball cap on top. She was out and in her car within fifteen minutes, heading toward the Debussy house.

Blanche greeted her at the door with an enormous bear hug. "Dear God, girlfriend, what are we going to do with you?"

"Okay, I won't lie. I was never so scared in my life."

"Not even when that crazy chick kidnapped you and took you to the desert?"

"More than that, believe it or not. Every second, I thought I was going to fall, and when that train went by, well, thank God for Benny Needles."

"Never thought I'd hear those words."

Peri laughed. "Never thought I'd say them."

Nick hopped down the stairs. "Hey, Aunt Peri. Lemme grab some juice and we'll go." He disappeared around the corner, toward the kitchen.

"He is a good guy," Peri told Blanche.

"I know. He's trying. Sometimes he tries my patience, but I think he'll be okay now. We've got him talking to a counselor about Alex. That seems to be helping." She shrugged. "Families. Crazy, huh?"

Peri grimaced, thinking of her brother. "Yeah. Crazy."

Blanche stared at her. "What's that about?"

"My brother, Dev." She shook her head. "I haven't heard from him in years. I decided to track him down. He might be dead, Beebs."

"Oh, God, Peri."

Nick returned, a half-eaten bagel in one hand and a bottle of orange juice in the other. "Okay," he said through his chewing. "I'm ready."

"You got the thing?" Peri asked as she reached out and gave Blanche's arm a squeeze.

Nick patted his jeans pocket and nodded.

After hugging her best friend one more time, and whispering, "We can talk later," Peri left with Nick to run an important errand.

Benny was still living at his Aunt Esmy's house, chafing at her rules and lack of Dean Martin music. Peri and Nick pulled up to the curb and saw the black Caddy in the driveway, looking splendorous as usual. They walked past the dainty flowerbeds and rang the bell.

A few minutes later, Benny opened the door.

"Hey, Benny," Peri said. "Where's your aunt today?"

"She went out. She goes out a lot lately. Says I stress her." He looked at Nick. "What's he doing here?"

She tried to remember her gratitude toward him and not his annoying quirks. "Nick came to give you a present."

314

Nick stepped forward, holding something in his hand. "I wanted to find a way to show you how sorry I am. Aunt Peri suggested this."

Benny took the small, rectangular object, and looked it over. "What is it?"

"It's an iPod, Ben," Peri told him. "Nick has loaded it with all Dean Martin, all the time."

Nick reached out and unlocked it. The device leapt to life, displaying its options. "See, Mr. Needles, I put all the songs I could find of Dean Martin on here, plus all the movies I could find. Plus, I found some TV shows, so I put those on." He showed Benny how to select videos or songs.

Benny's face went from confusion to wonder as he saw the selections before him. He quickly pressed one of the Dean Martin variety shows, plugged in his earbuds, and played. His expression told the story. It wasn't just marvelous. It was Dino-licious.

Peri tapped him from his viewing. "Benny, we have to go."

He nodded at first, then jerked his head up. "No, no, Miss Peri, wait." He disappeared into the house and returned with a handful of cash, which he thrust at her. "I want to hire you."

"To do what?"

He looked at her as if she'd forgotten some agreement they had. "To find my father, of course."

She reached out and took his money, then returned it to his hand. "This one's no charge. You saved my life. That's worth solving at least one case for you, pro bono."

"And Phil says you can help him with my house. I don't know how to build it again. Phil knows. He says you know too."

"Remind me to thank Phil," she told him. "Maybe when we find your dad, he can help."

"When are you going to find him?"

"I'll start work on it this afternoon."

"What time?"

Peri laughed. She could always count on Benny. "I'll let you know. I have to get Nick home now. Go have fun with your new gadget."

Benny waved the iPod at her, then restarted his TV show and put the earbuds back in, shutting the door behind him.

"That was good," Nick said. "He really liked it."

"Trust me, anything with Dino, he likes."

They got back into the car and drove to Yorba Linda. The radio played the oldies station. Peri hoped it wasn't too ancient for her young friend's tender ears.

"Aunt Peri, what do you think I'd need to become a policeman?"

"I know you need some college courses in criminal justice. I think you can't have a history of arrests or trouble with the law, or mental problems. Skip would know more. You should talk to him if you're interested."

He nodded. "I might do that. I'm not much into engineering, like Dad, or dead bodies, like Mom. But maybe I'd like to, I don't know, keep everyone safe."

"Not a bad career choice, if you ask me."

She pulled up in their drive. "Thanks, Nick. I think you and Benny will be BFFs now."

"Thank you, Aunt Peri. You really helped smooth things over with him." He opened the passenger door, then reached over to give her a small quick kiss on the cheek before leaping from the car. "Later."

She drove toward home, her heart a little lighter from their exchange. It was almost noon, and traffic was starting to clog the avenues. She missed the left-turn arrow at Bradford Street and Yorba Linda Boulevard, so she fiddled with the radio, waiting for the next cycle. Her phone rang, prompting the lady in her Bluetooth to ask if she wanted to answer. She tapped on the earpiece and said hello.

The voice was male, unmistakable, and as casual as if they'd spoken yesterday.

"Hi, Sis. What did you want?"

THE END

ABOUT THE AUTHOR

Gayle Carline is a typical Californian, meaning that she was born somewhere else. She moved to Orange County from Illinois in 1978, and landed in Placentia a few years later.

Her husband, Dale, bought her a laptop for Christmas in 1999 because she wanted to write. A year after that, he gave her horseback riding lessons. When she bought her first horse, she finally started writing.

These days, she divides her days between writing humor columns for her local newspaper and writing mysteries for a larger audience.

In her spare time, Gayle likes to sit down with friends and laugh over a glass of wine. And maybe plan a little murder and mayhem.

For more merriment, visit her at **http://gaylecarline.com**.